TRUST ME

BOOK FIVE IN THE HOLMES BROTHERS SERIES

FARRAH ROCHON

Copyright © 2017 by Farrah Roybiskie

Cover Design by Mae Phillips of CoverFreshDesigns.com

Cover Image by Delvin Dickerson of Super Dads Photography

All rights reserved.

No part of this book may be reproduced in any form or by any electronic or mechanical means, including information storage and retrieval systems, without written permission from the author, except for the use of brief quotations in a book review.

ISBN: 9781521422885

TRUST ME

Farrah Rochon

CHAPTER 1

Poison?
Hit man?
Staged car accident?

Mackenna Arnold massaged the bridge of her nose as she contemplated the various methods she could use to commit murder. Convincing a jury to side with her shouldn't be all that difficult. She simply had to present footage from tonight's city council meeting. Who would possibly convict her once they witnessed the bullshit she'd been subjected to for the past two hours?

Mack lifted the stack of papers that had been waiting at her designated seat on the raised, semi-circular dais and scrolled through the remaining agenda items. As she listened to Cecil Washington wax poetic about the need for a new gas turbine, she resisted the overwhelming urge to reach over and grab the gavel from her fellow New Orleans City Council member and bang him in the head with it. It had only been a month since Cecil was named council president, and the power had already swollen that melon size head of his. There was no way Mack would get through the remainder of his six-month term without telling him off.

She motioned to the deputy clerk.

"Councilmember Arnold wishes to be recognized," the clerk stated.

"Proceed, Councilmember Arnold," Cecil said. Mack knew she didn't mistake the frustration she heard in his voice.

Tough shit.

Cecil and his minions decided to ram this gas turbine down everyone's throat on the assumption that they wouldn't get any pushback. They should have known better.

"While I appreciate the council's commitment to improving the city's infrastructure, I vehemently protest the proposed site of this new utility plant," Mack started. "Furthermore, if we're even going to discuss the idea of this new facility, it is incumbent upon us all to revisit the city charter, where it states—"

"We all know what the charter states, Councilmember Arnold," Cecil said, cutting her off. "The charter can be amended."

"Not without just cause."

"And a new gas turbine that will bring a much needed additional power source to thousands of residents *is* just cause," he said.

"It will bring an additional power source to thousands of residents in District B, yet the proposed site is in District D. *My* district. Where *my* constituents will be subjected to the environmental and noise pollution associated with this new facility. If the residents of District B need a new power plant to generate electricity for their million dollar mansions, they should build it in their neighborhood. I refuse—"

Now Cecil chose to bang his gavel.

"We still have a number of items on tonight's agenda," he said, cutting her off again. "I propose we table this discussion and move on."

Mack clenched the pen in her hand as she pleaded with herself to settle down. She could sense that she was on the verge of losing it. She drew in a deep, calming breath and started to count to ten. She knew by the time she reached eight that it wasn't working.

She raised her hand. "I'd like to take a vote on how many members would like to move on, as oppose to those who would like to continue because they, like I, feel this discussion is too important to put on the back burner. Because they understand that the people who live in District D deserve the same air quality as those in the Uptown area, and that the amount one pays in property taxes should not determine one's quality of life in the city of New Orleans."

Cecil banged his gavel again. "You're grandstanding, Ms. Arnold."

His condescending tone was like a ball of rusty steel wool abrading her very last nerve.

"I'm stating the case for my constituents because the council-member-at-large will not allow me to do so any other way," she said.

"Forgive me for speaking out of order, but I happen to agree with Councilmember Arnold."

Mack peered over to the other end of the dais where her routine adversary, Russell Babin, sat with his hands folded and the usual air of superiority permeating the space around him. She was immediately suspicious.

Since being elected four years ago, she had gone head-to-head with the councilmember from District C more than any other on the council. This was the first time Babin had ever so readily agreed with her.

"I think we need to have a lot more discussion before allowing this to fall to the bottom of the agenda," Babin continued. "There are a number of new homes on the market in the Uptown area, and the promise of this new power source can only attract buyers. I, for one, believe that we need to do whatever we can to make sure the zoning is approved as soon as possible. The sooner the plant is built, the better."

If her eyes could shoot bullets both Russell and Cecil's families would be preparing for funerals tomorrow. Mack didn't know what she had been thinking earlier. Poison was much too kind for these two. She wanted to bring back medieval torture devices. A mace upside the head was the only way to go.

"I agree with you, Councilmember Babin, however—" Cecil started, but this time *she* cut *him* off.

"Before you attempt to table this discussion yet again, I'd like to point out that Mayor Warner has already stated his adamant disapproval of the proposed power plant," Mack said. "The council will have a hard time convincing the public to go along with this plan if the mayor isn't backing it."

The smug grin that curled up the side of Cecil's mouth made the hairs on Mack's arm stand on end. The council president held up a sheet of paper.

"Actually, in this memo, Mayor Warner expresses his

wholehearted *approval* for both the power plant and the proposed site," he said. "Now, I must insist we move on."

A knot of shock and dismay clawed its way up Mack's throat. Disappointment pounded within her chest, rendering her speechless.

She tried her hardest to listen as the deputy clerk called the next agenda item to the floor, but she was so stunned at the thought of Lucien Warner doing a complete one-eighty on the new utility plant that Mack barely heard what was being said in the chamber. This was the second time this month Mayor Warner had changed course on pledges he'd made to constituents. He'd backtracked at least a half dozen times this year, reversing his stance on issues he'd held firm on for as long as Mack could remember.

"Councilmember Arnold? Councilmember Arnold!"

"What? I…I'm sorry," Mack said. "What was that?"

Cecil's irritation was evident in his tightened jaw and clipped words. "I asked if you mind if we take a vote by general consent on your proposal for the new playground equipment in Pontchartrain Park?"

"No, no. Of course not," she said.

The proposal went through and Cecil adjourned the meeting with his usual flare for the dramatic. Mack couldn't help but roll her eyes. She tried to keep her distaste for some of her fellow councilmembers from showing on her face, but it wasn't easy. It especially wasn't easy after a night like tonight, when she'd been blindsided by her mentor.

As Mack packed up her materials, Juliette Cannon, the only other woman on the council, came up to her.

"I'm sorry about what they did to you tonight, Mackenna. I distinctly remember the mayor stating that he would not support the gas turbine being built in your district. I don't know what Cecil did to convince him to go against his initial wishes, but he must have been very persuasive."

"I don't know what he said to the mayor either," Mack said. "But I'm not giving up without a fight."

"You never do," Juliette said. "That's why you won your last race by a sixty point margin."

"I'm still convinced those other people only voted for Tom Shepard because he looks good in a suit. I nearly voted for him for that same reason," she said with a playful wink.

Juliette burst out laughing and patted Mack on the arm. "I'll see you tomorrow. You promised you'd help with the French Quarter noise ordinance, remember?"

"I'll be there."

She pasted on a smile for Juliette's sake, but inside Mack was still reeling from the mayor's reversal. His reasons for first opposing the power plant's construction aligned with hers, and they were damn good reasons. There was zero upside to building the plant in her district. The utility company had already stated that the facility would be manned by current employees, so the prospect of new jobs—something that would have been welcomed in some of the more depressed areas—wasn't even on the table.

The mayor had been raised in the Gentilly Woods neighborhood. He understood the longstanding obstacles those residents continued to face. How could he turn his back on his own people?

The only thing Mack could think of that would

make him go back on his word was that he'd been given some kind of incentive.

A possible financial incentive?

She shook her head. She would not—*could* not—go there. She'd been Lucien Warner's staunchest supporter since the day she'd walked into his *Theories of Argumentation* class back in her first year of law at Tulane University. He was one of the most upstanding men she'd ever known. Mack refused to believe that man would ever turn his back on the people of this city just to pad his own pockets.

Yet, as she rushed through the rain to her car, the nagging voice in the back of her head that insisted something was off with Mayor Warner refused to be silenced. She'd begun to question his motives months ago, when it appeared that he would relent on his opposition to holding internet-based vehicle-for-hire companies to the same standard as taxi companies in the city. He was the one who had first convinced her that the rights of the taxi drivers needed to be protected.

He'd made the same assertions regarding the residents in her district when it came to this new gas turbine. What could have changed? Why did he feel *they* no longer needed to be protected?

"This is why you need to run," Mack whispered as she turned onto St. Charles Avenue.

When she'd first considered challenging Lucien in the next mayoral race, Mack was honest enough with herself to admit that her reasons were not the most altruistic. That relentless compulsion to prove herself remained the driving force behind every step she'd ever taken regarding her career, but this felt different.

Over these last four years, she'd come to care about

the people of her district so much more than she ever thought possible. Their stories touched her. Their resilience inspired her. They deserved a champion. Every single person in this city deserved a champion.

You can be their champion.

Mack tensed as nervous flutters took flight in her belly, but she quickly quelled the sensation. She'd never been one to fall victim to fear. Whenever it reared its head, that's when she surged forward, daring anything to stop her. She sure as hell wasn't going to let fear overcome her now.

She had a class to teach tomorrow—the student who had now become the professor—and the meeting with Juliette, but Mack was determined to carve out some time to meet with Mayor Warner. She wanted to hear from his mouth just why he'd changed course on the gas turbine.

Mack pulled up to the curb in front of Griffin Sims's galleried cottage-style house. The handsome engineer and her best friend, Indina Holmes, had been carrying on a co-workers-with-benefits relationship for nearly a year, yet Mack had only learned about it a couple of months ago. She still hadn't forgiven Indina for keeping such a juicy secret from her.

Griffin had persuaded Indina to turn their purely physical arrangement into the real thing, a fact that continued to astonish Mack whenever she thought about it. She'd been convinced her best friend was done with relationships.

Mack knew for certain she sure as hell was done with them. After the implosion of her fifteen-year marriage, she'd rather light her own hair on fire than reenter the dating scene. The occasional bouts of loneliness she'd encountered since her divorce were preferable to the utter misery she'd faced during those last few years with Carter. Her eye twitched just at the thought of her ex-husband. That bastard could stand right next to Cecil and Russell if she ever got that firing squad primed and ready.

Just as she reached for the door handle, a loud crack of thunder resonated from above and a torrent of water poured from the sky.

"Shit," Mack cursed as she searched for her umbrella. She thumped her head on the headrest, recalling last Thursday's downpour, when she'd last used the umbrella. The damn thing was still in her office at City Hall. *Shit.*

She pulled her ringing phone from her purse, spotting Indina's number on the screen. "Hey," Mack answered. "I'm right outside."

"I know you are," her friend said. "I'm watching you through the front window."

Mack looked to the house and saw Indina peeking out from behind sheer curtains. She waved.

"I was about to call the police," Indina continued. "I forgot you were driving that rental car."

"Mine is still sitting at the mechanic's shop waiting for a part," Mack said. "I'll come in as soon as the rain slacks. I forgot my umbrella."

"I'll send someone out to get you," she said.

"No, that's okay—" Mack started, but Indina had already disconnected the call. A minute later, the front door opened and her worst nightmare walked out.

"You have *got* to be kidding me," Mack muttered.

Of all the people…

If there was one person who worked on her nerves

more than her two adversaries on the city council, it was Ezra Holmes. She didn't hate him enough to shove him in front of the firing squad, but it was pretty damn close.

Indina's younger brother had worked for years as an investigative reporter for the city's now defunct major newspaper. For reasons Mack had yet to figure out, Ezra had gotten it in his head that she was engaged in some kind of nefarious activity. He'd spent the past four months sniffing around her office at City Hall, pestering her assistants and the deputy clerks with all kinds of questions. Basically being a giant pain in her ass.

Everything had come to a head a couple of months ago, when Mack had breakfast with her former brother-in-law—a man she was convinced had been adopted. She'd told Charles, a longtime officer with the NOPD, about Ezra's annoying harassment and, without her knowledge, Charles took it upon himself to arrest Ezra for stalking.

Charles had hoped to scare Ezra into leaving Mack alone, but his plan backfired. The arrest only fueled Ezra's insane idea that she had something to hide. He'd become even *more* dogged in his pursuit to "uncover Mack's web of corruption."

As he rounded the rental's front bumper, she was tempted to start the car and drive away. But it was Griffin's birthday, and Mack had promised Indina she'd come over to help them celebrate. She owed it to her friend after cancelling on her the last few times they'd made plans. But if she had to spend any significant amount of time in the same space as Ezra, Mack considered her debt to Indina paid in full.

The thunderous boom that shattered the sky

symbolized her sudden mood shift. She'd stay, but she couldn't promise she'd be here for long.

Ezra tapped on the driver's side window. Mack fixed the glower she knew her face held and opened the car door. She would at least try to be nice.

"*You?*" Ezra balked, seeming to recoil just at the sight of her.

Okay, forget being nice. This jerk didn't deserve it.

"Yes, me," Mack bit out. "Care to get out of the rain?"

He growled a curse as he held the door wide and stepped out of the way so she could exit the car. They remained silent as they hurried up the stone walkway. Halfway to the front door, the heel of Mack's favorite taupe Giuseppe Zanottis got caught between two stones. She pitched forward, but Ezra halted her fall, hooking his free arm around her.

"You okay?" he asked, still holding her.

Mack sucked in a breath as she nodded. She refused to read into the disconcerting sensation that resonated from where his muscled forearm rested underneath her breasts. It illustrated just how hard up she was when Ezra Holmes of all people could elicit such a reaction from her.

"Yeah. Thanks," she muttered, disengaging from his hold.

"Come on out of the rain," Indina called from the front door.

Ezra allowed Mack to enter ahead of him, proving that annoying bastards could also be gentlemen.

"I was afraid you wouldn't be able to make it after you texted that the meeting was running long." Indina enveloped Mack in a hug. "How did it go with the city council tonight?"

Mack rolled her eyes. "Be grateful I didn't have to call you to bail me out of jail," she said. "Where's the bar? I need a drink."

"Everything's set up in the dining room. You'll have to settle for wine, though."

"This is why I should start traveling with scotch," Mack said. She started for the dining room, stopping to give Griffin a quick kiss on the cheek. "Happy birthday. You'll get a proper hug after I've gotten some food and liquor in me."

"I plan to collect on that," he called after her.

She arrived at the dining room table, where dainty platters of charmingly arranged hors d'oeuvres jockeyed with several bottles of wine for her attention.

"Someone has been scouring the party planning boards on Pinterest," Mack teased as she popped a mushroom cap stuffed with something gooey into her mouth. "Oh, good Lord, this is good," she mumbled around the food.

"Guess you don't mind my mad Pinterest skills now, do you?" Indina said.

Mack shook her head, chasing a second mushroom with a deep swallow of red wine. It wasn't her drink of choice, but it would do.

"You want to tell me why I almost had to bail you out of jail tonight?" Indina asked.

"Don't worry, you'll get your chance to bail her out of jail soon enough," Ezra said as he strolled up to the table, grabbing a handful of cheese cubes and popping one in his mouth.

"Kiss my ass," Mack said. She was *so* not in the mood for his bullshit.

"Ezra, don't start," Indina chastised him.

Contempt shimmered in his intense gaze. "Just preparing the councilwoman for her eventual fate."

"How long have you been searching for dirt on me?" Mack asked. "If you haven't found anything yet, maybe that should tell you something."

"That you're better than most at hiding your dirt?"

"You're fucking insane," Mack sneered.

Indina stepped between them. "And that's the end of round one. In your respective corners, please."

Ezra released a derisive snort as he popped another cheese cube in his mouth and sauntered away. Mack changed her mind about the firing squad. She would shove his ass in front of one without batting an eye.

"Why didn't you remind me that he would be here tonight?" she asked Indina.

"So you could cancel on me again?" She cast a dismissive wave toward her brother. "Don't let Ezra get to you. He'll eventually realize he's wasting his time with whatever story he's pursuing. Now, tell me what happened at the meeting tonight. It must have been pretty heated to have you so riled up."

"I'm not talking about tonight's meeting," Mack said. "This is supposed to be a happy occasion. I refuse to ruin Griffin's party by bitching about the city council."

"Fine, but you *will* tell me later," Indina said. "One of the perks of my best friend being on the city council is that I get to hear all the inside dirt. You know I find that stuff fascinating."

Mack shook her head, huffing out a laugh. "You're so weird."

"But you love me anyway."

"Of course I do. Would I remain in the same house with your pain-in-the-ass brother if I didn't love you?"

Indina barked out a laugh as she enveloped Mack in another hug. "I owe you one."

Mack took a sip of her wine and scanned the room. Her gaze arrested at the sight of Ezra staring at her from an arched entryway. His cold eyes were trained on her, his expression redolent with distaste.

Oh, yeah, Indina definitely owed her one.

~

"You planning to stay in this one spot all night?"

Ezra Holmes looked over his shoulder and grunted as his cousin, Toby, approached the curved doorway where Ezra had sequestered himself. The spot afforded him a view of the dining room and half of the living room, where the dozen or so people who'd gathered for Griffin's birthday all congregated.

Toby sidled up to him, a foil-covered plate in one hand and car keys in the other.

"You heading out already?" Ezra asked him.

He held up the plate. "My wife wants dinner. She gets mean when she's hungry."

Ezra managed to laugh despite the sulky mood he'd been in for the past half hour. He gestured to his own eyes then pointed at Toby's. "I'm guessing that new baby is responsible for those bags under your eyes?"

Toby dropped his head back and groaned at the ceiling. "That little sucker wakes up every hour on the hour. I can't remember what it feels like to get a full night's sleep."

"It shows."

His cousin elbowed him on the arm. "At least I have a good excuse for the sour look on my face. What's yours?" He looked over to where Ezra had been staring. "Ah, I see. Be careful with that, man. You don't want to end up in handcuffs again." Toby tapped him on the shoulder. "I'll see you later."

The reminder of his arrest sent Ezra's mood on another downward spiral.

He'd suffered his share of humiliating moments during his thirty-nine years. Tripping over his own feet while walking across the stage at his high school graduation, getting numerous drinks thrown in his face during his disastrous college partying years, losing his job; all had given him reason to want to curl into a ball and just disappear.

But being handcuffed and shoved into the back of a police cruiser in front of his entire family?

That shit made his body shudder with shame to this day.

Growing up in New Orleans, it was easy for young black males to get caught up in the street life. But that had never happened to any of the Holmes boys. It was a testament to his mom and dad's strength and determination that they, along with his Aunt Margo and Uncle Wesley, had raised six males in this city and not one of them had ever seen the inside of a jail cell. That is, until Mackenna Arnold sicced her brother-in-law on him. That arrest was, without a doubt, the single most humiliating moment of his life.

Ezra clenched his jaw so hard he feared it might break. Disgust throbbed through his veins as he regarded the woman responsible for that mortifying episode.

She stood next to the fireplace, laughing at something his cousin Eli had just said. Eli's wife, Monica, who still wore her scrubs from the hospital where she worked as an ER physician, made exaggerated hand gestures as she added to the conversation, setting off another round of laughter.

It chapped his ass to stand there and watch Mack enjoying herself, as if she didn't have a care in the world.

But Ezra knew it was all an act. She was scared as hell that he would expose all the skeletons crowding up her closet. He knew they were there. And he knew he was close to finding them. *So* close. He felt it in his bones. Ezra would stake his entire career on the hunch that Mackenna was involved in some kind of shady dealings with the company that landed the city's huge garbage disposal contract earlier this year. He'd found everything but the smoking gun to tie her to it.

And that's what chapped his ass the most. He knew it was out there. That one piece of information linking her to BDF Disposal, Inc. But damn if he could put his finger on it.

It had been months since he'd received that anonymous tip from the phone number that always followed his byline. During that time, Ezra had uncovered a link between her ex-husband, Carter Arnold, and BDF Disposal's parent company. It was just one entity Carter had his finger in. The prominent divorce attorney was as much a businessman as he was a man of the law. The web of connections was so convoluted it had taken Ezra months to piece it all together. If only he could find that missing puzzle piece that would prove that Mackenna had knowledge of her husband's holding interest when she approved the city contract.

She *had* to have known. How could she not?

"Would you please stop staring at my best friend like you want to chew her head off?"

Ezra jolted at his sister's voice. Indina handed him a fresh glass of ginger ale on the rocks and then snaked her arm around his waist.

"Can you at least pretend to be the sweet younger brother I once knew and loved?"

"I was never sweet," Ezra said.

"That's why I emphasized *pretend*. Stop brooding for five minutes and enjoy yourself."

Ezra didn't promise her anything. He was still upset that she hadn't bothered to tell him Mack would be here.

It shouldn't have come as a surprise. Mack and Indina had been best friends since the first year they roomed together at Grambling State. Mack had taken part in countless Holmes family gatherings over the span of their twenty-year friendship. Although she didn't make as many once she got married, and even less once she won a seat on the city council, Ezra should have expected to see her here tonight.

If he were being honest with himself he could admit that he was *hoping* to see her. His hand still itched from where he'd touched her earlier when she'd tripped on her way up the walkway.

Dammit. Was there a bigger fool?

In those few moments when he'd held her warm body snug against his side, he'd forgotten all about his investigation. His entire focus had centered on his long-standing infatuation with her. An infatuation that continued to thrive, no matter how hard he tried to fight it.

Ezra nearly choked on the self-loathing that climbed up his throat.

It started the first time he laid eyes on her. She'd come home with Indina for winter break back when they were juniors in college. Ezra had just started his freshman year at the University of New Orleans, and thought he was the hottest shit walking the streets. Mackenna had walked through the door of his parents' home and he'd damn near lost his mind.

He'd tried everything he could think of to impress her, yet for the first two days she'd mistakenly called him Evan. She couldn't even get his damn name right, but did that stop him from obsessing over her for years? Hell no. It wasn't until she married Carter Arnold that Ezra accepted there would never be anything between them.

Or had he?

Last year, when he learned that her marriage was ending, his first thought was that maybe he could finally get his chance.

He shook his head, grimacing at his own ridiculousness. Was there anything more pathetic than the torch he still carried for this woman?

More than once he'd questioned if his pursuit of this corruption story against her stemmed from anger over years of unrequited attraction, but Ezra had managed to convince himself that his complicated feelings for Mackenna Arnold had nothing to do with this. He wanted to expose her for the fraud she was. Period.

And because it would be the kind of story that could

finally propel him into the same national spotlight Lindsey Marshall was basking in at the moment.

Ezra peered down at his glass and wished it held whiskey instead of ginger ale. He needed something strong and inebriating to wipe his mind clear of the image of Lindsey's byline in the *Washington Post* earlier today.

It's not that he wasn't happy for his former co-worker. He and Lindsey had been friendly rivals back when they worked together at the paper, pushing each other to do better instead of competing with each other. But the reality that Lindsey had made it to a national publication while he was still here busting his ass to get his stories picked up by local outfits was more demoralizing than Ezra could stomach at the moment.

He needed the kind of story that would catapult him into the national spotlight; a juicy political scandal the city—the *nation*—could sink its teeth into. Like exposing the corruption of a popular sitting member of the New Orleans City Council.

Ezra finished his drink in one swallow and walked over to the table for another. He'd just finished pouring when he heard, "So, are you done harassing me?"

A barrage of conflicting sensations traveled up his spine at the sound of her voice. Ezra dialed his expression to indifferent before turning to face her, cursing the brief tinge of longing that still pinged him in the chest. *Pathetic.*

"You done giving city contracts to companies you have a business interest in?" he asked, mentally patting himself on the back for keeping his tone emotionless.

Her shoulders wilted with her exasperated sigh. "You are exhausting," Mack said. "How many times do

I have to tell you that I have no idea what you are talking about?"

"You can cut the innocent act," Ezra told her. "Just because I haven't found the direct tie to you, doesn't mean there isn't one. The deeper you try to bury it, that's the deeper I'll dig. Nothing's going to stop me from exposing you."

She rolled her eyes. "You need to find a new hobby."

Hobby?

Now *that* pissed him off. This wasn't a damn hobby. This was his *job*.

If Ezra hadn't heard the same kind of talk from some of his friends—some of his own family members—after he'd been let go from the paper, it probably wouldn't have rankled as much as it did.

He didn't spend hours researching public records and crosschecking sources to pass the time. He was a journalist. Hell, he taught young students how to become journalists. He didn't have to stand here while some corrupt politician insulted him.

"Let's see what you think about my *hobby* once you're the one being taken away in handcuffs," Ezra snarled.

"Is that what this is all about?" Mack asked. "You're still upset over that incident?"

"Incident? You had me arrested in front of my entire family."

"I already told you Charles did that just to scare you. No charges were ever filed."

"Must be nice to have an NOPD officer you can call on to help do your dirty work."

Her eyes narrowed. "Are you insinuating that my ex-brother-in-law is a dirty cop?"

Ezra shrugged. "If the tarnished badge fits."

Her deep brown eyes shot daggers at him. "You are one sick son of a bitch," Mackenna spat.

"Call me names all you want." He stepped up to her, getting right in that gorgeous face. "But know that I *will* expose your ass."

"You can *kiss* my ass!"

"Whoa, whoa, whoa." Indina slipped between them, holding her hands up. "If you two are going to have this fight in public, at least let me charge people for the show."

"There is no show," Ezra said, backing away. "But give me time. I'll give everybody something to gawk at when it comes to the councilwoman here."

Mack released another exasperated sigh. "I am so tired of going back and forth with you. For the last time, Ezra, I have absolutely no connection to that garbage company."

"You hear that?" Indina said. She gave him a playful slap. "Now leave Mack alone. Please."

Ezra waited until his sister walked away before closing the distance between himself and Mackenna again. Years of experience had taught him that it was stupid to show his hand, but he was fed up with her continued denials.

"You really don't have anything to do with BDF Disposal?" he asked.

"Nothing, Ezra. I have never had any connection with them."

"Oh, no?" He leaned in close. "I have two words for you: Starlight Enterprises."

She jerked her head back, as if he'd landed a physical hit, her eyes rounded with shock. The stunned look on her face was pretty convincing, but Ezra wasn't buying it. She was a politician. She'd probably perfected that look and a dozen others so she could pull them out when the need arose.

Nope, he wasn't buying this wide-eyed innocent act.

Yet, as he made his excuses to Indina and Griffin and walked out of the house, Ezra couldn't shake the feeling in his gut that a hint of the surprise he'd witnessed on Mackenna's face had been real.

CHAPTER 2

EZRA PARKED his navy Chrysler 300 next to the chain-link fence at the corner of Octavia and Fontainebleau Drive. As he navigated the jagged slabs of uneven sidewalk, courtesy of the protruding roots of century old oaks underneath, he picked up a metal Holmes Construction sign that had apparently fallen off the fencing, probably during last night's downpour. The light but persistent rain that had fallen earlier in the evening had turned into a raging storm in the wee hours of the morning, ripping off tree branches and scattering them and other debris all around the city.

He entered the construction site, nodding at a worker who looked familiar, but whose name Ezra couldn't remember.

"Hey, is Reid around?" he called.

A second guy in a hardhat gestured to the mobile trailer just to the right of a row of wooden pallets piled high with cinderblocks. "He's in there with the boss man."

"Thanks," Ezra said. He held up the sign. "This

must have fallen off the fence last night. I found it on the sidewalk." After handing the guy the sign, he climbed the metal steps and rapped twice on the door before entering the trailer. "Hey, hey. Y'all in here?"

Ezra closed the door behind him and stopped short.

His cousin, Alex, who owned Holmes Construction, sat behind a desk cluttered with unfurled blueprints, two computer monitors, and at least a half-dozen paper coffee cups. Ezra's younger brother, Reid, who worked as a plumber for Alex's company, occupied one of two chairs that faced the desk. One steel-toe booted foot bounced rapidly atop his knee, a clear indication his brother was agitated.

The tension in the air was so thick Ezra was certain he could reach out and grab it with his hands.

"Uh, did I come at a bad time?" he asked.

Alex motioned for him to come in. "We were just finishing up here."

"Were we?" Reid asked.

A thick vein stood out in stark relief on Alex's forehead as he levied a frustrated scowl at Reid. "We'll talk about this later."

"Before or after you fire Jessie?"

"Reid—"

"Jessie Jacobs is one of the best plumbers we have, Alex. You'd be crazy to let him go. So he comes in late every now and then." Reid shrugged. "When he's here, he does good work and the guys on the crew respect him."

"That's the problem. They *shouldn't* respect someone with such a bad work ethic. If I reward Jessie by keeping him on, they'll think I condone that behavior, which I don't."

Reid dropped his head back and growled at the ceiling. "You're making a mistake, man. It took you over a month to find a new foreman after Mike up and quit on you. How long do you think it'll take you to find someone to replace Jessie?"

"You let me worry about that. And Mike didn't just up and quit. He gave me several weeks' notice."

"Yet it still took you a month to replace him. It'll be even longer to find someone who can fill Jessie's shoes." Reid held his hands out in a pleading gesture. "You're not out in the field every day, Alex. You don't understand how hard it is to build camaraderie on the job site. You can't just stick someone new out there and expect the rest of the crew to just be on board."

Alex looked over at Ezra. "What's up?" he asked, making it clear he was done with his conversation with Reid.

"Actually, I'm here to see him," Ezra said, tipping his head toward his brother. He pulled the envelope from his back pocket and handed it to Reid.

"You came through on the Pelicans tickets?" Reid asked, hopping out of the chair.

"Luxury box seats," Ezra replied.

"Dude, I didn't know you still had this kind of pull." He cast an annoyed frown at Alex. "I was going to bring this honey I met at The Hard Court last week, but I think I'll take Jessie instead. He's going to need some cheering up tonight if this one here goes through with what he's threatening."

"I don't make threats," Alex said. "Remember that when I finally get tired of your shit and send you packing. Now get back out there and find out why I don't hear that air compressor humming."

Reid started to speak, but apparently thought better of it. Smart move. Ezra had no doubt that if his brother pushed too hard, he'd find himself out of a job. Reid started working for Holmes Construction right out of high school, but Alex hadn't built the top-rated, black-owned construction company in New Orleans by giving his workers passes just because the same blood ran through their veins. Reid was treated like every other carpenter, bricklayer and plumber who wore an orange Holmes Construction safety vest. He would be fired like one too.

"Remember, we're meeting later this week at Harrison's to talk about Mama's foundation," Ezra told his brother as he headed for the door.

"I'll be there," Reid called.

Ezra started to leave out after him, but Alex stopped him. "Hey, Ezra, you mind sticking around for a minute?"

"Yeah, sure," he said. He took the seat Reid had just vacated. He tipped his head toward the door. "Is he in danger of losing his job?"

"No." Alex shook his head. "But that boy knows how to test me. He doesn't understand that I don't have the luxury of becoming buddies with everyone that works under me. If someone isn't doing their job, they have to go."

"You gotta do what you gotta do," Ezra said. "It's your reputation on the line. So, what's up?"

"This is about your *other* brother," Alex said.

"Harrison?"

Alex nodded. "He came over last night to help Jasmine with a report she's working on for Career Day. She wants to be a lawyer."

"She's got the mouth for it," Ezra said of his cousin's twelve-year-old.

"Tell me about it." Alex huffed out a weary laugh. "Anyway, once he and Jasmine were done, I followed Harrison out to his car, thinking we'd catch up since I hadn't seen him since the last family picnic. You know, the one where—"

"I know," Ezra said. The one where he was arrested.

"Yeah, well, Harrison and I are just shooting the breeze, and I happen to ask how Willow is doing."

"Oh shit," Ezra muttered.

"He went off on a ten minute rant about how her expectations are too high and he's tired of not being enough for her and all kinds of other crazy shit. What's going on with those two?"

"Hell if I know," Ezra said. He pitched his head back and ran both hands down his face. There was definitely something troubling going on between Harrison and his wife of sixteen years.

"It wasn't until Indina pointed it out on the family reunion cruise that I noticed how little they even spoke to each other the entire time we were on that ship," Ezra admitted. "I tried talking to Harrison, but he just blew me off."

"He sure was in a talkative mood last night. He hung around at my place for almost an hour after he and Jasmine were done. I think he was trying to avoid going home."

"Shit," Ezra said again.

"Whatever's going on, it's stressing him out. Somebody needs to talk to him."

"Who? *Me?* I just told you that he blew me off."

"Well, somebody has to. We can't sit around waiting

for this train wreck to happen and not try to do something to stop it. Maybe we can put together a dominoes night and see if we can't get him to open up about it?"

"You know Harrison won't appreciate us staging an intervention into his marriage."

Alex put both hands up. "I didn't say anything about an intervention. I'm just trying to figure out a way to let him know that he's got family here to help. I know how stubborn your brother can be."

"We're *all* stubborn," Ezra pointed out.

"You're damn right. And I'm the oldest, so I've been stubborn for longer than any of you."

Ezra huffed out a laugh. "You say that like it's a badge of honor or something."

"No, I say that like someone who knows how that Holmes stubbornness can come back to bite you in the ass. I don't want that to happen to Harrison. Just…think it over. If you have a better idea, I'm all for it."

"I get what you're saying," Ezra said. He reached over and clasped Alex's outstretched hand. "I'll catch up with you later. I've got to get back to work."

His cousin narrowed his eyes. "You're not still pestering the councilwoman, are you?"

"If by 'pestering' you mean am I still *investigating* her business dealings, then yes," Ezra said. "And they're called council *members* now. None of that gendering shit."

"Thanks for telling me before I made the mistake of saying it in front of the mini-feminist I'm raising. I suggested pink border for her science fair project board and got an earful about my sexism and wanting to put her in a box. I blame Beyonce."

Ezra burst out laughing. "I should get on my knees

every day and thank God that I never had kids. I saw Toby last night. He looked like a zombie. I don't know how you guys handle it."

Alex waved that off with a dismissive snort as he rose from behind the desk.

"Babies are easy. Pre-teens are a different story," his cousin said as he followed Ezra out of the trailer. "Hey, try not to get yourself arrested again with whatever this story is that has you investigating Mackenna Arnold. I don't think Uncle Clark will be as understanding next time somebody has to go down to the police station to pick you up."

Ezra chuckled at Alex's good-natured ribbing, but being reminded of the humiliation he'd experienced at Mack's attempt to "teach him a lesson" only fueled the animosity that had been simmering since his run-in with her at Griffin and Indina's last night.

Yeah, that's why you're so pissed.

That episode with her overzealous ex-brother-in-law happened over a month ago. Sure, he was still angry about it, but Ezra knew damn well that wasn't the reason his temper had been on such a short fuse most of the day. It was his reaction to seeing her last night that continued to gnaw at him.

Contempt was the only thing Mackenna Arnold should stir within him. But it wasn't contempt that had him wide awake last night, staring at the ceiling, thinking about the way that gray skirt had followed the curve of her ass, or how amazing her legs looked in those sheer stockings, or how the heels she wore made those legs look a mile long. No, that definitely wasn't contempt he'd felt last night.

It was hell. That's what it was.

Ezra jerked at his car door's handle so hard he was surprised he didn't rip the damn thing off.

It didn't matter how nice her ass looked in a skirt. Exposing said ass was still his top priority. His mouth twisted in a derisive sneer at his memory of the shocked expression she'd tried to fool him with when he mentioned Starlight Enterprises last night. He could only speculate that she wanted him to think she was confused or even innocent. It hadn't worked.

Even though he had yet to find anything that directly tied Mack to Starlight Enterprises, he'd found several documents linking Carter Arnold to the company. The two were now divorced, but they had not been back when, as a city council member, Mack had voted to approve a multimillion-dollar contract with a subsidiary of Starlight Enterprises. One of the reasons he became a journalist was to expose that kind of corruption.

If only he could find that damn smoking gun connecting *her* to Starlight.

"You will," Ezra said as he started up the ignition.

He pulled away from the curb and made a U-turn. He had a date with the Orleans Parish Court Directory. And unlike the last two dates he'd had with a couple of women his friends had tried to hook him up with, this was one date he was determined to keep.

∽

Mack shoveled a forkful of tuna straight from the pouch and into her mouth as she motioned for John to continue. Her former law school debate partner scrunched up his nose.

"You know, it tastes a lot better if you add a little mayo and relish to the tuna. Maybe some salt and pepper?"

"I don't have time for mayo or pepper," Mack said. "I'm due in court in less than an hour and still have to prep for my class tonight." She made a *get on with it* gesture with her fork.

"You're going to eventually have to give up one of these careers if you decide to run for mayor, Mack. You can't run the city *and* practice law *and* teach law."

Mack shushed him. "Not so loud," she whispered. She rose from behind her desk and walked over to the door of her City Hall office, shutting it. "I don't want to start the rumor mill churning, especially since I haven't decided if I *am* running yet."

"That's why I'm here. It's time to weigh the pros and cons and figure out if you really want to do this." John reached over and grabbed a legal pad from her desk. He flipped the sheet where Mack had been jotting down notes for the *Intro to Intellectual Property* class she taught two nights a week at Loyola Law School and looked up at her, his pen poised. "Let's start with the cons. What do you see as your biggest one?"

"That's easy. It's my loyalty to Mayor Warner," Mack said. "I owe that man a lot."

"We both do," John said. "He taught me nearly everything I know about law. But it goes without saying that in a head-to-head, I'd support you over Lucien Warner every day of the week and twice on Sundays."

Mack smiled. Her affection for John Darbonne still ran deep. She often wondered how different her life would have been if she hadn't dismissed the brief fling they'd had back in law school. She hadn't considered

John a serious contender for the role of significant other. She'd allowed her family's entrenched racism to cloud her judgment, knowing that if she brought home a blond-haired, blue-eyed boyfriend her grandmother would have had a heart attack.

Instead, Mack had fallen for the lying asshole with rich dark skin and a charming smile that she eventually married and wasted fifteen years of her life on. Meanwhile, John and his wife Anna now had two kids and a marriage that was still going strong. Add a check in the regret column on that one.

"I'm still weighing the pros and cons," Mack said as she picked up a yellow highlighter and swept the closed cap along the edge of the framed thirty-year-old picture of herself and her baby sister, Alicia. Their crooked-tooth smiles still made Mack laugh. There was very little that made Mack laugh when she thought of her sister these days.

She tossed the highlighter on the desk. "This is a big decision," she told John.

John put his hands up. "Hey, you don't have to tell me. I don't blame you for taking your time. Being responsible for just your district is a lot to handle. The thought of being responsible for the largest city in the state is nothing to take lightly. Which is why I need you to make sure you've thought this through, Mack." He shifted in his chair. "Tell me this, what would you do if Lucien Warner wasn't in the picture at all? If you didn't have to consider him, one way or the other?"

"I would still run."

"Even though you're also opening yourself up to a new level of scrutiny?"

She grinned. "You think I have something to hide?"

"No, but Mayor Warner's opposition team will search every nook and cranny of your life trying to find whatever they can to use against you."

Mack sat back in her chair and stretched her arms wide. "Let them look."

When she first moved to New Orleans for law school, Mack had considered hiding her past, but she quickly realized that she was sitting on an empathy goldmine. The public ate up a good pull-yourself-up-by-the-bootstraps story. Growing up poor in the boondocks of North Louisiana, being raised by her grandmother, going to bed hungry most nights. Who would have thought all the shit she'd been through as a kid could be used to her advantage? But use it she did. People loved to root for the underdog, and she had no qualms about playing to their desires.

Had she shared everything? No. There were still some parts of her past she had yet to share with even her closest friends, and Mack knew if someone searched the right places, it would be uncovered. But she'd already come up with a counter story just in case that happened. She would not be caught with her pants down by anyone.

She had her defense already in place for anyone who approached her about her mother, who lost custody of her children when Mack was only seven years old. Or her younger sister, whose battle with drug addiction had broken their grandmother's heart more times than Mack could count. She'd spent thousands on rehab for Alicia, but there was only so much money could do.

Mack didn't have control over her birth mother or her sister, and if anyone tried to place the blame at her feet, she was prepared to defend the choices she'd made in regards to her family.

"Don't worry," Mack said. "I don't have any big skeletons in my closet."

"Yeah, well, make sure the small ones aren't the kind that can turn into a big deal," John warned. "When I ran Louis Champagne's run for senate, an arrest for possession of marijuana when he was nineteen years old nearly took him down. You didn't have any real opposition during your run for the City Council, Mackenna, but a mayoral run is an entirely different animal. These things can get ugly."

"Thankfully, I will have a campaign manager who understands how the system works, right?" she asked.

"You know I'm here for anything you need, including being your campaign manager," John answered.

Those regrets over breaking up with John all those years ago were really rearing their annoying heads right now. Mack brushed it off as being lonely. She would not in any way, shape, or form even consider attempting to cozy up to John in a romantic way. Having been the victim of an adulterous affair by a spouse, she knew all too well the hurt that caused. She would never inflict it on another woman. She'd just have to find another way to work through her loneliness.

"I need to get going," John said. "I have a meeting with Annabeth's school principal."

"Uh oh," Mack said as she rose from behind her desk and walked John to the door. "Hope she's not in too much trouble."

"Trouble is that kid's middle name," John said. "She, unfortunately, has a mouth like her father. Her teacher overheard Annabeth saying that the principal has a stick up his ass."

Mack burst out laughing, but her humor quickly faded when John opened her office door and she discovered Russell Babin waiting on the other side.

Mack's heart skipped a beat. Had he been listening at her door as they talked about her possibly running for mayor?

"I'll see you later, John," Mack said, giving him a friendly kiss on the cheek. She turned her attention to Russell. "Are you here to talk about last night's ambush?"

"It wasn't an ambush," Babin said, walking past her and entering her office without an invitation. If she wanted to be a bitch she could have called a security guard to come escort him out. They all loved her way more than they liked Babin. But she didn't have time for a scene. She had too much on her plate today.

"I have ten minutes before I need to leave for court, Councilmember Babin. What do you need?"

"Mackenna, you need to come around on this gas turbine."

"I'm not talking about this—"

"The argument that the turbine needs to go in the neighborhood that will utilize the electricity is asinine. Can you imagine a utility plant in the middle of St. Charles Avenue? Forget the fact that there isn't room for one, but property values in that area would plummet."

"Why exactly should the people in my district be concerned about the effects on property values on St. Charles Avenue?"

"You're smarter than this, Mackenna. You know how this world works."

"I know that poor people are continually expected to endanger their own well-beings so that the rich are not inconvenienced. Guess what, it's not happening on my watch."

Babin's smug sneer was like a cheese grater sliding along Mack's last nerve.

"You're going to lose on this," he said. "The mayor is on our side, and it won't be long before we convince Johnson and Collingswood to come on board too. You can save face if you just admit you're wrong about this before you get humiliated in front of the entire council, Mackenna."

"I have to go," Mack said, grabbing her purse from her desk drawer.

Russell lifted his shoulders in a hapless shrug. "Don't say I didn't warn you. And don't expect anyone to wipe the egg off your face when the gas turbine is approved."

Mack didn't reply. She remained silent as she followed her fellow councilmember out the door, locked up her office and rushed to her rental car. Despite her attempt to shake off Babin's words, her mind refused. She tried to focus on what would take place before the Honorable Judge Mabel Winters in a few minutes, but this was a simple petition filing on behalf of a client from the Arts Council. Mack could present this case in her sleep.

Instead, her mind drifted to the warning John had given her before leaving her office.

She wasn't naive. She knew stepping into the mayoral race would lead to greater scrutiny of her past. She was prepared to answer anything regarding those skeletons John was so concerned about.

But what about the skeletons even *she* didn't know about?

Ever since her run-in with Ezra at Griffin's birthday get-together last night, something about that company he'd mentioned, Starlight Enterprises, continued to gnaw at her. She couldn't pinpoint exactly what it was, but every time she tried to brush it off, something stopped her.

"It's probably nothing," Mack said.

But what if it is?

She damned that annoying voice in her head to hell. And while she was at it, decided to do the same with Ezra Holmes.

He'd been a thorn in her side for the past four months, and nothing she said to him seemed to matter. He was determined to find *some*thing to justify his witch-hunt.

"He's such a pest," Mack growled.

Her irritation wasn't reserved entirely for Ezra. Mack placed some of it squarely in her own lap. Because, for a second last night, she'd actually thought he looked cute in that charcoal gray newsboy cap he always wore. But then he'd opened his mouth and all Mack could see was the rage he managed to induce whenever she thought about him these past few months. There was nothing *cute* about Ezra Holmes.

Well, except for the obvious. Like the rest of those Holmes men, his handsomeness couldn't be denied. But his stank attitude of late completely obliterated the handsomeness factor.

"Forget about Ezra," Mack said to the empty car. She had enough to worry about.

Just the thought of having to decide whether or not

she should even consider making a run for mayor had Mack wanting to bury her head in the sand and not emerge until Thanksgiving. There were just too many anxiety-inducing items on her plate to worry about whatever Ezra had dreamed up.

Yet, as she pulled into a parking spot in front of the district court building, Mack picked up her phone and set a reminder for herself to Google Starlight Enterprises after she was done with class tonight.

CHAPTER 3

MACK THREW the onions she'd bought pre-diced from the grocery store into the hot skillet and gave them a stir, making sure to coat every piece with the olive oil and butter combination. She scrolled down on her iPad, skimming the recipe she'd looked up earlier today. It was a rare night that she made it home in time to actually cook herself a full meal, but after her class was cancelled because of a busted water main, she suddenly had several free hours on her hands.

She grabbed the container of fresh scallops she'd picked up on the drive home, and ran them under a stream of cold water. Just as she was about to add the scallops to the skillet, Mack stopped.

Seaside.

That's what she remembered, not Starlight or whatever it was Ezra had mentioned. It *was* Seaside, wasn't it?

"No. Wait."

Mack set the scallops on the counter and raced to the linen closet in her back hallway. She flipped on the light and peered up in the corner, spotting the boxes she'd repeatedly asked Carter to pick up. She grabbed the stepladder she kept in the closet, but just as she reached for the first box, she caught a whiff of burning onions.

"Shit!"

Mack raced back to the kitchen. Smoke billowed from the skillet.

"Dammit," she cursed. *The one time I attempt to cook.*

She set the skillet in the sink and tried to scrape the little black chunks of burnt onion that were stuck to the bottom of the pan. It was useless. Putting dinner out of her head, Mack returned to the linen closet and climbed the stepladder again.

She pulled down the first of three cardboard boxes and set it on the floor. She'd skimmed through the boxes just a few weeks ago, ready to toss them out to make room for boxes of her own papers from her office in City Hall.

She uncovered the box, but quickly recognized that it wasn't the one she was looking for. This one had all Carter's Atlanta Falcons crap. She should have known something was wrong with him when she discovered he was a closet Falcons fan, but was too afraid to wear any of it outside the house for fear of losing business from local diehard Saints fans.

She pushed that box to the side and climbed up for the second one. She took the lid off and felt around. Feeling the various file folders, Mack slid the heavy box to the edge and gently brought it down. She carried it over to her circular dining room table and started going through the files.

She knew she wouldn't rest until she confirmed that

it wasn't Starlight Enterprises that she'd glimpsed while going through these files. She needed it to be something else, *anything* else. Ezra could not be right about this.

Mack's fingers stilled as she came upon a light blue file folder.

There it was. Starlight Enterprises.

"I'll be damned," she whispered.

She took a seat and opened the folder flat on the table. Her anxiety level rose with each minute that passed as she read over the documents. Mack drew the laptop from her briefcase and did a web search on Starlight Enterprises. She skimmed over a dozen sites before she finally made the connection.

"That son of a bitch."

She grabbed the file folder and tucked it underneath her arm, hauling her purse strap over her shoulder before tearing out of the condo. Twenty minutes later, Mack pulled up to the gated driveway of the home she'd lived in before her ex-husband decided he was ready for "something new." She jammed her finger on the buzzer.

"Carter, let me in right now," Mack said.

Her request was met with silence, but a few seconds later the electronic gate slid open. Mack swerved her car around the circular driveway, threw it in park and stomped across the walkway and up the marble steps of her one-time home. Carter stood in the open door, his hands braced on his hips.

"What are you doing here, Mackenna?" her ex-husband asked.

Mack slapped the file folder to his chest. "You are one low-down dirty bastard, you know that?"

He let out an exasperated sigh. "Don't you ever grow tired of insulting me?"

"Don't you ever grow tired of giving me a reason to insult you?" she threw back.

"Carter, is everything alright?"

Mack looked beyond her ex-husband's broad frame and caught his new wife, Leanne, entering the foyer. Leanne had been a paralegal in Carter's law firm for years, had attended Christmas and Super Bowl watch parties in Mack's house. Little did Mack know the heifer had been sleeping with her husband.

Leanne could have Carter. Mack was more than happy to be rid of that rat bastard. But it *did* piss Mack off that this pencil-thin, stringy-haired bitch got to live in this house. This was *her* house, dammit. *She* was the one who'd put all the time and effort into decorating it.

"Everything's fine," Carter called over his shoulder. "I'll be done here in a minute. " He turned back to Mack. "What do you want? We were just about to have dinner."

She was reminded of her aborted dinner, and the smoke filling up her kitchen, *and* the damn scallops she'd forgotten to put back in the refrigerator that would probably now spoil.

Dammit!

Her rage ratcheted up another level.

Mack pointed to the file folder Carter still held against his chest. "What is Starlight Enterprises?" she asked him.

The flash of shock on his face was brief, but Mack caught it all the same. She shook her head, unable to keep the derision from her voice. Not as if Carter was due any courtesy from her. He deserved every bit of derision she threw his way.

"You really are an asshole," Mack said. "Did you think I would never find out about this? Why did you hide it; so that I wouldn't get a piece of it in the divorce?"

Carter's jaw ticked, a telltale sign that he was angry. He had some damn nerve. He wasn't the injured party here.

"You screwed me out of everything else in that divorce," Mack pointed out. "Did you really think it would be any different if I knew about this little side deal you had going?"

He set the folder on the brushed chrome foyer table she'd found at an estate sale years ago. She loved that table.

Carter folded his arms over his chest. "If it's no big deal, why are you bringing it up right now?"

She took several steps forward, until only inches separated them. With a sneer, she said, "Because Starlight Enterprises has an interest in BDF Disposal, the same company that won the city garbage collection contract earlier this year. And I've had an investigative reporter up my ass for months because he discovered *your* connection to Starlight Enterprises and thought I knew about it."

If she didn't know him as well as she did, Mack would have thought she'd spotted a flash of guilt cross Carter's face. But he remained silent. The only reaction was that damn tick in his jaw, as if he was growing more and more irritated with her.

"Do you know the kind of shit storm it would cause if this got out? It doesn't matter that I had no idea your scheming ass owned part of this company. The only thing that matters is that, as a sitting council member, I voted to accept the bid of a company that my husband at the time had an interest in."

"I wasn't thinking about you or your little seat on the council when I bought into Starlight Enterprises," he said.

"Of course you weren't. You only think about your damn self." Mack gestured to the file folder. "You do realize I could take you to court over this, right? You purposely hid assets in our divorce. Your buddy is no longer on the bench, so you wouldn't get the same sweet deal you did in the original settlement."

It still pissed her off that one of Carter's law school friends presided over their divorce proceedings. The two of them used every tactic they could to screw her out of every single thing they could.

Except for his precious boat. She still had his speedboat. That boat could rot for all she cared.

"You're not taking me to court over this," Carter said. "If you do, it will just bring more attention to you. People will question whether or not you knew about my investment in Starlight the entire time." He leaned forward, and in a hushed voice, said, "I won't say a single word. I'll let them speculate. Just think of the stink it will cause, Councilmember Arnold."

What she wouldn't give for the chance to slap that cocky smirk off his face.

"I hate you so fucking much," Mack said.

Carter tipped his head to the side. "Now, if you want to work out a deal with my speedboat, maybe we can talk."

"I'd set that boat on fire before I let you have it," Mack said. She poked him in the chest. "You better let me know if there's any other bullshit you were involved in that can be tied to me. And if you want that crap you left at the condo, you have one day to pick it up. Otherwise, it's going in the trash."

"I did you a favor." He slid the folder from the table and held it up to her, that smug grin tilting up one corner of his mouth. "If I'd picked up those boxes when you first asked, you never would have found this."

Mack had never had the urge to spit on another human being before this very moment, but she wouldn't stoop to this bastard's level. She snatched the file folder out of his hand.

"Fuck you, Carter," she said before turning and stomping down the steps.

She got behind the wheel of her car and tore out of the driveway. Five minutes later, Mack pulled into the parking lot of a dry cleaner on Metairie Road. Her hands were shaking so much she could barely grip the steering wheel.

What if the scenario she'd just laid out for Carter had actually happened? What if Ezra had decided to run with whatever information he'd been able to find so far on the connection between Starlight Enterprises and BDF Disposal? Mack knew there was no direct connection that he could make between her and the companies, but that didn't matter in this age of click-bait headline reporting. All it would take was the insinuation that she'd somehow had knowledge that Carter had an interest in Starlight. They'd been married for fifteen years. One of New Orleans's power couples. Of course people would assume she knew.

The scandal it would cause made Mack's breath hitch. Everything she'd worked so hard for; it would all be gone. Her mayoral run? Yeah, right! It would be over before she could ever get it off the ground.

"All because of that asshole."

Mack lowered her head onto the steering wheel and sucked in several deep breaths.

For the first time in months she actually had something to be grateful for when it came to Ezra Holmes. Most journalists would have run with the story. At least he'd practiced some restraint and taken the time to do his due diligence.

Goodness, she actually owed Ezra an apology. And a thank you.

All this time he hadn't been on a witch-hunt at all. She wasn't sure who or what had tipped him off, but he'd had a legitimate reason to look into her background. Ezra had simply been doing his job.

And doing a damn fine job at that. He'd done a better job than both she and her lawyers did back during her divorce. She was sure they'd uncovered every business dealing Carter had been involved in for the past decade, yet this Starlight Enterprises had flown right past them.

Yes, she owed Ezra an apology.

Mack blew out a disgusted breath.

"Well, this should be fun."

*

Ezra's knee bobbed up and down, hitting the underside of the small round table as he checked his watch for the tenth time in the last three minutes. He was giving her thirty more seconds and then he was out of here. He'd told himself not to do this. What possible good could come from meeting with Mackenna Arnold?

Unless she was ready to confess.

"You wish," Ezra mumbled to himself.

It was foolish to even entertain the thought that Mack would cave. She'd fought him tooth and nail since the minute he started investigating her, never backing down from her claims of innocence. Ezra was convinced that even if he displayed all the evidence against her on the jumbo screens in the Super Dome in the middle of a Saints game, she'd continue to deny it. The problem was that he still hadn't found evidence directly tying her to BDF Disposal.

But you're close.

He'd touched a nerve when he mentioned Starlight Enterprises the other night. He'd seen it in her eyes. The way those deep brown orbs had widened with shock had been the confirmation he'd needed. Not only was he on the right track, he was close to pulling into the station.

He wouldn't be surprised if she'd spent these last couple of days trying to figure out how she could spin this story so that she didn't look like the crooked politician she was. But there was no spinning. He'd caught her. Maybe she *was* on her way here to confess. Maybe he wouldn't even have to find the proverbial smoking gun.

Despite the vindication that surged through him at the thought of finally getting a confession out of Mack, Ezra couldn't deny that a part of him was disappointed. Sure, he'd spent all these months investigating her, banking on outing her for using her influence on the city council for her own personal gain. But there was another part of him that had hoped he was wrong about the entire thing.

For years he'd thought Mack was one of the good ones. From the first day he'd met her, when she'd walked into his parents' home wearing a red, black and green sweatshirt with an outline of the African continent on it, Ezra had known she was down for the cause. It didn't matter what the cause was, he just liked knowing that she stood for something. It was disheartening to uncover that even one of the good ones could be turned by the seedy world of politics.

He checked his watch again. He stared at it as the second hand ticked by and the time changed from 10:59 to 11:00.

That's it. He'd sat here for a half hour without hearing a word from her. Ezra was willing to wait for a story, but he expected people to respect his time. The least she could have done was call or text when she realized she wouldn't be here for their scheduled 10:30 a.m. meeting—a meeting time which *she'd* set.

Ezra was halfway to the door when something occurred to him. She hadn't called him to ask for this meeting. She'd sent an email to the public email address that followed his stories. Hell, he didn't know if Mack even knew his phone number.

He returned to the table he'd occupied for the past half hour and clicked into his email app.

"Shit," Ezra muttered.

She'd sent an email forty-five minutes ago, letting him know that she was stuck in court and asking if he could meet her at 11:00 a.m. instead of their agreed upon 10:30 a.m. Not even a minute later, Mackenna walked through the door of the coffee shop. She spotted him immediately and made her way to his table.

"Sorry I'm a few minutes late," she said. "You did get my email, didn't you?"

Ezra held up the phone and nodded. "Yeah, I got it."

"Oh, good," she said with a relieved smiled. "I'd hate to think of you sitting here waiting for me all this time."

"Nope. I'm good," he said. "Just wondering what this is all about."

She pointed to the counter. "You mind if I get a coffee first? My morning has been ridiculous."

He stood. "I'll get it."

Her perfectly arched eyebrows dipped with her frown. "You sure?"

Could he blame her for being suspect? For the past four months he had not extended her a single bit of courtesy. Ezra could practically see his mother shaking her finger at him from heaven. When it came to Mack, his behavior of late did not reflect his upbringing.

"I'm sure," Ezra answered her. "What can I get you?"

"Large coffee. Black."

She reached for her purse, but he waved off her money.

"I've got it," Ezra said. He went up to the counter and returned a couple of minutes later to find her typing furiously on her phone.

"Give me just a minute," Mack said. "I promised my assistant I would get her these instructions before she leaves for lunch." She typed in a few more words then set the phone on the table. "Thank you," she said, smiling as she picked up the cup he'd placed in front of her and took a sip.

That was the second time she'd smiled at him since she got here. It made the hairs on the back of Ezra's neck stand on end.

"Thanks again for agreeing to meet with me," she started.

"No problem," Ezra said. "I assume you called because you're ready to confess?"

"Confess? What is this, church?" she said with a light chuckle. "I have nothing to confess. I was telling the truth when I told you I have nothing to do with Starlight Enterprises. It was all Carter."

His lips twisted in a skeptical smirk. "Come on, Councilmember Arnold. You can do better than that."

"You can stop calling me that, Ezra. You knew me long before I was a member of the city council."

True, but he needed that professional buffer. With the buffer, his mind wouldn't be so quick to wander to places it sure as hell shouldn't be wandering, like how she could make a simple navy skirt and peach button down shirt look like sex.

Don't go there.

Ezra rerouted his thoughts, bringing them back to this woman who very likely had used her influence on the city council to put money into her own pocket. It was his job to expose such corruption. *That's* what he should be thinking about right now.

"You were right," Mack continued. "My ex-husband has an interest in Starlight, but I had no knowledge of it. He hid it from me."

Bullshit.

"Do you really expect me to believe that?" Ezra asked.

"It's the truth. When you mentioned the company's name at Griffin and Indina's the other night, something about it sounded familiar. I remembered running across documents with that name in some of Carter's old paperwork that's been sitting in my condo, but I didn't know exactly what it was about. I thought it was maybe work for a client."

She held her hands out. "Think about it, Ezra. This is a community property state. If I'd known about Carter's interest in Starlight, don't you think I would have brought it up during our divorce proceedings? Why would I knowingly allow him to hide one of his assets?"

Dammit, why was she making so much sense right now?

"So you really didn't know your ex had an interest in Starlight Enterprises, even though the two of you were married for what, ten years?"

"Fifteen," she said.

"Really?" He jerked his head back. He didn't realize it had been *that* long.

"Yes," she confirmed with a nod. "Carter and I were married for fifteen long years, and if you think it's impossible for me not to know everything my husband was involved in, think again.

"Carter and I both had very demanding careers. We kept our business dealings separate, not only for financial and tax reasons, but also simply because it was too complicated. I didn't have the time or desire to be concerned with his practice once we got it off the ground. I had my own career to worry about."

She folded her hands on the table and released a

heavy breath. "I confronted Carter with the paperwork tying him to Starlight Enterprises yesterday."

Ezra leaned forward. "What did he say?"

"He was typical Carter. Cocky. Arrogant. He's built a career out of making sure his clients get all they can in a divorce. He knows every trick there is."

"So why did he hide this from you?"

She shrugged. "Because he could. Who knows, he probably hid all kinds of money from me. I just so happened to learn about this one because you found it." Her mouth twisted up in a small smile. "So, as much as it pains me to say this, thank you for being so tenacious."

Ezra made a production of looking toward the ceiling and over both his shoulders.

"What are you doing?" Mack asked.

"Searching for the four horsemen. Always thought I'd die before you ever thanked me for anything."

She shook her head as she huffed out a laugh. "Don't get me wrong, that apology was *not* easy. But I believe in owning up to my mistakes, and I now realize it was a mistake to accuse you of investigating me for no reason. You had just cause."

"Councilmember Arnold, I didn't want—"

"Mack, or even Mackenna if you still want to be formal," she said.

"Mack," Ezra corrected. "This was never personal. I'm an investigative reporter. As a member of the free press, my job is to root out corruption. That's why I became a journalist."

"I understand that," she said. "And I also understand that your work is a vital part of our democracy. We need people like you to hold politicians accountable."

Ezra put his hands up. "That's all I was trying to do."

"So, does this mean you're done investigating me?" She leaned forward and Ezra's eyes automatically zeroed in on the small gap in her shirt. He saw a bit of white lace and, within an instant, his pants became uncomfortably snug.

"Um, yes," he said. He tore his gaze away from her chest and looked her in the eyes. "If you truly didn't know anything about Starlight Enterprises, there's nothing more for me to investigate."

No matter how much he tried to dismiss it, Ezra couldn't deny the melancholy that suddenly overwhelmed him. He didn't want to stop learning about her. His reasons for investigating Mack had nothing to do with his personal feelings toward her, but as he'd probed into her professional life, he'd learned things that left little doubt about the kind of person she was.

Now that the cloud of suspicion had been lifted, he could acknowledge the admiration he'd begun to feel toward her. She worked hard for the people of her district, especially the children. She was still a politician, but maybe—*maybe*—she was one of the very few good ones out there.

She stuck her hand out to him. "We're good here, right?"

Ezra stared at her hand for a moment before clasping it. "We're good," he said.

"Maybe the next story you write about me can focus on the work I've done as a member of the city council," she said as she rose from the table. Ezra quickly stood. "It's not the juicy political scandal you were hoping for, but I think it's important."

"I'm sure there's a juicy political scandal out there somewhere," he said. "But I can do a write-up on the work you've done for District D, as well."

"Maybe we can set up a meeting sometime in the near future," she said with yet another smile.

Three genuine smiles from Mackenna Arnold.

Guess he shouldn't bother to pick up his clothes from the dry cleaners. The end of the world must be near.

"You've got my email," Ezra said. "I'm ready whenever you are."

She dipped her head in a brief nod before leaving the coffeehouse. Ezra knew he had a list of things to do today, but for the life of him he couldn't remember a single one. He sat back down. He needed a few minutes to process everything that had just happened in the last fifteen minutes. Now that his investigation into Mackenna's wrongdoings was officially over, he needed to think about his next steps.

~

Mack directed her attention to the large monitor fixed to the wall just to her right, where the proposed amendments to the city budget stood out in bright red font. She'd known this afternoon's budget meeting would get heated. Anthony Accorso, the council member from District A, adamantly opposed cuts to his district's recreation department.

Mack understood his frustration, but there were more important items on the council's plate than using taxpayer money to build a new splash park for an area of the city that already had several public swimming pools. She sat back and listened as two of the council members went back and forth, knowing already that the budget item would not be approved.

The door opened and Mayor Lucien Warner, along with the deputy mayor, entered the room. The mayor usually presided over the budget meetings, but he had been delayed by an emergency call with the governor. Mayor Warner nodded toward the council members before taking his seat at the long polished walnut table that faced the raised dais where the council sat.

The discussion over the splash park lasted another ten minutes before Cecil finally banged his gavel.

"Councilmember Accorso, while we can appreciate your desire to provide this attraction to the people of your district, it is simply not in the budget for this year. We must move on to the next item. However, before we do, I'd like to acknowledge Mayor Warner, who now joins us. Mayor, we hope you had a productive call with the governor. We're just about to move into the budgetary concerns surrounding the criminal justice system.

"Speaking of those budget concerns," Cecil continued. He then motion for one of the deputy clerks to come forward. "We have a slight change to the amendments you were previously given."

The deputy clerk distributed several stapled papers to the council members, the people present at the mayor's table, and the one citizen who'd been brave enough to sit in on this afternoon's meeting.

"I move the council accepts—" Cecil started, but Mack cut him off.

"Excuse me, but can we please have a few minutes to look over these new changes?"

Mack ignored his pinched expression and went back to perusing the documents she'd been handed. She squinted at the small print, frowning as she caught what had to be a mistake. Mack picked up the original budget amendments and compared the two documents.

She raised her hand. "I'm sorry, Councilmember Washington, but there seems to be a mistake regarding the budget for the DA's office. The operating budget has been reduced by..." Mack paused to do the quick math in her head. "By nearly fifteen percent."

"That isn't a mistake, Councilmember Arnold."

Her mouth fell open as she looked over at Cecil. "What is the justification for reducing the DA's budget by such a significant amount? Their department is stretched thin as it is."

"The reduction is specifically for the Internal Affairs department," Cecil said. He pointed to Mayor Warner. "Some of us, including the mayor, believe that the DA's office has more pertinent objectives to focus on."

"*Excuse me?*" Mack screeched.

Cecil banged his gavel. "Councilmember Arnold, we will not have a repeat of the last council meeting."

"You will if you think I'll approve this budget cut," she said.

Mayor Warner spoke into his microphone. "Cecil, if I may speak," he started.

Mack turned her attention to her mentor. She did her best to keep her face neutral, but inside she was pleading with him not to break her heart by siding with this ridiculous move.

"The DA's office spends enough time as it is

conducting witch hunts on its own department," Lucien started, and Mack was certain she heard her heart crack in two. She barely heard the rest of his explanation. It was as if he spoke from the other end of a long, foggy tunnel, his words muddled by the silent screams suddenly rioting through her brain.

She could not believe this was the same man who had a framed copy of a front-page news article celebrating his takedown of several corrupt detectives years ago when he worked as an assistant district attorney. What had happened to him? Why was he now coming out as a proponent of less scrutiny for public officials? Something didn't add up.

"With all due respect, Mayor Warner, the Internal Affairs and Public Integrity divisions both serve a very important role in ensuring the constituency that public servants are being held accountable," Mack said. "It is imperative that we dedicate resources to these departments."

"Of course, of course," the mayor said. "It's very important that the DA's office polices itself."

"Yet you support this budget reduction?" she asked.

Cecil cut in. "Councilmember Arnold, we are here to discuss the entire budget. Can you save your argument for when we get to this particular line item?"

Mack put her hands up. "Fine, I'll wait."

As they worked their way through the budget amendments, Mack's attention remained on Mayor Warner. He, at times, seemed disinterested, gazing off at the empty space in front of the table where he and his staff sat. He would occasionally focus on whoever was speaking, but his attention seemed to again drift, as if he had something more important than the city budget to think about, or had somewhere else to be.

The council got so caught up on a discussion about the proposed cuts to the new traffic safety cameras—the budget item the lone citizen had apparently come to discuss—that they had to table the rest of the budget meeting until next week. The moment Cecil banged the gavel, bringing the meeting to a close, Mayor Warner rose from the table and walked straight out of the council chambers, not saying a single word to anyone.

Tremors traveled down Mack's spine.

Something wasn't right here. This was not the man she knew. Mack didn't want to speculate on what could be behind the mayor's odd behavior, but asking her inquisitive mind not to search for an answer was like asking the sun not to rise in the east. And the more she thought about it, the more troubled she became by the answer that was all too obvious.

When she added up the changes she'd observed in him over the previous months—siding with big business instead of the common citizen, his complete reversal on so many issues, and now favoring less scrutiny by the DA's office? There was only one conclusion that made sense.

Lucien Warner, her mentor, her friend, must be involved in some type of corruption.

A sharp pain twisted in the pit of Mack's stomach as she walked to her car, which she'd finally gotten back from the mechanic. She settled in behind the wheel, but couldn't bring herself to turn over the ignition. She was too distracted to drive.

What other explanation could there be for the mayor's bizarre behavior of late? It wasn't as if a corrupt politician was some kind of anomaly. These days, it seemed more common to find someone who *wasn't* on the take than the reverse.

But Lucien? The most upstanding man she'd ever known?

In her internal war over whether or not she wanted to run for mayor, the only thing stopping her was her loyalty to her longtime mentor. But if Lucien Warner was involved in some type of misconduct, not only would she not hesitate to put her name in the ring for mayor, Mack would do everything humanly possible to win.

She knew firsthand what happened when local officials cared more about lining their pockets than serving their constituents. Her family had been forced to leave her great-grandfather's land, having it ripped from under them for the sake of a new highway that now ran through her small northern Louisiana hometown. A highway that hadn't been needed, but that Mack later learned had been a financial boon for the contractor who'd built it. A contractor who happened to be a friend of her small town's local mayor. Their lives had been upended by the same man her grandmother had spent her Saturdays going door-to-door to help get elected.

If Lucien had turned his back on the citizens of New Orleans in order to make a buck, then he'd better get ready for a fight.

"Not so fast," Mack whispered.

Before she made any decisions about running for mayor, she had to know if Lucien was really involved in some kind of corruption. How she would go about doing that, she had no idea.

Maybe you should get Ezra on the case.

Mack snorted a laugh, but then she sat up straight. "No." Mack shook her head. "Don't be ridiculous."

The idea *was* ridiculous, wasn't it?

Yes, of course it was ridiculous. Ezra Holmes would help her off a cliff, or into a jail cell. He sure as hell wouldn't help her look into whatever was going on with the mayor.

Or…maybe he would.

Back at the coffee house, Ezra said he would be on the lookout for the next big political scandal. If the mayor really were into something underhanded, it would be the story of the year.

Mack shook her head as she started the ignition up and put the car in drive.

"Don't be a fool, Mackenna."

Inviting Ezra Holmes into her world was just asking for trouble, and Lord knows she didn't need any more of that in her life.

CHAPTER 4

Mack released a massive sigh of relief when her phone dinged with a text message from Ezra, saying he was at the streetlight at St. Charles and Louisiana Avenues, about ten blocks away. She'd tried to keep herself busy by grading essays, but the entire time her mind had been fully aware of the minutes that continued to tick by with no answer from the text she'd sent him earlier.

She'd called Indina for his number, eliciting a barrage of questions from her best friend, who was afraid Mack wanted to have her brother arrested again. As much as she loved her ex-brother-in-law, Mack was sorrier than ever that Charles had made good on his ill-advised promise to bring in that annoying reporter if he continued harassing her. That incident would only make things more difficult now that she was trying to get Ezra to work with her.

Mack still wasn't convinced she'd fully earned his trust. He'd agreed there was no reason to continue investigating her, but she'd sensed Ezra's lingering skepticism. That was just one reason she wasn't sure how she should approach their upcoming conversation.

Should she lay out her entire case against the mayor and risk Ezra taking the information and abandoning her? Or should she give him just enough to intrigue his investigative nature, but be vague enough that he'd have no choice but to partner with her?

Mack wasn't interested in being a mere tipster, or some anonymous source for Ezra's next big story. She needed a collaborator. Someone who would join her on a deep dive into the mayor's dealings so she could figure out just why the closest thing she'd had to a father figure since her grandfather passed away thirty years ago had suddenly turned his back on so much of what he once believed in.

Her door buzzer sounded, and Mack's heart nearly burst through her chest like the Kool-Aid Man from that old commercial.

Shit! She had to calm down. She was wound way too tight these days.

She made her way to the keypad and spoke into the intercom system.

"Mackenna Arnold."

A second of faint static came through the speaker, followed by, "Hi. It's Ezra."

She told him the condo number and buzzed him in. A few minutes later, there were two sharp knocks on her door.

Mack opened it and had to forcibly ignore the sensation that began to swirl in her stomach. She'd felt it when she spotted him at the coffee house yesterday morning. Hell, she felt it every time she was around Ezra Holmes.

And wasn't that the most ridiculous thing in the universe?

The man had been a thorn in her side for months. He'd doggedly pursued a story meant to take her down, hell-bent on destroying her career—her *life*. But did that stop the millions of tingles cascading along her skin whenever he was around? *Noooo.*

Mack noticed a hint of an after-five shadow covering his jaw that hadn't been there yesterday morning and her knees grew a little weak.

Ugh. *Get it together, girl!* Weak knees were so twenty years ago.

"Thanks for coming," she said, moving aside so he could enter.

Why did her foyer seem to shrink the minute he walked in? Oh yeah, because Ezra Holmes was built like a linebacker, with broad shoulders that seemed as if they could hold the weight of the world without yielding an inch. Yet, when it came to his personality, he was the complete opposite of the stereotypical muscle-bound type. It's the one thing that had always fascinated her about him.

He wore his usual newsboy cap, this one a rich navy to match his navy slacks, with the buttoned front brim cocked slightly to the left. Wire-rimmed glasses sat atop the bridge of his broad nose.

Suspicion emanated from him in waves, his gaze cutting from one spot over her shoulder to another, as if he expected someone to jump out of the shadows and pounce on him. That wouldn't work. She needed him to trust her if they were going to work together. And Mack was determined that they *would* work together on this.

She held her hands up. "Before we get into why I asked you to come here—"

"Why *did* you ask me to come here?"

"I'm getting to that," she said. "But before I do, can we please establish that we both may have said some things to each other over the past few months that we regret?"

"Do you regret any of the things you said to me?"

"I regret calling you psychotic," Mack said.

His forehead furrowed. "You never called me psychotic."

"Not to your face."

One corner of his mouth tipped up in a grin, and some of the tension began to ease.

"I regret calling you a crooked politician," he said. "That label is unfair now that the issue with BDF Disposal has been put to rest."

"Thank you," Mack said. She hadn't realized how much she needed to hear him say that. Of all the things she could be accused of, corruption was the one that Mack just could not abide. She despised corrupt politicians.

She gestured to the living room. "Come in," she said. "And you can stop looking around as if you're waiting for the boogeyman to jump out at you. No one else is here."

"Can you blame me?" Ezra asked.

She wished she could, but after considering things from his point of view, Mack understood why he would still be suspicious. He'd taken her word for it when she told him that she'd had no knowledge of Carter's involvement with Starlight Enterprises, but if the tables were turned, Mack doubted she would have been so quick to forgive and forget.

"No, I can't blame you," she answered. "But I hope you now recognize that you can trust me. All I'm asking is that you hear me out."

"I still don't know what it is you want me to hear, Mackenna."

She noticed that he didn't say anything about trusting her. Mack pointed again to the living room. "Let's sit. Then we'll talk."

He gave her the barest nod before they set out for her living room. As he walked alongside her, Mack watched as he overtly sized up her apartment.

"I used to drive past this place every day when I worked for the paper. I watched the outside transform from an old abandoned warehouse to this swanky complex, but this is my first time seeing it on the inside. This is nice."

"Thanks. Carter bought it three years ago so that he could have a place in the city. Because, you know, that five minute drive from Old Metairie was just too long a commute," Mack said with a snort.

"Tell me how you really feel about the ex," he said as he studied the original George Rodrigue Blue Dog painting on the wall.

"Believe me, you do *not* want me to get into that." Mack laughed. "We'd be here all night and into the morning."

In a distracted murmur, Ezra said, "That sounds good to me." His eyes immediately shot to hers. "I mean...uh. I wouldn't mind listening to you *talk* until the morning. Wait, that doesn't sound any better, does it?"

Mack waved her hand and laughed in an attempt to

lighten the suddenly intense air around them. "I know what you meant," she said.

That didn't stop a barrage of butterflies from fluttering in her belly. She did a mental eye roll. She felt like such a damn teenager.

Mack wrapped her palms around the back of a dining room chair, squeezing the brushed aluminum bar in an attempt to release the pent up adrenalin racing through her bloodstream.

"So, can I get you anything to drink?" She peered up at the clock above the built-in wet bar. "I didn't realize it was so close to dinner. Have you eaten? I can order something."

"Will whatever you have to tell me take that long?"

"Uh, no. It doesn't have to," she said.

"Not that I mind," Ezra quickly interjected. "I'm done with work for the day, so I don't have to rush off or anything."

"Well, in that case, it may take a while," Mack said. "It all depends on what you think about my theory."

The curiosity clouding his expression intensified. "I'm definitely intrigued."

"I'd hoped you would say that." She pointed to the phone. "Are you sure I can't order something? There are several restaurants nearby."

"I had a big lunch." He patted his taut stomach. Mack stopped just short of licking her lips. "But you can go ahead and order dinner for yourself."

"Actually, I don't need anything heavy either, but I am a bit hungry." She gestured to the stack of papers on her dining room table. "I've been grading essays since I got home and I completely forgot about dinner. Can you give me just a few minutes?" Mack tilted her head toward the couch. "Have a seat."

She went into the kitchen and pulled out a wedge of pecorino romano and the sliced smoked prosciutto she'd picked up at the deli yesterday from the fridge. She broke off a few chunks of cheese and added them to a small plate with the meat, some green olives, and a few crackers. Then she poured a glass of the Malbec she'd received as a gift from a grateful photographer she'd represented on a copyright infringement case and carried it all over to the couch.

She set the plate and wineglass on the sofa table and folded her legs underneath her. Mack had never recognized just how small her sofa was until faced with the limited space remaining between her and Ezra.

"What, no scotch?" Ezra asked, gesturing to the glass she'd just brought to her lips.

She looked at him with a raised brow. "You know my usual drink?"

"Only because you don't typically run across a woman who's a scotch drinker."

She took a sip of the dry red wine and said, "I'm not your typical woman."

"You don't have to tell me that."

If she'd received his response in a text or email, she could have mistaken his words for an insult. But there was nothing insulting about the low timbre of his voice or the way his gaze dipped to her lips. Mack's tongue darted out and passed over her bottom lip, and Ezra's stare grew even more intense.

Awareness pulsed in the air, thick and sultry and shockingly potent.

Mack jumped up from the couch. It was suddenly too intimate a setting.

"Why don't we move to the table?" she asked.

She went over to the dining area and, with one hand, gathered the essays scattered across the circular glass table. She arranged them into a haphazard pile. Ezra arrived with the plate she'd left on the sofa table. He took the glass from her hand and set both on the table.

"Thanks," Mack said. She motioned to the seat across from where she'd been grading papers. "This is better, right?"

He hunched his shoulders. "Sure. This is fine."

She nodded, sucking in a deep breath. She was usually more put together than this. The fact that Ezra Holmes had her this flustered was something Mack knew she'd chew on for the rest of the night. This was *not* her.

"So," Ezra said. "Are you finally ready to tell me what this is about?"

"Yes," Mack said with more enthusiasm than the question deserved. She needed to remember just why she'd brought him here. Gulping down the remainder of her wine, she started, "When we met at the coffee house, you said you were on the lookout for the next big political scandal."

Ezra nodded. "There's always a scandal lurking somewhere. It's whether or not it's a *big* scandal that's usually up for debate."

"What if I told you that I could deliver a scandal bigger than anything this city has seen in years?"

"I'd say that's a pretty big order to fill considering we currently have an ex-mayor who's still serving time in a federal prison." Ezra's eyes narrowed. "Does this have something to do with our current mayor?"

She didn't confirm or deny, she just continued to stare at him.

"Do you have something on Mayor Warner, Mackenna?"

She held her hands up. "I don't have anything concrete just yet, but I have my suspicions."

"Based on?"

"Based on his actions of the last six months or so," she said. "To be honest, it's been a little longer than that. I'd say more like a year."

"What are you talking about?"

She folded her hands on the table. "I first noticed that something was off with the mayor during a news conference last fall, when he expressed support for a new riverboat casino near the Poland Avenue Wharf."

"I was at that news conference. What's wrong with him supporting a new casino?"

"I know for a fact that Lucien Warner has never supported the idea of a second casino. He was firmly against both the riverboat and land based casinos when they first began to sprout up in south Louisiana. I received emails from a few of my former law school classmates after they heard of his reversal on the matter, because he was just that strongly opposed to it back when we were all in school."

Ezra shrugged. "People change their viewpoints. The casinos have been a good revenue stream for the city."

"You don't have to tell me that. The city council just went through a budget meeting. But this issue with the casino is just the start. A number of the positions Mayor

Warner has taken this past year have me scratching my head. I don't know if it would be as noticeable to someone who hasn't known him for as long as I have, but he isn't behaving like the man I've known since law school."

Ezra leaned back in his chair and crossed his arms over his chest. "There has to be more than flip-flopping on a couple of issues," he said. "Mayor Warner has a seventy-one percent approval rating. Why would he jeopardize that by doing something that would raise people's suspicions?"

"That's just it. His flip-flops haven't been on issues that would draw much attention. But when I start to add them up, it's glaringly obvious that something is going on." She slid over a legal pad she'd been working on earlier. "I jotted down a list of the things I could think of just off the top of my head that the mayor has changed course on over this past year."

As she read the list to Ezra, Mack noticed how his expression shifted from skeptical to wary to thoughtful.

"I hadn't heard about the changes to the evacuation routes," he said.

"That's because the item was scrapped before it ever made it to the city council's agenda, but there was a lot of discussion going on behind closed doors to improve evacuation routes out of the city. Mayor Warner did a complete one-eighty on it."

Ezra leaned forward and put his elbows on the tabletop. He folded his hands and lightly tapped his lips with his fingers, his expression both confused and contemplative. With a hunch of his shoulders, he said, "There are only two things I can think of that would cause the mayor to change course so drastically. Either he's getting paid to do it, or he's being forced to do it by someone who has something really damaging against him that he doesn't want to come out." He looked over at her. "Those are pretty serious accusations to make against a sitting mayor, but based on what you just laid out, it seems reasonable."

Mack wasn't sure if she was relieved that Ezra had reached the same conclusion she had, or if she was heartbroken. The hollow feeling in her chest indicated the latter.

"I thought the same," she said. "The final straw for me was this gas turbine the council has been debating in my district. I'm firmly against it, as is the mayor. Or, I should say, he *was* against it. I discovered the other night that he wrote a memo that he now supports the construction of the new utility plant. I came straight from that council meeting to Griffin's birthday party."

"Ah," Ezra nodded. "So that's why you were in such a mood that night."

"I was not in a mood that night," she argued. "You were provoking me, as usual."

"Me?"

Mack rolled her eyes. "Ezra, you've spent the last four months provoking me."

"I had good reason."

"Yes, you did," she acknowledged with a sigh.

"You do know that I was only doing my job, right?"

She nodded. "I do." She rolled a slice of prosciutto around a chunk of cheese and popped it in her mouth. She chewed for several seconds, swallowed, and asked, "Do you now believe that I wasn't involved in any wrongdoing?"

"Haven't we been over this already?"

"You never said whether or not you believe I had nothing to do with it," she said.

His eyes locked with hers. "You've convinced me."

Mack studied him for a moment. She thought about pushing just a bit further and asking if he trusted her, but decided against it. Instead, she said, "I don't remember if I said this before, but I'm sorry about that thing with Charles."

"You mean when he barged in on our family picnic, slapped handcuffs on me and shoved me in the back of a police cruiser? That thing?"

"Yes," Mack said. She felt her cheeks heat up. "Charles thought he was helping. He's always been overprotective of me."

Ezra reached over and picked up a piece of Romano from her plate. "It sounds as if your brother-in-law is more protective of you than your husband," he said before biting down on the hard cheese.

"Ex-husband," she corrected him. "And that has always been the case. I was happy to divorced Carter, but I don't think Charles would let me divorce him. Not that I would ever want to. It's nice to know he always has my back," she said. "However, he can get a little heavy-handed with the brotherly love. Again, I apologize that the whole thing ever happened, especially in front of your family."

"Apology accepted," Ezra said. He dusted his fingers off on his shirt and resumed his reclined pose. "It did open up a dialogue with my eight-year-old nephew about how I never want him to see the inside of a police cruiser, but Athens and I could have had that conversation without me actually seeing the inside of one myself."

She rolled her eyes. "It's going to take a lot for me to make this up to you, isn't it?" Mack asked.

"He did clamp those cuffs on pretty tight," Ezra said.

Chuckling at the playful smirk edging up the corners of his lips, Mack asked, "Is there anything I can ever do to make this right?"

The lighthearted vibe in the air evaporated as Ezra's eyes dropped to her lips. A current of electricity crackled between them, stimulating Mack's nerve endings.

Neither spoke, the only sounds were the hum of her air-conditioning unit turning on and faint ambulance sirens coming somewhere from street level. Ezra's eyes continued to study her lips, then they traveled up her face until they connected with her eyes.

He was the first one to break eye contact.

"I, uh, I should be going," he said. He slapped his hands on his thighs and rose.

Mack stood so abruptly she sent her chair rocking back. Ezra's reflexes were quick. He caught the chair before it crashed to the floor.

"Thank you," she said. "I don't know when I became so clumsy. Maybe it's the wine."

"You're a scotch drinker. I think you can handle one glass of wine just fine," Ezra replied.

Mack knew her clumsiness had nothing to do with the wine, but acknowledging the perplexing feelings reverberating throughout her brain was not on the table. She'd save that for later, when Ezra's keen gaze was no longer studying every inch of her face.

"So, what do you think?" she asked as she led him to the foyer. "Am I being paranoid about Mayor Warner? Do you think maybe these are all just coincidences?"

"You're a smart woman, Mackenna. I think you know the answer to that."

She nodded. "It's not just paranoia."

"I doubt it," Ezra said in agreement. "I've worked in this business long enough to know that when things seem like coincidences, they usually aren't. There's at least something here that warrants digging a little deeper."

Mack released a relieved sigh. "I was hoping you would say that. In case you hadn't realized it, that's the reason I asked you to come over."

"You want me to look into the mayor," Ezra said.

She hunched her shoulders. "Well, you were able to uncover information about Carter that my team of lawyers all missed. You obviously have superior investigation skills."

His brow cocked and a mischievous glint sparkled in his eyes. "Why Councilmember Arnold, did you just give me a compliment?"

Mack had the horrifying suspicion that she was blushing. What in the heck was the matter with her? She hadn't blushed in years.

"I just figured if anyone could find out what's going on with the mayor, it's you," she said.

He fitted the cap back on his head and pulled the brim down to where it cast a shadow over the upper half of his face.

"I'll check out a few sources and see what I can find. Whether this turns out to be a big scandal or not, it's worth looking into it. I'll be in touch."

"Thank you, Ezra."

"You're welcome," he said. He waved good night as he crossed the hallway and boarded the elevator.

Mack waited until the elevator doors closed before going back into her apartment. She closed her front door, thumped the back of her head against it and slid down to the floor. Cradling her head in her hands, she took several deep breaths and tried to convince herself that she was doing the right thing.

~

*E*zra stood on the sidewalk, facing the steel and glass doors outside Mack's condo building. Was it really less than twenty-four hours since he'd last stood here, debating whether or not to press the button next to her name?

His stomach twisted in a dozen different ways, just as it had yesterday. He'd been taken aback by his readiness to fall hook, line and sinker for the scenario she'd proposed. It wasn't until he got home last night that it even occurred to him that he should at least question what she said about the mayor.

He'd stayed up half the night fact-checking the different issues Mackenna claimed Lucien Warner had flip-flopped on. It hadn't taken Ezra long to recognize that her suspicions had merit. Just as she'd pointed out, the mayor's numerous reversals weren't on hot button topics that would garner a lot of attention, which is probably why they had all flown under the radar.

Ezra had texted her a half hour ago, asking Mack if she could meet with him to discuss a couple of things he'd found in his initial search on the mayor. She'd asked if he wanted to come over so they could go through it, and he'd answered yes so fast he nearly broke his damn finger in his haste to respond.

That's what had given him pause.

Forget the stuff he'd uncovered about the mayor. It was his inability to curb the excitement that sprouted in his gut just at the thought of seeing Mack again that was, by far, the most troubling discovery of the last twenty-four hours. Especially when just a few days ago it was the mental image of her being led down the steps of City Hall in handcuffs that conjured that kind of excitement within him.

Seeing Mackenna Arnold in handcuffs was no longer his goal. Ezra was now convinced that whoever had sent the anonymous tip insinuating that she had knowledge of BDF Disposal's ties to Starlight Enterprises had made the same mistake he'd made.

She may not be guilty of wrongdoing, but that didn't mean he should be so quick to let go of the healthy skepticism he brought to every story either. He'd done that once before, and it had bitten him in the ass.

Just remember, you're here for work.

And therein lay a huge piece of this messy, problematic puzzle. There was no good reason for him to be here at all. He could have easily emailed Mack the bits of information he'd uncovered so far. Meeting her in her apartment for the second night in a row wasn't necessary.

Then again, when it came to his preferred journalistic style, Ezra favored face-to-face encounters over electronic ones. It was harder for him to gauge a person's attitude over email. He relied on nuance. He wanted to look into a person's eyes when he questioned them, or when he imparted information he'd discovered.

Sure, that's why you're here.

He could throw out every excuse in the book, but

the truth remained. When it came to Mackenna, he just liked seeing her face. Period.

Ezra threw his head back and released a frustrated curse. He wasn't sure if he was up to bearing the burden of dealing with this insatiable attraction to her. It would require willpower he doubted he possessed. It had been hard enough to fight it back when he thought she was a crooked politician. Now that that barrier had been removed, what was there to stop his overactive imagination from conjuring things he damn sure shouldn't be thinking about when it came to Mack?

"You're here to do a job," Ezra reminded himself.

Sucking in a fortifying breath, he pressed the button next to her name, calling up to her condo. He stood there for a full two minutes waiting for her to answer. Nothing happened.

He pressed the button again. And waited.

Just as he reached into his pocket for his phone, he heard her sexy voice just to the right of him, "Ezra?"

He turned to find her a couple of steps away, carting a brown shopping bag in each hand.

"I was hoping I could make it back before you got here," she said. She held up the bags. "I went to August Moon. I didn't want to invite you here at dinner time and not have anything to feed you the way I did last night."

"You didn't have to do that," Ezra said, taking both bags from her hands.

"Yes, I did," she said as she punched in a code and held the door open for him. They boarded the elevator to her seventh-floor condo.

When they entered the apartment, Ezra noticed at least a half dozen boxes stacked by the door.

"You moving?" he asked.

"No, my ex-husband is finally sending someone over to get the rest of his crap," she said. "I've been asking him to do so for over a year. I guess me finding those files on his little side business finally lit a fire under his ass. I'll bet he's hiding a bunch of other stuff in there."

"Maybe you should have a look before he comes to get them," Ezra said.

She waved off his suggestion. "I don't care anymore. Carter can have a million dollars stashed away in the Caymans, and I still wouldn't want it. He doesn't seem to understand that the only thing I want is to be rid of him."

"I would have thought you *were* rid of him," Ezra said as he set the bags containing the Chinese food on the table. "He was the one who filed for divorce, right? I remember when it happened. It was kind of a big deal around the city."

"New Orleans's power couple's big split. You don't have to remind me," Mack said. "I lived it."

All of New Orleans had lived it. Ezra was still at the paper when news broke about Carter Arnold telling his wife he wanted a divorce while the two were dining at one of the French Quarter's most popular restaurants. According to those who witnessed it first hand, Carter didn't even make an attempt at discretion. It was as if he wanted to embarrass Mackenna in the grandest way possible.

It had always been Ezra's opinion that she never should have married that son of a bitch in the first place, but what did he know?

He folded his arms across his chest. "So, if the

divorce was your ex's idea, why is he still bothering you?"

"Because he's an asshole," she answered. "Carter likes to win. He screwed me over in our divorce, not because he needed the money, but because in his mind screwing me over means he won. It's all a game to him. That's why he was still cocky as ever when I confronted him about his connection to Starlight Enterprises. He knows there's nothing I can do about it because I would never jeopardize my position on the city council. It's his way of showing me that he can still win whenever he wants to."

Ezra shook his head. "I'm surprised you stayed with him for as long as you did."

"Carter may have sucked as a husband, but he was good for my career." She hunched her shoulders. "There are perks to being one half of New Orleans's power couple."

"You seem to be doing just fine without being a part of a power couple," he said. "I think you give him more credit than he deserves."

A small smile tipped up the corner of her mouth. "You're probably right."

"No 'probably' about it."

"If I could do it all over again, I would have been the one to ask for the divorce, and I would have done it a few years ago, back when I first suspected he was messing around." Mack cocked her head to the side. "How did we get on the subject of my ex-husband and his side-piece turned wife?"

Ezra pointed to yet another cardboard box, this one next to the sofa. "His crap is crowding your apartment. I'm happy to change the subject if you are."

"Yes, please," she said. "Let's get to why you're really here." She shoved the paper bags toward him. "You start pulling out these cartons and I'll get us some plates and drinks. Bottled water okay? Or maybe some wine?"

"Water's fine," he said.

Ezra began unpacking the Chinese food. "You think you ordered enough?" he asked as he set the fifth carton on the table.

Mack returned with two plates, two sets of chopsticks and two bottles of water.

"I wasn't sure what you liked, so I ordered a bunch of stuff. I figure whatever we don't finish tonight will be lunch and dinner for me tomorrow."

She dished out the food, and five minutes later, they were both deep into the sesame chicken and vegetable stir-fry while Ezra reviewed the bits he'd been able to piece together about the mayor so far.

"In my initial search, I was mostly concerned with finding out what the mayor has done in the past, compared to how he has been voting over the last two years. Earlier today I covered the walls in my living room with butcher paper. I plan to build a huge timeline where I can physically chart Lucien Warner's voting habits since he became mayor. I'll color-code it so that I can get a better picture of how much his habits have changed over the years."

"That's brilliant."

He shrugged. "It's the way my brain works. I need to see the visual for things to sink in." He hefted the leather messenger bag his mother had bought him ten years ago, when he first started at the paper, onto the table. "For now, I think we should start by going back to when the mayor worked as a prosecutor at the DA's office."

Ezra pulled out several file folders. "These are all the public statements I could find from Mayor Warner's early days working for the city. You never know what a person has said in the past that will prove to be significant later."

A smile drew across Mackenna's face. "I knew I'd found the right man for this job."

"Pace yourself, Councilwoman. That's two compliments in two days' time. I'm not sure I can handle many more."

She burst out laughing as she gathered the remnants of their dinner, then invited him to join her in the living room. Ezra was about to sit on the sofa, but she pushed him out of the way and began to spread the transcripts out. She picked up the first one, and slid down onto the floor with her back against the sofa.

Ezra moved her coffee table by two feet, because there was no way in hell his big body would comfortably fit between it and the sofa. Then he followed suit, sitting on the floor next to Mack. Together they scoured the documents. After about an hour, Ezra stood so he could stretch his legs.

"Are you bored yet?" he asked her.

"Oh, my God, yes!" Mack said. "I'm dying here. This is worse than pre-trial discovery. I should have my students read through these so they can get a taste of what it's *really* like to be an attorney." She yawned as she stretched her arms above her head. "Most of them think being a lawyer is like what they see on television. If you go in expecting to recreate your favorite *Law and Order* episodes, you're in for a rude awakening."

"Is that what happened to you?"

She grinned. The sight was so stunning it damn near killed him.

"Do you remember that old TV show *Matlock*?" she asked.

"It rings a bell," Ezra said, reclaiming his spot on the floor between the sofa and coffee table.

"My grandmother loved it. I watched it with her every week and wanted nothing more than to help people the way Ben Matlock did. But I knew television was make-believe. I had ample opportunity to witness how real lawyers operated." She uncapped her water bottle and peered over at him as she took a drink. "I was raised by my grandparents. They fought my mother for custody, so I had a firsthand view of the way the process works."

That single revelation set off a swarm of questions in his head. Why didn't her grandparents trust her birth mother to raise her? Did she know her birth mother at all? How had that entire episode influence her life? Had it played any part in the person she was today? It had to. You didn't go through something like that as a child without it affecting you.

He'd known her for nearly twenty years, yet there was still so much Ezra didn't know about her. But he got the sense that she wasn't ready to share, so instead of seeking answers to his multitude of questions, he asked, "So when did the turn from law to politics happen?"

She did another of those arms-above-the-head stretches. The motion caused her cotton top to pull taunt across her breasts and, for a moment, Ezra forgot how to breathe. He sat there transfixed as she tilted her head from side to side, working out the muscles in her neck. The light overhead cast shadows on her smooth, chestnut-brown skin. It begged him to reach out and touch it. The barest brush of his fingertips would be enough. He just wanted to know if her skin felt as soft as it looked.

"The move to politics was gradual, but probably inevitable," she said, jerking his attention back to their conversation. "Lucien Warner had a lot to do with it."

"He was somewhat of a mentor to you during your years at Tulane, right?"

She nodded. "I once heard him argue for both the negative and affirmative in a mock discussion on corporal punishment in schools, and for months later I couldn't decide if I was for or against it. I knew I wanted to follow in his footsteps, so when he stepped into politics, I naturally gravitated to it."

"He still doesn't seem like the law school professor type," Ezra said.

With an amused lilt in her voice, she asked, "And what exactly is the law school professor type?"

"When I think 'law school professor' I picture some old guy with gray hair, elbow patches on his jacket and a pipe hanging out of the side of his mouth."

Mack laughed. "I'm sure that's what my students see when they look at me."

"We both know that's not the case with you. You're the exception to the rule."

Her full, decadent mouth eased into a slow, mischievous smile. "Now who's the one handing out compliments?"

"Just calling it as I see it," Ezra murmured.

The temperature in the room spiked as Mack's gaze dropped to his lips. Arousal pulsed between them, thickening the air. Ezra was captivated by its hypnotic allure as her tempting smile continued to draw him in, and he realized he liked it a lot better when he wasn't her adversary.

A voice in his head picked that particular moment to remind him that he wasn't her friend either. He was here to do a job.

Ezra cleared his throat and sat up straight. "Yeah, so I think we're off to a good start when it comes to digging into the mayor's background."

"Yes." She nodded. "This is a good start."

Ezra pushed himself up off the floor and began collecting the transcripts. He didn't need to be here right now. He shouldn't be here at all.

Just because he'd agreed to work with Mack on this investigation, it didn't mean he had to be around her. In fact, it was probably better if he kept his distance. That way he could concentrate on the task at hand instead of focusing on the way the light played against her skin or how her glorious head of thick, brown hair framed her perfect face.

There was one significant thing that had become alarmingly clear to him tonight. Now that he no longer looked at her as a criminal, it made it easier to look at her as a woman.

And *that* scared the hell out of him.

CHAPTER 5

"Hey, Uncle Ezra! Wanna see my crossover?"

Ezra walked up his brother's driveway and stopped underneath the basketball goal where his nephew, Athens, stood with an NBA regulation Spaulding.

"What do you know about a crossover?"

"I know I can do one. I learned it on YouTube. Look!" He tried bouncing the ball through his chubby legs—baby fat according to his sister-in-law—but didn't quite make it, losing control of the ball as he reached for it behind his back. The basketball bounced toward Ezra, who stopped it with his foot.

"Close," Ezra said. He handed the ball to his nephew. "Keep practicing. LeBron didn't become LeBron overnight. It takes time." He pointed to the house. "Your dad in there?"

He nodded. "Aunt Indina too."

"Uncle Reid isn't here yet, is he?"

"Nope."

Thank God. It was good to know at least some things were still operating as normal. After spending half the week texting and emailing Mackenna, Ezra had forgotten what normal felt like. If Reid had managed to make it somewhere on time, Ezra would question whether or not he was living in an alternate universe.

He rubbed Athens on the head and said, "Keep at it," before walking up to the front door of Harrison's two-story brick home in New Orleans's Lakeview area. It was the kind of house and neighborhood their mom and dad had always dreamed of for their kids. Ezra didn't tell him enough, but he was damn proud of the home Harrison had built for his family.

"Hello?" Ezra called as he entered the front door.

"We're in here," came Indina's voice from somewhere in the vicinity of the kitchen.

At the same time he heard Reid's booming laugh not too far behind him. No doubt Athens was trying to wow him with his sweet basketball moves. Ezra turned and waited for his younger brother to join him at the front door.

"What's up?" he said, accepting Reid's handshake/half-hug greeting. "How was the game the other night?"

"Pelicans lost, but that suite was nice." Reid leaned over and murmured in a loud whisper. "Even nicer was hooking up with the girl who refilled the refreshments." He released a low whistle. "She taught me some stuff even I didn't know."

Ezra just shook his head. His younger brother was the very definition of a man-whore, and at twenty-nine Reid showed no interest in changing his ways.

"What about that issue you were having with Alex?" he asked as they made their way to the huge kitchen and breakfast area.

Reid snorted. "He's still being a hard ass, but that's Alex for you."

"Did he let that guy go?"

"Jessie?" Reid nodded. "Yeah. To be honest, I can't really blame him. Jessie's a good plumber, but his work ethic ain't worth shit. Maybe losing a good job with benefits will force him to get his act together."

"What are you two gossiping about?" their older brother asked as Reid and Ezra entered the kitchen.

Ezra went straight to Indina and gave her a kiss on the cheek before walking over to the breakfast bar and greeting Harrison in the same way he had Reid.

"Just some drama that's been happening at Holmes Construction," Ezra said.

"Everything okay?" Harrison's forehead creased in concern as he poured coffee into a mug and handed it to Ezra without him even having to ask.

Reid waved that off. "It's all good. At least it is for now. If Alex decides to bring in some chump and mess up the vibe the plumbers have going, it won't be pretty."

"It's his company," Harrison said.

"That's exactly what I told him," Ezra said.

Indina butted in. "And now I'm bored with this conversation. Can we please get down to business? I have to meet Griffin in an hour."

"What, he's going to paint your toenails or something?" Reid laughed. "Talk about a man that's whipped."

"No, I promised him we could try out the new vibrator I got from this adult store in the French Quarter."

The three men in the room all groaned with such ferocity it shook the walls.

"Would you stop that shit," Reid said. "Nobody wants to hear about that!"

"Seriously, Indina!" Harrison said. He tossed the bagel he'd been eating in the trash, as if Indina had spoiled his appetite. Ezra stared down at his cup of coffee and realized that she'd spoiled his. It was his default to remain prepared for any outrageous thing that came out of his sister's mouth, but Indina had a knack for shocking the hell out of him. She thrived on it.

A loud crash came from outside.

"What in the hell was that?" Indina asked.

"A basketball hitting the garage door," Harrison said.

"I wondered where all those dents came from," Reid said.

"Athens suddenly thinks he's going to play in the NBA one day, but his coordination is worse than mine." Harrison chuckled. "Give me a few minutes. It's time for him to come in and take his bath anyway."

As Harrison headed for the front door, Reid headed for the refrigerator.

"Can you grab me a bottle of water while you're in there," Ezra asked.

"You need anything, Deenie?" Reid called.

"For you to stop calling me Deenie," she answered. Then she turned to Ezra. "So, what did Mackenna want with you the other day? It didn't sound as if she wanted to murder you, which was a surprise."

He shrugged. "It's nothing."

"Really? After all the months you spent being a pain in her ass? Come on, Ezra. What did she want?"

"It's—"

"Okay, where were we?" Harrison asked as he came

back into the room. He put up a hand and yelled toward the stairs. "I want to hear water running." He shook his head. "Was it so damn hard to get us to take showers when we were his age?"

"Yes," Indina said. "For some reason boys just love smelling like the outside. I don't understand it."

"It's the caveman in all of us," Reid said. "Smelling like sweat and dirt means you don't mind getting your hands dirty. That shit appeals to women."

"And that's why you will grow old and alone with nothing but a bunch of venereal diseases to keep you company," Indina said.

Ezra and Harrison both laughed. Reid didn't seem to find their sister's prediction funny.

"When are we going to discuss Mama's foundation?" Reid asked. "That's what we're here to talk about, right?"

"Right," Harrison said. "I filed the paperwork for the 501(c)(3)."

"What's that?" Reid asked.

"It designates the Diane Holmes Foundation as a non-profit and gives it tax-exempt status."

"Damn, I need to get me one of those," Reid said. "Half my paycheck goes to taxes."

Ezra snapped a dishtowel, catching Reid behind the ear. "It's not for individuals, fool."

"Ow!" Reid reached back and jerked the towel from his hand.

"Don't start," Indina told them both. She turned to Harrison. "The last time I met with Willow, she jotted down some criteria we should use for the scholarship essay on a yellow notepad. You don't know where she put that notepad, do you?"

Harrison shook his head.

"Hey, where is Willow anyway?" Reid asked. "I haven't seen her since the picnic where this one got thrown in the slammer." He hooked a thumb in Ezra's direction.

"She's in Pensacola visiting her sister," Harrison answered.

"So who's watching the kids?" Reid asked.

"They're my damn kids. Who do you think is watching them?"

Reid put his hands up in mock surrender. "Damn, man, don't take my head off. I was just asking a question."

"When is Willow coming back?" Indina asked.

Harrison shrugged. "How in the hell am I supposed to know?"

"What do you mean by that?" Ezra asked. "You don't know when your own wife will be back home?"

"Mommy's not coming back?"

They all turned to find Athens standing at the base of the stairs in his Ironman briefs, a bath towel draped over his shoulders. The tortured look on his face reminded Ezra of how he used to feel whenever his mom would leave. He loved his dad, but he'd been a mama's boy through and through.

"Didn't I tell you that mom would be back by the weekend?" Harrison said as he walked over to Athens. He took the towel from his son and used it to dry his hair, which was now cut in a short mohawk. "Go get in your pajamas. I'll put the meatloaf and mashed potatoes in the fridge and order pizza for dinner instead."

"Extra pepperoni," Athens said. "And no green stuff."

"They're called peppers," Harrison said. "And I said I was putting away the meatloaf and potatoes, but you still have to eat some of the broccoli."

Ezra laughed at the way Athens's face scrunched up. He couldn't blame him. Pizza and broccoli were not his idea of an appetizing dinner either.

Indina, however, wasn't laughing. She wasn't even smiling. Her face held the same expression it held that time she caught Ezra chopping the hair off her Barbie dolls back when they were kids. At least the look was directed at Harrison this time around.

"How long has Willow been at her sister's?" Indina asked as soon as Athens was out of the room.

"None of your business," Harrison answered.

"Harrison—"

He sighed. "Indina, please, just stay out of this."

"What am I missing?" Reid asked around a mouthful of the meatloaf and white bread sandwich he'd just taken a bite of.

"Nothing," Harrison said. "Let's get back to the foundation.

Ezra kept his eyes on Indina. He hadn't expected her to relent, but she must have recognized that stubborn set to Harrison's jaw. They all knew that look. Once his older brother adopted it, you could forget about getting anything out of him.

Harrison continued. "As it currently stands, Indina and I are the two primary signatories for all official documents regarding the foundation, but if you or Reid would like to be added, I don't see a problem with that."

"I'm good," Reid said.

"Same here," Ezra said. "I'm here for whatever the

foundation needs, but I don't have to sign anything. The simpler, the better."

"That was my way of thinking when I asked Jake to set it up," Harrison said. "It's not as if any of us have experience running a foundation. It would just add to the confusion if there's too many in charge."

"Actually, that's something I wanted to talk to you all about," Indina said. "I was talking to one of my sorority sisters the other day and she volunteered to step in and run the foundation until we raise enough money to hire someone. Sheena has been the head of several non-profits. She's in Lake Charles, but she's planning to move to New Orleans soon to work as the finance manager for Mack's election campaign."

Ezra's head jerked back. "Election campaign?"

"Oh, shit," Indina said. "Don't say anything." She looked at Ezra. "Well, I assume you already know that it's top secret, but you two need to keep a lid on it."

Reid put both hands up. "I have no idea what you're talking about."

"Neither do I," Ezra admitted. "Why would Mack need a campaign manager? She just won her second term on the city council. She has another four years."

Indina frowned at him. "Wait? You don't know about her considering a run for mayor?"

Ezra's entire body went numb with shock.

"Mayor?" Harrison asked. He nodded. "I'm surprised she'd run against Warner, but she's probably the only politician in this city who has the chance to beat him."

The numbness swept through Ezra's his bloodstream, shutting down every thought as if systematically flipping off a light switch on his emotions.

"You really didn't know?" Indina asked him.

Ezra shook his head.

"I just assumed that's the reason Mack wanted your number the other day. She didn't go into detail about *why* she wanted it, but I couldn't see any other reason."

Ezra thought he'd known the reason she wanted him to work with her, but apparently he'd been mistaken. She wanted him to do her dirty work for her. And like a damn fool, he'd jumped all over the chance, thinking that her only intention was to uncover corruption.

He should have known better. Mackenna Arnold was a politician. Didn't he know better than to trust a damn politician to look out for anyone but herself?

The moment they were done at Harrison's, Ezra headed for Mack's Warehouse District condo. It wasn't until he was parking his car at the curb that it occurred to him that he should, at minimum, check to see if she was even home. She was. She answered his text message in a matter of seconds, and buzzed him up as soon as he rang the doorbell. She was waiting for him when he emerged from the elevator on her floor.

"Hey there," she greeted. "What's up?"

"You're running for mayor?" Ezra asked, striding past her and into her apartment.

"Who told you? Indina?"

"Is it true?" he asked her.

She closed the door and turned to face him. Crossing her arms over her chest, she answered, "Yes."

Ezra was certain he'd reached his limit when it came to the amount of rage that had built up on the drive over, but he was wrong.

"So all that stuff you fed me before was just a load of bullshit. This has nothing to do with you wanting to root out corruption. This is about me helping you find dirt on the mayor so you can use it against him in a political campaign."

"No," she said.

"Do I look stupid to you, Mackenna?"

"If you would stop talking for a minute so I can explain."

"I don't want your explanation." He ran a hand down his face. "I should have expected this shit from the very beginning. An honest politician is like a damn unicorn."

"I haven't lied to you."

"Really?"

She threw her hands up and let them flap down on her hips. "Fine, if you want to say that I lied by omission, then sure, go ahead. I concede that I could have been a little more forthcoming, but, Ezra, I swear that nothing I asked you to do has anything to do with me wanting to run for mayor. I don't even know if I *do* want to run for mayor. I'm still trying to decide."

"So exactly what *is* my role in all this? If I find enough dirt for you, then you'll decide to run?"

She gestured to the living room. "Can we please sit down and talk about this?"

He folded his arms over his chest and widened his stance. "No."

She tipped her head back and groaned at the ceiling. "Can I at least get you to agree to hear me out?"

He was too pissed to answer her verbally. The most Ezra could manage was a curt nod.

"Thank you," she said. She brought her fingers up to her temples and rubbed. "I already told you how much I love and respect Lucien Warner."

"I don't need to hear this song again."

Anger flashed in her eyes. Despite the fury she'd stirred within him, Ezra couldn't help but notice how glorious those deep brown eyes appeared when she was angry.

"I won't say that I've never considered running for mayor, because that would be a lie. But I never thought I'd consider doing so this soon. In my mind, I've always envisioned it as a peaceful passing of the baton once Lucien was done with politics."

"What changed?"

"You know what changed," she said. "Lucien changed. The only thing that would make me consider running against him is if I thought Lucien was no longer in the job for the right reasons. His actions over the last year point to that."

"So you're running for mayor out of some altruistic sense of duty? That's the story you're going with?"

"It's not a story," she said. "And I haven't made up my mind about whether or not I'll run. I haven't even set up an exploratory team yet. I've only talked to a few people about it." She blew out a weary breath. "Ezra, don't you see how hard this is for me? Whether you believe me or not, I don't want to run against Lucien Warner. Nothing would make me happier than to discover that this has all been a mixture of coincidence and paranoia on my part."

He wanted to believe her. Damn did he want to believe her. But he would be a fool to let this woman dupe him. He'd learned the hard way what could happen when he put his trust in the wrong person. It had cost him his job. It could have cost his old newspaper a lot more if his editor hadn't caught the mistake in time.

Ezra moved past her, and captured the door handle. Before turning it, he called over his shoulder, "You'll have to find someone else to do your dirty work for you. I'm not the guy for the job."

He walked out, closing the door behind him. By some miracle, he managed not to slam it.

~

Decked out in the expensive workout gear she'd bought earlier this year when she made a pact with Indina to start going to a gym, Mack grabbed a muffin from the stash she kept just for days like today, and carried it, along with a mug of coffee, over to the couch. She wasn't in the mood for working out on a good day. She sure as hell wasn't going to attempt to do it today.

Setting the coffee on the table in front of her, she lifted the stack of papers Ezra had left—transcripts from some of the mayor's past speeches—and started perusing them. Pride overwhelmed her as she read the words, mentally hearing them in Lucien's soaring, eloquent voice.

How could a man who spoke words of such hope possibly be on the take? It defied explanation. Lucien loved the people of this city too much to hurt them. There had to be another reason for his behavior over the past year.

Mack tried to read more of the transcript, but tossed it on the sofa cushion after a few minutes. It was only a distraction from the issue that had been plaguing her for the past three days, and not a very good distraction at that.

She'd first donned these workout clothes as a way to tear her mind away from what took place with Ezra just a few yards from where she sat, hoping some time on the treadmill or elliptical would give her something else to concentrate on. Maybe she *should* have gone to the gym, though she doubted that would have worked either. Mack wasn't sure what it would take to free her mind of Ezra's words and the look of complete and utter distrust she'd witnessed on his face.

If she'd been forthcoming about her potential mayoral run, all of this could have been avoided. Now, Ezra was right back to thinking she was nothing but a crooked politician.

"Dammit," Mack cursed.

Why hadn't she come clean from the very beginning?

She'd asked herself that question a thousand times since Ezra walked out of this apartment. The answer was simple: she hadn't thought about it. Even though the deadline to declare loomed in her not-so-distant future, she was still so unsure whether she would mount a mayoral run that it simply had not occurred to her that she should mention it to him.

Yet, as she looked at things from his point of view, Mack realized she would have had the same reaction Ezra had. She'd just started to gain his trust after months of him thinking she'd been engaged in corruption. Then she goes and asks him to investigate the man whose job she wanted to take?

Yeah, definitely not the smartest thing she'd ever done.

She cradled her coffee mug in her hands, contemplating her next move. She had to figure out how she was going to investigate Lucien now that she was back to doing it on her own. Maybe she could get another reporter?

Mack shook her head. Ezra Holmes may have been a pain in her ass these past four months, but it's because he took his job seriously. He was a damn fine reporter. She wasn't willing to put her trust in anyone else in the media. Not with something this sensitive.

"Looks as if you really are on your own," Mack murmured.

And now that she *was* on her own, she would have to work twice as hard. She had about six weeks before the qualifying period where she would have to declare her candidacy for mayor. She had to contend with the very real possibility that she wouldn't uncover substantial evidence against Lucien before the deadline.

You could always go back to being just a lawyer.

Mack mentally chided herself. She'd engaged in this argument with herself too many times before. It was her go-to whenever she started feeling overwhelmed. When constituents started breathing down her neck, or her fellow council members gave her grief, she'd start fantasizing about how much simpler life would be if she just returned to practicing law full-time.

But she was way too invested in this city to ever turn her back on its people. There was too much work to do. The people in District D had put their trust in her. They'd put the hopes and dreams of their children in her hands. She couldn't trust anyone else to step in and finish the work she'd started.

That's why, whether or not she had Ezra Holmes by

her side, she had to find out if Lucien was engaged in activity that would harm the people they'd both sworn to serve.

Her phone rang, and for the barest second, Mack hoped it would be Ezra. Her hopes were dashed when she saw it was Juliette Cannon.

"Hi Juliette," Mack answered. "Do you need me to look over the noise ordinance again?"

But that wasn't why Juliette had called. As Mack listened to her fellow council member, her blood pressure steadily rose until it reached a boiling point. Mack grabbed her laptop from where she'd left it charging on the dining room table and logged into the secured email system the council used to communicate.

She saw red.

"Where are they?" she asked Juliette.

She ended the call, and headed straight for her bedroom. She changed into her favorite charcoal gray suit with the pleats at the hem, the one that made her feel like a total badass. Instead of carting her laptop with her, she snapped a picture of the email on her phone before leaving her condo.

Twenty minutes later, Mack pulled into the driveway of Cecil Washington's Mid-City Victorian. She recognized Russell Babin's black BMW and came as close to snarling as she ever had in her life.

These bastards were actually plotting against her.

She marched up to the front door, but took a moment to catch her breath before knocking. She couldn't allow them to see her rattled. Appearing cool, calm and unshakable would unnerve Cecil and Russell way more than if she stalked in raging against them.

Mack knocked on the door. A few moments passed

before Cecil's wife, Adele, answered it. Mack usually liked Adele, but right now all she saw was fault in the woman's choice of husband. Recalling whom she'd been married to for fifteen years, Mack decided she had no room to fault anyone their spousal choice.

"Hi Adele," Mack said. "I believe a couple of my fellow council members are holding a meeting here. I'd like to join them."

Adele Washington looked like a deer caught in headlights. She shook her head, but moved to the side. "I... uh...I guess that's okay. They're in the library. Here, let me show you."

As she followed Adele through the house, Mack couldn't help but notice how beautifully and expensively decorated it was. Before retiring and joining the city council, Cecil worked as an attorney at the same firm that first recruited Mack years ago. She'd turned them down, something she believed her fellow council member still held against her.

Mack often wondered if she hadn't made a mistake back then. She was never officially on the payroll at her ex-husband's firm, but she'd spent the first few years of their marriage helping him to lay the groundwork for it. If she hadn't spent so much of her energy helping Carter build his firm, maybe her world wouldn't have been so tied up in him for all those years.

When they arrived at the door to the library, Adele knocked twice and waited for her husband's answer.

"It's Adele," she said. "There's someone here to see you." Adele opened the door and Mack walked in.

"Good evening, Cecil. Russ." She nodded to both men. "I have to say, I'm feeling a little left out."

Cecil quickly stood. "What are you doing here, Councilmember Arnold? This is a private matter."

She held up her phone with the snapshot of the email. "Sorry to be the one to break this to you, but it isn't a private matter. Just a tip, the next time you plan a secret meeting to discuss *my* district, make sure you don't just hit 'reply all' on an old email. Those emails go to the entire council."

"Shit," Russell Babin said, shaking his head.

Mack took a seat in the wingback chair that faced Cecil's rich, cherrywood desk. She crossed her legs and folded her hands in her lap.

"Okay, gentlemen," she said, infusing extra cheerfulness into her voice. "Let's continue."

"This has nothing to do with you, Ms. Arnold," Russell said, though Mack wasn't sure how he managed to get the words out through his clenched jaw.

She gave him a nonchalant wave. "Oh, we're not in the council chamber right now. No need to be so formal, Russ. And, again, if you're discussing District D, which is what this email you sent to Cecil says you wanted to discuss, then it *is* my business. Now, I want to know what was so pressing about my district that it warranted a private meeting with the head of the city council at his home?"

"I'll remind you that even though District D is your district, it is still a part of this city, and our job as members of the council is to do what is best for the *entire* city, not just our individual districts," Cecil said.

"And what do you think is best for the entire city?" she asked.

"The gas turbine."

She'd been expecting that answer, yet her body still tensed with a combination of anger and annoyance.

"You know what, I'm happy you two decided to have this little powwow away from an official city council meeting," Mack said. "We need to drill down to the heart of this without the formalities getting in the way. Tell me right here, right now, why you feel so strongly about them building this gas turbine in *my* district?"

"We've been over this already, Mackenna. It needs to be close to a water supply, and there's land just north of Leon C. Simon Boulevard that the energy company believes will be ideal."

Mack straightened up in her chair.

"Wait a minute," she said. "The area north of Leon C. Simon was never discussed as a potential site."

"That's the reason Russell and I are meeting right now," Cecil said.

She mentally mapped out the neighborhoods in her district. "There isn't any available space north of Leon C. Simon," she said.

"We can make space," Russell said.

A light bulb went off in her head. Mack released a low chuckle. "Sometimes I'm still struck by my own naïveté," she said. "You're going after the senior center, aren't you?"

She should have known. Russell Babin had been making noise about the senior citizen center on the northern edge of her district since before Mack had been elected to the council. He considered it an eyesore, and wanted a new one built. But the center held sentimental value for the people in her district. There was a huge mural painted by a local activist who'd been gunned down several years ago. Knocking down the building would mean getting rid of the mural, and Mack refused to do it. And she wouldn't allow anyone else to do it either.

There had to be more to this than Babin finally getting rid of the senior center. These two wouldn't be pushing so hard for this new utility plant if there weren't something in it for them.

"What are you both getting out of this?" Mack asked.

"What are you insinuating, Councilmember Arnold?" Cecil asked.

"I'm not *insinuating* anything. I'm straight up asking what kickback are you both getting from this? Is this a favor for a longtime client? What is it?"

Cecil leaned forward in his chair. "Despite what you may think of yourself, you're still relatively new to the politics of this town, so maybe you don't know how business is done in this city. If one of the largest companies in New Orleans—one that employs hundreds and helps to keep this city afloat—wants the council to consider a new gas turbine, then we owe it to them to at least explore the idea."

"And I don't have to remind you the benefit this would bring to the homes and businesses in the Uptown area," Russell added.

"And I don't have to remind *you* that the homes and businesses in the Uptown area are not my first concern. Since when is it appropriate to weigh one set of constituents' needs over another? That's not how this works."

"That's exactly how this works, Mackenna. Stop being so damn naive. The revenue generated by the businesses in the Uptown area, and the property value of those mansions on St. Charles Avenue, mean more to this city than the people in your district. Deal with it."

She couldn't have been more stunned if he'd walked up to her and slapped her across the face. "The fact that you have the gall to say that out loud tells me just the kind of person you really are, Russell. Not that I didn't already know."

"This plant *will* happen, Ms. Arnold," Babin said.

Mack stood. "I'm done here," she said. If she spent another minute with these people she may just lose it. "If you thought I was opposed to the gas turbine before, you haven't seen anything yet."

She was positively shaking with anger as she marched out of the library and out of Cecil Washington's house. If they wanted a fight, they'd just found themselves one.

CHAPTER 6

As HE STOOD in line behind a group of high school girls in their plaid skirts and black and white saddle oxford shoes, Ezra kept an eye on his usual table at the coffee shop where he sometimes worked. It was the last remaining table with an available outlet. He'd allowed the battery on his laptop to drain down to hardly anything, a clear indication that he wasn't in his right mind. His laptop was his most important tool. He never left himself in this kind of predicament.

Thankfully, his table was still available after he'd picked up his cafe au lait. As he unpacked the laptop from his messenger bag and plugged it into the wall outlet, he noticed a copy of the Advocate someone had left on the table next to his. Disappointment squeezed his chest as he caught the name of a former colleague on the byline, above the fold.

That used to be *his* spot.

Before his misguided decision to put all his trust in one source—a source Ezra had known in his gut he shouldn't have trusted—he had been the one who enjoyed having that prime spot most days of the week. He was the go-to journalist at his old paper, the one that colleagues had come to expect to get the big stories because he'd built his name and career from the ground up. He'd been on his way to being editor-in-chief.

He'd had it all yanked away because of the stupid mistake of trusting a liar who'd fed him bad information in an attempt to get even with an old business partner.

The top on his coffee cup popped off, splashing hot coffee on his fingers. "Dammit," Ezra cursed. He hadn't realized he'd been squeezing the paper cup.

He adjusted his chair so that his back was to the wall, then opened the laptop. He first went to Twitter to see what was trending nationally. It had taken Ezra a while to warm up to the platform—he couldn't wrap his brain around why people would want to get their news in 140 character chunks—but after he got the hang of it, he was all in.

He scrolled through his Twitter feed, scanning the mix of news, sports scores, horoscopes and memes about this past weekend's episode of *The Walking Dead*. A tweet from a local neighborhood watchdog group made Ezra sit up straight.

NOLA Mayor Warner Changes Course on School Voucher Program.

Ezra clicked on the group's Twitter handle, then again on a link to an article that had been posted to the group's stellar blog. It recapped statements the mayor had made last night at a dinner celebrating the 100th anniversary of one of the city's high schools. While there, the mayor announced that he no longer opposed the governor's school voucher program, which allowed parents to send students to schools outside of their district.

It was a complete about-face from an issue the mayor had placed at the center of his election campaign. He'd vowed to champion all schools—making them better so that parents wouldn't have to choose. He railed against how the voucher program gave state money to for-profit institutions, instead of using that money to fix what was broken in public schools. His commitment to elevating all schools, especially those in poorer districts, was one of the reasons Ezra had supported the guy. Now he was for the vouchers?

Unease trickled along Ezra's spine. Something wasn't right here.

Why would the mayor all of a sudden champion a program he so adamantly opposed for years? Could it be that he'd bowed to the demands of those businessmen and women who invested in those for-profit schools? Could it be that he now had something to gain from them, something financial?

Could it be that Mackenna was right?

"Shit," Ezra muttered as he powered down his laptop and slipped it back into the leather messenger bag.

He considered sending Mack a head's up, but then thought better of it. With the way he'd left things the other night, he wouldn't be surprised if she cursed him out over text message. It wouldn't be any less than he deserved. As he thought about it over these last few days, Ezra realized how harsh he'd been. He could make the case for his behavior being warranted, but it was a weak argument at best. She hadn't outright lied to him. She didn't owe him any explanation. But he did owe her an apology.

Ezra headed for City Hall, but when he got there, her assistant informed him that Mackenna was at the Arts Council of New Orleans. Indina had told him a while ago that Mack took part in a program that provided pro bono legal help for struggling artists, musicians and writers. He was impressed as hell that, despite all the things on her plate, she still made time to help out those in need. It squared with so many other things he'd read about her while investigating her connection to that garbage company.

Over the past four months, the only thing that had kept him from falling head-over-heels in love with this woman was his insistence that she was into something shady. Now that he knew she wasn't a corrupt politician—that she really was as upstanding and courageous as she'd been painted in the numerous articles he'd read about her—Ezra had no doubt he was a goner.

But he couldn't think about his ever-increasing infatuation with Mack right now. He needed to focus on the mayor, and what uncovering a corruption scandal involving the city's top politician would mean for his own career.

Feverish anticipation bubbled up inside him.

Ever since the incident that had led to the implosion of his credibility with the paper, Ezra had been seeking that one story that would jumpstart his career again. This could be it. Exposing the well-known, well-respected mayor of a major American city as a fraud was the type of news story that put a journalist's name on the Pulitzer list.

Pie in the sky? Maybe. But it wasn't out of the realm of possibility.

He just needed to stay focused on the true goal here. This was about investigating the mayor, not getting lost in Mackenna's deep brown eyes or fantasizing about how soft her skin must feel. As long as he kept his head on straight and concentrated on the job at hand, he didn't have anything to worry about.

He pulled into an available parking spot on Gravier Street and took the elevator up to the building's eighth floor. He confirmed with the Art Council's receptionist that Mack was the in-house legal council for today and, thankfully, that she wasn't with a client.

"The phone lines are being worked on right now, so I can't buzz her," the receptionist said. "If you give me a minute I can run back there and see if she's busy."

"Can I just go back there?" Ezra asked.

"I can—" the receptionist started, but a trio of musicians who entered the suite, all carrying their instruments, interrupted her.

"Just point me in the right direction," Ezra said.

The receptionist graced him with a grateful smile and gestured to the hallway. "It's the last door on the right."

He made his way to the office and rapped twice on the door before opening it just a crack. The minute he saw the tears streaming down Mack's cheeks, Ezra rushed into the room.

"What happened?" he asked, closing the door behind him. She looked up at him with surprised eyes. They were glistening and gorgeous as hell.

Focus, Man!

"Mackenna, what's wrong," Ezra asked. He walked around her desk and put a hand on her shoulder.

She pointed at the computer. On the screen was the same blog post he'd read this morning.

"I just talked to a fellow council member who was at the event last night," she said. "He confirmed that the mayor had a 'change of heart' about the voucher program." She used air quotes and snorted in disgust.

She looked up at him, her brown eyes luminous with the tears she'd shed. "I didn't want to believe it was true," she said. "This entire time, I've been praying that I was being overly paranoid. That all these flip-flops were just a bunch of coincidences, and that my mind was somehow inflating them." She shook her head. "But I can no longer deny what's right in front of me."

She pulled a tissue from the box on her desk and held it up to her nose. She looked so sad, so vulnerable. It gutted him.

Fighting the urge to wrap her up in his arms, Ezra took a couple of steps back and perched on the old building's deep windowsill.

Mack looked over at him and tilted her head to the side, confusion blanketing her face. "What are you doing here?"

Ezra gestured to her computer. "I read that same article this morning. Like you said, it's hard to deny what's right in front of you."

She shook her head, softly blowing her nose into the tissue. "I still can't wrap my head around all of this. It's as if corruption is everywhere around me."

Ezra frowned. "What do you mean by that?"

"I'm having…issues…with a couple of city council

members over a new utility plant they want to build in my district. I just found out last night that they want to knock down a senior center to make room for it. It's something Russell Babin has been advocating for a long time, and I suspect it's because an old family friend is a building contractor who could very likely get the building contract."

"So the utility plant is just a front?"

"Oh, no, they definitely want the new utility plant in District D, even though all the power from it will go to District B. Babin finally getting his way with the senior center is just an added bonus." She picked up the wadded tissues and tossed them into the wire wastebasket next to the desk. "As for Mayor Warner, this business with the voucher program solidifies it for me. He has to be on the take."

"You really think so?" Ezra asked.

She hunched her shoulders. "What other explanation is there? I worked on the official letter he sent to the governor's office opposing the voucher program. If there was one thing I never thought he would change his mind on, this is the one. He has been adamantly against the program from the very beginning." She sniffed. "Either someone is blackmailing him, or he's on the take. There's no other explanation for it."

Another stream of tears began to roll down her cheeks. Ezra pushed away from the windowsill and stooped so that he was eye-level with her. He brushed her tears away with his thumbs.

"I'm sorry," he whispered.

She turned to look at him and Ezra nearly lost the ability to breathe. Her tear-stained cheeks made her look even more vulnerable. Vulnerability was not a word often used to describe Mackenna Arnold. Capable, steadfast, no-nonsense. Never vulnerable.

But that was the only description that came to mind as he stared into her luminous eyes. She was hurting right now. And all Ezra wanted to do was make it better. He cupped her jaw in his palm and slowly brushed his thumb over her soft skin. He heard her swift intake of breath. The sound sent a tremble down his back, stopping at the base of his spine.

"Does...does this mean you're willing to help me again?" she asked in a hushed voice.

He nodded. "I think you're onto something with the mayor."

"What about me using you for my own political gain?"

He dropped his hand and stood. After a second, he said, "I still don't know what to believe about that."

Mack's eyelids slid shut. "Dammit, Ezra," she muttered.

"It doesn't matter," he said.

"Of course it matters." She stood, pushing the chair back so hard that it hit the wall behind her. "You need to trust me if we're going to do this."

"I don't trust easily, Mackenna." He folded his arms over his chest. "Whether or not I believe you intended for me to help you find dirt on the mayor so that you can run against him has nothing to do with this. Your intent doesn't change the fact that the mayor is possibly involved in some kind of corruption. That's what I plan to focus on."

"So we're going to investigate the mayor together, even though you think I was purposely trying to use you?"

He hunched a shoulder. "I'm okay with that if you are."

She pitched her head back and let out an exasperated sigh. Ezra knew he was being a hard ass, but that's the way things had to be. He was willing to work with her, as long as she understood that whatever she shared would be met with skepticism until he could independently verify it. His name had been tarnished enough. He wouldn't allow it to happen again.

"We'll figure out a way to work together," he said. "We may not have the same goal in mind, but we both have something to gain from figuring out just what the mayor is up to."

"And what's your goal?"

"The same goal I had when I was investigating you. Political corruption sells papers. Or, in this day and age, I guess you can say it gets clicks." He rounded the desk and sat in one of the mismatched chairs facing her. "It also gets you noticed on a national stage. I want to break the kind of story that will make my old bosses at the paper sorry they ever let me go."

"So this is about revenge for you. Or is it about getting your old job back?"

"There is no old job to go back to," he said. "The paper folded, remember?"

"But we have *The Advocate* now. They took on some of the reporters from the old paper."

"I'm looking beyond the local level. I want a national paper or magazine. I also feel it's my moral obligation as a journalist to expose corruption, especially when it has the potential to affect so many vulnerable citizens."

Mack stared at him from across the desk. Her eyes

still held a hint of that sheen from her earlier tears. The sight had the same gut-punch affect that it had on him earlier.

This was going to be so damn hard. The effort it would take to detach his emotions from what he was doing would be monumental. But he would do it. All he had to do was remember what was at stake.

His career.

Being romantically involved with Mack would compromise everything he stood for as a journalist. It would cloud his judgment. He knew this for a fact, which was why he had to nip these feelings in the bud.

Wait a minute. Who said that *she* would want anything to do with *him* romantically?

Yeah, there was a mutual attraction. He was done denying that. But it didn't mean that Mack wanted there to be anything more meaningful between them. This was about exposing the mayor.

"Are we good here?" Ezra asked.

"Can you at least consider that I wasn't trying to use you before?" Mack asked.

"Will it really make a difference to you?"

"Yes," she said. "I would own up to it if it were true, but it isn't, Ezra. I didn't intentionally set out to use you to do my dirty work for me."

Several heavy moments slipped by before he finally nodded. "Okay. I believe you."

Those eyes he couldn't help but obsess over lit up.

"Good." She leaned forward and stuck her hand out to him.

Ezra debated the wisdom of touching her. His overactive imagination had already put too many enticing scenarios in his head. But if they were going to do this, he would have to learn how to deal.

He captured her outstretched palm.

"Let's get to work."

~

Mack scooped the last of the documents from the printer bed, and then arranged them in order by subject on her dining room table. She and Ezra had agreed to start with the mayor's most startling and controversial reversals over the past year, and work their way back from there. They'd been at it for a week already. Mack had a feeling that when she finally looked deep enough, she was going to find that these changes with the mayor had started happening a long time ago.

She thought back to when it first occurred to her that something wasn't quite right. It was the mayor's abrupt dismissal of the head of the sewage and water board—a longtime colleague who, as far as Mack was concerned, had done a fine job. When Mayor Warner replaced him with the son-in-law of a disgraced businessman who was currently serving time for fraud, it had struck Mack and several of her fellow council members as strange. But she'd trusted Lucien too much to question his judgment.

Not anymore.

She felt like the biggest fool for not speaking up sooner. Throughout the year, as the mayor made questionable move after questionable move, she'd made excuses, because she couldn't bring herself to face what had been right in front of her. Now it seemed as if she was on a collision course to having an all-out battle with the one man she'd trusted above all others—even above her own husband, back *before* she learned Carter was a lying, cheating sack of shit.

"Goodness, is there any man you can trust?"

Ezra Holmes's face immediately popped into her head.

Mack tried to block out the image of his whiskey brown eyes rimmed with a hint of light hazel, and the way they looked in those wire-rimmed glasses that drove her downright crazy. Just because the man was sexier than sin, it didn't mean she should let her guard down. But she also recognized that it would be just as bad to equate Ezra with Carter and Lucien. She should at least give him the chance to show he was untrustworthy before lumping him in with all the other men who had let her down.

Her door buzzer sounded, scaring the shit out of her. With a hand to her heart, Mack went over to the security panel and buzzed Ezra into the building. She was waiting for him at her front door when he stepped off the elevator. He wore khaki slacks, a white button down shirt with a navy vest over it, and his signature newsboy style cap. She was coming to love that cap.

He held up a plastic bag. "I brought dinner this time," he said. "Po'boys from Mother's."

"That sounds perfect," Mack said. It had been ages since she'd visited the world-renowned eatery.

"And dessert." He held up the second bag. "Mini chocolate ganache cakes from Sucré."

"You had me at dessert," she said. She gestured for him to come in. "We'll have to find somewhere else to eat. The dining room table has become Research Central."

"It's a po'boy. We can eat them standing up if necessary. But wherever we eat them, let's do it now. I didn't have lunch and I'm starving."

She got plates, napkins and a couple of cans of soda, and brought them into the living room. Ezra had already unwrapped the sandwiches from their brown paper wrapping.

"I was feeling the fried shrimp, but went instead with roast beef because I didn't know if you were allergic to seafood."

"You could have called or texted me," she said.

"I wanted dinner to be a surprise." His smile was almost too much for her to handle. "Consider it my apology for being a bit of an ass last week."

"I'm not entirely sure an apology is necessary," Mack said, stuffing some of the meat that had fallen onto the paper back into her sandwich. "You had your reasons for behaving the way you did."

"Would you please just allow me to be the gentleman my mother raised and seek your forgiveness?"

Mack couldn't help but laugh at his frustrated expression. "Forgiveness granted," she said. "I'm ready to wipe the slate clean and start fresh if you are."

"I am," Ezra said. "From here on out, we're partners in this. Let's just leave what happened in the past behind us."

Once they were done with their sandwiches, Mack brewed a pot of coffee and served it with the mini chocolate cakes Ezra had picked up from one of the city's premier bakeries.

She sat in her favorite spot on the floor, with her back against the sofa, poring over the first batch of documents Ezra had received through the Freedom of Information Act.

"Lucien's reversal on the voucher program still stands out as the most shocking," she said. "There wasn't any indication that he'd changed his mind, and nothing I'm seeing in these transcripts of past school board meetings would refute that."

"That's why we can't rely on just the school board meetings when it comes to this voucher program," Ezra said. "I teach my students that the first rule of investigative journalism is to look beyond the obvious. Maybe we dig a little deeper into the backgrounds of those running these for-profit schools and try to figure out who stands to profit the most from all of this."

She acknowledged his plan with a nod as she took a sip of her soda. She pointed the can at him and asked, "You teach?"

Ezra nodded. "It's actually my full-time job now that I'm no longer with the paper. I still freelance as a reporter, of course, but teaching provides a steady income."

He took a bite of the decadent cake. Mack squeezed her thighs together at the sight of him licking chocolate from his finger.

Sweet Jesus.

She could use some air. And a cold shower. And some sex. A little sex wouldn't hurt one damn bit.

"You, however," Ezra continued, "have a steady stream of income as a member of the city council. Why do you still choose to teach? Just the paperwork alone must take up a lot of your time."

Mack cleared her throat. If he ate any more of that cake in front of her she just might start whimpering.

"It's only one class a week," she said. "I remember how important it was for me to have a good mentor while going through law school, and figure this is my way to give back. The students I teach are gaining practical experience through the pro bono program at the Arts Council." She braced her elbow on the sofa cushion and rested her head against her fist. "It's not the easiest job I've had, but it's the most rewarding."

"Is that what you tell yourself when you're seconds away from strangling one of your students?"

She barked out a laugh. "You understand the struggle."

"Hell yes, I understand it." He chuckled. "Not a week goes by that I don't talk myself out of flipping a desk."

"Indina tells me that I'm saving their future clients from headaches."

Ezra snorted. "She must have told you that pre-Griffin, because these days she doesn't talk about anything else."

"Those two are so sweet together it's sickening, isn't it?" Mack said. "But I'm happy for them both. I like Griffin. He's good for her."

"Yeah, I like him too. He fits in well with the rest of us Holmes boys."

"I can see that." She ran her finger along the rim of her coffee mug. "You know, I've always been so jealous of you Holmeses."

Ezra's brow wrinkled. "Why would you have to be jealous of us? Most of the Holmeses consider you to be a part of the family."

She could have taken that as a compliment if not for that *most* he'd tacked on. Mack considered letting it pass, but something compelled her to say, "So, am I reading too much into your words, or am I right to think that you aren't included in the 'most' that considers me to be a part of the family?"

The answer was obvious in the guilt-ridden look he shot her way.

"Wow, Ezra," Mack murmured. "I knew I wasn't your favorite person, but I didn't realize just how deep it ran."

He balanced his wrist on his up-drawn knee, toying with a bit of loose string he'd plucked from her carpet. "It's not as if I've always hated you. I just…"

"*Hate?* Okay, so it's even worse than I first thought."

Ezra blew out an exasperated breath. "Hate isn't the right word," he said. Then he shrugged. "But, if we're being honest, I have to admit that for a long time my feelings toward you have been…complicated." He glanced over at her before returning his attention to the string. "It was hard for me to even look at you after you married Carter."

"Don't use Carter as your excuse," she said. "You didn't like me even before Carter stepped into the picture."

He turned stunned eyes on her. "Says who?"

"Stop with the pretense. This has been going on since my college days when Indina and I would come to visit. You would walk out of the room as soon as I walked in."

He dropped his head back onto the sofa cushion and exhaled a deep sigh toward the ceiling. "Not liking you wasn't the reason I always walked out of the room, Mackenna."

"Then why?"

He lolled his head to the side, one brow cocked.

"Oh." She frowned. Then her eyes widened as understanding dawned. "Oh!"

"Yeah." His gruff laugh didn't hold much humor. "The minute you entered a room my body pretty much reacted on its own. It was better for me to leave than to embarrass myself."

Mack thought back to those days and how hurt and confused she'd felt that Indina's younger brother didn't seem to like her.

"Why didn't you say anything back then?"

He held his hands out. "What was I supposed to say? I was a sophomore in college who hadn't even decided on a major yet and you were this gorgeous, brilliant law student, blowing everyone away with that sharp mind of yours. You were so far out of my league, there was nothing I *could* say to you."

"You could have said 'Hi Mack, I think you're gorgeous and brilliant. Maybe we should go out some time.'"

He snorted. "You would have shot me down in an instant."

"How do you know that? You never gave me a chance."

He sat up straight, his eyes zeroing in on her. "You couldn't even get my name right," he accused.

"What?"

"That first time you came down from Grambling with Indina, you called me Evan for the first two days you were here."

Mack rolled her eyes. "That was a joke, Ezra. Indina said she used to call you Evan when you guys were younger because it used to annoy you. It was my attempt at being funny. Ha, ha," she deadpanned. "Guess the joke was on me."

A pregnant paused filled the air before he said, "It didn't come across as a joke. It made it seem as if I didn't rate high enough for you to even remember my name."

Mack's heart pinched at the despondence she heard in his voice.

"That wasn't the case at all," she said. A small, regretful smile tugged at the corner of her mouth. "I thought you were kinda cute back then. It frustrated me that you didn't like me."

"I liked you too damn much." His eyes dropped to her lips. In a whisper, he said, "That's always been the case when it comes to you."

The air vacated her lungs, leaving her breathless as his brown eyes grew darker with every second that ticked by. Desire gathered deep within her belly, the heavy sensation eddying around her body, setting off tiny bursts of awareness along her nerve endings.

"Why do you look like you want to kiss me?" Mack asked in a hushed voice.

"Because I do," Ezra answered, leaning toward her.

"That's probably not smart."

"No, it isn't."

"But it won't stop you, will it?"

He slowly shook his head. "You're the only one who can stop me." His voice was so soft she could barely hear it. "If you say you don't want me to kiss you, that'll stop me."

"What if I don't say that?"

Satisfaction gleamed in his eyes as he narrowed the distance between them, cupped her jaw in his palm and connected his mouth to hers. The first brush of his lips felt like heaven. Mack closed her eyes and focused on the sensation of his gentle touch as it moved across her mouth. Her breath caught in her lungs as his tongue probed tentatively at her lips. Slowly, she opened her mouth, taking him inside.

A moan escaped as she lost herself in the incredible passion sweeping through her. He tasted so damn good. Like chocolate and coffee and something with a hint of spice. He plunged his tongue inside her mouth, over and over and over again, and Mack soaked up every bit of his flavor.

Her breasts grew heavy and desire pooled between her legs. It had been much too long since she'd experienced the feverish excitement currently overloading her senses. Every erotic thrust of Ezra's tongue propelled her to another level of pleasure. It throbbed through her bloodstream, coaxing another moan from her lips.

With one last swipe of his tongue inside her mouth, Ezra ended the kiss. But he didn't let go of her face. He continued to hold her jaw in his hand as he rested his forehead against hers.

"Maybe we should have done that from the very beginning, just to get it out of our systems and be done with it."

"*Are* you done?" Mack asked him.

"I don't want to be," he said. He lifted his head and stared into her eyes. "But it's probably best if that doesn't happen again."

She ignored the sharp ache that struck her chest at

his words. He was right. Getting involved with him on anything but a professional level would only muddy the waters. She had too much at stake to allow Ezra Holmes's drugging kisses to distract her.

He pushed himself up from the floor. "I should probably head home."

Mack nodded, but remained on the floor. She couldn't stand if she tried. Her knees were still too weak from his mouth's erotic assault on her senses.

He stuffed his hands in his pockets. "I'll…uh…lock the door on my way out."

"Hey," she called out after him. She waited until he turned before she winked, and with a cheeky smile, said, "See you later, Evan."

CHAPTER 7

Ezra stood at the crosswalk where Decatur collided with Frenchmen Street, waiting while a fire truck pulled out of the Engine no. 9 firehouse. He crossed to Esplanade Avenue, shouldering his way through the crowd of people who had descended on the French Quarter for Satchmo Summer Fest, the annual event celebrating New Orleans's native son, Louis "Satchmo" Armstrong and his contribution to jazz music.

It wasn't as if the city needed a reason to have a festival, but this was one Ezra heartily approved of. It began as a one-day commemoration, but over the years had grown into a full-blown three-day conflagration of music, food and booze, the hallmarks of a good time in the Crescent City.

Ezra turned the corner from Esplanade and onto Elysian Fields, and spotted Mack standing exactly where she said she would be. He had to stop to take a breath at the sight of her. The peach sundress she wore, as innocent as it may have seemed at first glance, draped seductively over her nicely-shaped hips and that perfect ass.

Her ass really was perfect. There was no other way to describe it. Her bare arms were toned and sexy as hell. And that desirable dip at her collarbones? That spot just screamed for his tongue to skim it.

Damn, but he needed to get ahold of these feelings that he absolutely, without a doubt, should *not* be feeling right now. He was setting himself up for more trouble than his brain could fathom. She was a member of the city council, and could quite possibly become this city's next mayor. To harbor such feelings for a politician he would undoubtedly have to cover was unprofessional at best, and career suicide at worst.

It was just as stupid on a personal level. His ego was as healthy as the next guy's, but Ezra knew when a woman was out of his league. And Mack had always been out of his league.

That wasn't a knock against the smart, beautiful, cultured women he'd dated in the past. Some would argue—his brothers for instance—that quite a few of those women had been out of his league too.

His brothers would have been correct. Yet none of those women could hold a candle to Mack. She was on an entirely different level. He needed to remember that, especially when she turned on that smile that made him feel as if he was someone she'd be interested in for something other than his investigative skills.

Ezra walked up to her and said, "Hey there."

She turned and greeted him with that smile. For a second, every other thought vanished from his head. Her radiance commanded his undivided attention.

"You're here," she said, as if she'd expected him to stand her up.

"Of course I'm here. Although I'm still trying to

figure out exactly why you asked me to meet you at Satchmo Fest."

"I have to admit my reasons are completely selfish," she said. Ezra's brow cocked in inquiry. "I needed a break," she explained. "I got into it with Carter on the phone this morning, and then had a back and forth with Cecil Washington over email. I needed to get away from everything, if only for a few hours." She hunched her shoulders. "We've both been working nonstop. I figured you could probably use a break too. And, to be honest, I just need to be around someone I can trust right now."

Ezra couldn't help but laugh.

Her brow dipped with affront. "What's so funny about that?"

"Think back to a month ago. Could you have ever imagined that *I* would be that person for you?"

Her mouth curved in a slight grin. It had the same effect on him as her full-wattage smile.

"Okay, when you put it that way I guess it is somewhat amusing."

"Somewhat, huh?"

"I never would have predicted this, but, then again, life is unpredictable," Mack said. "When I consider some of the more unpredictable moments in my past, finding myself in a partnership with you falls in under the 'hashtag winning' category." She leaned forward, and in a conspiratorial whisper, said, "In case you're still keeping count, that's another compliment."

"You're going to spoil me," Ezra said.

With a laugh, she captured him by the wrist and tugged. "Come on. I want to listen to wonderful jazz music, eat amazing food, enjoy this beautiful weather and not worry that the person smiling in my face isn't really plotting something against me behind my back. Even if you *are* plotting something behind my back, let me just pretend for the day that you're being one hundred percent honest with me."

Ezra gave her hand a tug, halting her steps. He closed the distance between them and stared down into her warm brown eyes.

"Forget about your ex, the city council, the mayor, your students and anyone else driving you crazy at the moment. The only thing you have to worry about today is having a good time," he said. He tipped his head toward the crowd. "Allow me to show you how to do just that."

Her expression was a combination of gratitude, amusement and something else, something Ezra hesitated to qualify for fear that he was reading too much into it. As tempting as it would be to fall head-over-heels for Mackenna, Ezra reminded himself he had too much at stake to allow himself to be deterred. Breaking the political story of the year—possibly of the decade—and catapulting himself into the national spotlight as an investigative journalist was his ultimate goal. He could never lose sight of that.

They rounded the block and entered the old U.S. Mint. The historic building had been turned into a museum and stood as the centerpiece of the Satchmo Summer Fest. It had been years since Ezra had been here, not since one of his fraternity brothers had asked him if he could play tour guide for his parents, who'd come to town for their anniversary. Ezra had planned a day of museum stops and historical tours, only to discover that his friends' folks wanted to party on Bourbon Street with the rest of the tourists.

As they toured the collection of instruments played by some of the city's most notable musicians, Ezra had a hard time focusing on the artifacts. Much of his concentration rested on the woman standing next to him. He studied her as she stared at the last trumpet Louis Armstrong played before his death.

"I can't believe I've never been here before," Mack said, running her finger longingly against the Plexiglas case. "One would think a music buff would actually take the time to visit such an important museum, especially with it being so close by."

"I didn't know you were a music buff."

"Not as much as I once was, but music has always been a big part of my life. I was a member of my high school marching band for four years." She tipped her nose up in the air. "I have the distinction of being the first freshman to make first chair."

Ezra's eyes widened with surprise. "You were a band geek? Get the hell out of here."

She laughed. "Band geeks run shit. Don't let anyone tell you differently."

"I never would have pegged you for the marching band."

She shrugged that impossibly sexy bare shoulder. "It was one of the few extracurricular activities my very small high school offered."

"Which instrument?"

"Well, I wanted to play the trumpet," she said, bringing her eyes back to Armstrong's instrument. She released a sigh and looked back at Ezra. "But I had to settle for the clarinet."

He cocked his head to the side. "Why's that?"

"Misogyny and growing up poor," she answered in

the same longing voice. She smiled, but it didn't reach her eyes. "Our band teacher was adamant that girls could only play the flute or clarinet. I was lucky that I got to play at all. The only reason I did was because my grandmother found a used clarinet at a thrift store over in Ruston. There's no way she would have been able to afford a brand new instrument."

As he took in the doleful look in her usually expressive eyes, it suddenly occurred to Ezra just how much he didn't know about her. He'd never given much thought to her upbringing. The first time she came home with Indina, he'd been too enamored with her face to notice whether or not she'd worn designer clothes or anything like that. She hadn't needed any of that to stand out in a crowd. Apparently, she wouldn't have been able to afford designer clothes even if she had wanted any.

"I came to love the clarinet," Mack continued. "But I still envied those guys on trumpet."

"Did you play in college?"

"Oh, no," she said with a laugh. "Have you heard The World Famous Grambling State Marching Band? The university recruits as heavily for the band as they do for the football team." She shook her head. "Thankfully I was able to get in on grades alone. I didn't have to rely on a band scholarship to pay for school." She cast one last longing look at Satchmo's horn before turning to Ezra. "Are you ready for something to eat? I didn't have breakfast this morning, and I am *starving*."

Ezra didn't want food nearly as much as he wanted to learn more about *her*.

He wanted to ask her about her childhood, because based on the little she'd just shared, it was vastly different from what he'd envisioned. Even though he'd had nothing to base it on, he'd assumed she'd come from money. The way she'd carried herself, the way she fit so perfectly in with New Orleans's society scene—first as one half of one of the city's most high-powered couples, then in her own right as a member of the city council. It just seemed as if she'd been born into the role she'd played so far. To find out that she considered herself lucky to have played a secondhand clarinet in a small town marching band completely blew away so many of those notions he'd held about her.

Then again, it shouldn't surprise him in the least that Mack was intriguing as hell. She'd always intrigued him.

They exited the Old U.S. Mint and walked down to Jackson Square, where some of the city's premier restaurants had set up food booths.

"We *are* hitting the main stage, right?" Ezra asked, gesturing with his head in the direction of Barracks Street. He could hear a brass band playing second-line music. There was a time when he could decipher which one was playing, just by listening to the style. The fact that he couldn't anymore was telling. It had been a long time since he'd given himself permission to just enjoy himself. Not since he'd been let go from the paper. He'd felt as if he didn't deserve the right to enjoy himself.

"We are definitely hitting the main stage," Mack answered. "But I just got a whiff of fried chicken and my body will rebel if I don't get some of that in my belly in the next five minutes."

Instead of fried chicken, she chose the Blackened Shrimp over Gouda Grits, while Ezra tried pho from a Vietnamese booth. They both opted for Abita Beer, a local favorite.

Mack gestured to an available patch of green grass, just in the shadow of Andrew Jackson's statue in the center of the square. Ezra looked on in awe as she gracefully lowered herself to the ground, stretching her long, shapely legs out in front of her and crossing them at the ankles. Suddenly, his food didn't hold the same appeal it had just a few minutes ago. He'd much rather feast on her.

Stop that shit, Ezra chastised his overeager imagination.

Just because Mack had invited him to spend the day with her, it didn't mean she was inviting him into other parts of her life. He had to chill the hell out and just enjoy this time with her.

"So, did you play an instrument in high school?" she asked.

Ezra shook his head. "I was one of those assholes who made fun of the band geeks. I would have totally made fun of you."

She kicked at his leg with her sandaled foot. "All us band members ever wanted was to be appreciated," she said.

"I appreciated how you all gave us something to make fun of."

"You're awful. I can't believe I thought you were a nice guy."

Ezra caught her ankle. "I am a nice guy now, I promise. I stopped being an asshole back in high school."

The alluring glint in her eyes caused Ezra's breath to quicken.

"I guess I can believe that," Mack said. "My opinion of you has changed from what it was just a few months ago. Now that I know you actually had a reason for being such a pain in my ass." She tugged her leg out of his grasp and crossed her ankles again. "So, what else?" she asked.

"What else what?"

"What else did you do in high school? Besides stuff band members in the trash can," she said.

Ezra's head flew back with his laugh. "I promise I never stuffed a single band member in the trash."

"Well, that's certainly good to know," she said. "I still want to know which Holmes brother you were."

"We have labels?"

She nodded. "According to Indina, Harrison was the super smart one who got all the A's. Reid was the spoiled baby of the family who could get your parents to agree to just about anything. But she never really talked about you that much."

"Are you trying to hurt my feelings?" he asked. "It's like I'm the forgotten Holmes."

She laughed. "I swear I didn't mean to make you feel bad."

"I think you did. You're trying to get back at me for being mean to band geeks." He set aside his bowl and leaned back, bracing his hands on the grass. "I played football," Ezra said.

"Oh, right. How could I forget? You used to call Indina on Saturday mornings after your football games."

"Only because she wanted me to," he said. A wry grin curled up the edge of Mack's lips. Ezra's eyes narrowed as a matching smile crept along his lips. "Are you saying she *didn't* want a detailed explanation of every single tackle I made in every single game?"

She laughed. "She indulged you because you were her little brother. I thought it was adorable."

Ezra wasn't sure how he felt about Mack thinking of him in those terms. Adorable Little Brother usually didn't make it into the Potential Bed Partner category. Not that being her potential bed partner was anywhere on his radar.

He glanced up at the sky to make sure those thunderclouds he'd noticed earlier hadn't made their way here yet. Lightening was sure to strike him down after that lie.

"I remember now how much of a stir it caused when you decided not to enter into the NFL draft."

Ezra shrugged. "My draft chances weren't as great as the people in my family seemed to believe. Besides, it's not every football player's dream to play professionally. I had more interests."

"Like?"

"Books," he said. He grinned. "I used to make fun of the band geeks, but they would make fun of this here science fiction geek."

"You are *not* a sci-fi fan," she said.

He nodded. "Biggest one I know. I've read Gibson's *Neuromancer* so many times I can damn near recite it verbatim. And I've read just about everything Niven ever wrote."

"I devoured *Ringworld* the first time I read it," Mack said.

Ezra shook his head. "There you go, blowing my mind again. I would have guessed you'd be into legal thrillers or maybe even romance novels."

"Hey, I read those too. I've got more romances on my bookshelf than any other genre, but science fiction has always been my first love. Back when I was in high school, Octavia Butler was my escape."

"Butler is a legend. I have a paperback copy of *Parable of the Sower* that's being held together by paperclips and packing tape, but I refuse to replace it."

She slapped her hands to her chest. "That's one of my favorites. Second only to *Kindred*."

"*Kindred*," Ezra said at the same time. He grinned. "You look like a *Kindred* kind of girl."

"It's such a heartbreaking, eloquently written piece of fiction." They stared at each other, both grinning in their shared geekiness. "You know," Mack continued. "One of the biggest fights I ever had with Carter was over an autographed copy that I bought on eBay. It cost an obscene amount of money, but I'd pay it again in a heartbeat. I consider that signed book one of my most prized possessions."

"First edition?"

"You know it."

"Wow. I'd love to see it."

"I'll show it to you the next time you come over. The book," Mack hastily tacked on. "You're more than welcome to see the book."

It hadn't occurred to him that she'd meant anything else, but the fact that she thought she had to clarify her statement told Ezra what *she* had been thinking. It sent his already robust imagination on a journey it had no business taking in the middle of this crowded square.

Mack swallowed down a large gulp of beer and started to gather up their empty paper dishes. "Are you ready to head to the music stages?" she asked.

Ezra didn't want to go anywhere, unless it was somewhere quiet where he could learn more about her.

No. No!

Learning more about Mackenna Arnold should not be a part of his agenda. Knowing that she played clarinet in the school band, and that she found escape through the world of science fiction novels the way he had when he was younger, was already more than Ezra needed to know about her. It only invited him to want to learn more, when what he should be concentrating on is investigating the story that could reinvigorate his stagnant career.

Mack had handed him a golden opportunity with this lead on Lucien Warner. If there truly was something underhanded going on in the mayor's office, and *he* was the reporter to break the story, Ezra knew it would put him on the radar of news outlets from around the country.

That's what he needed to focus on.

Mack stood and dusted off her sundress. And just like that, Ezra's focus jumped from what he *should* be concentrating on to the only thing he *wanted* to concentrate on right now. The amazingly gorgeous woman who was turning out to be more of a surprise than he ever thought possible.

~

As she danced among the thousands of people crowding around the main stage, Mack was hyperaware of one person in particular. While her body's reaction to Ezra *shouldn't* have been a surprise, every slight brush of his arm against hers sent shockwaves racing through her bloodstream.

Today had been full of surprises. Mack had known there was more to Ezra than being a fierce—maybe even overzealous—investigative reporter. Today, she'd been granted a glimpse into the man underneath the hard-hitting exposés and newsboy cap.

She observed him as he swayed to the beat of the Rebirth Brass Band, one of the city's premier jazz ensembles, who were tearing up the stage with their signature style of play. Despite his sturdy, solid frame, Ezra moved with ease, exhibiting a laid-back suaveness that did interesting things to Mack's insides. There was something decidedly sexy about a man who could look so smooth while he danced.

When the band climbed down from the stage and into the crowd, leading a second-line march around the grounds, Ezra pointed at her and crooked his finger. Her first instinct was to say no, but where was the fun in that? After all, that's why she'd come here this afternoon, wasn't it? She'd been in much need of some fun in her life.

So, instead of following her first instinct, Mack placed her hand in his and allowed him to lead her to the dozens of people who were now following the band. Several festival-goers recognized her and started a "Go Councilwoman, Go Councilwoman" chant as Mack high-stepped to the rhythmic beats. Someone handed her a handkerchief, and she waved it in the air, rocking in time with the music.

"I know this will end up on YouTube, but I don't care," she said.

Ezra winked at her. "You're going to make people jealous of New Orleans. When people around the world see it, they'll wish they had a city council member as cool as you are."

The band played long past their allotted time, but there were no complaints from the crowd. Mack wouldn't mind if they played for the rest of the afternoon. This lazy, carefree feeling was one she didn't want to let go of. It felt so amazing to just be…free. Free of the strife down at City Hall and the court cases piled high on her desk at the Arts Council. Free of Carter and his continual bullshit. She could just be herself, if only for a few more hours.

As she and Ezra danced, Mack was hyperaware of every brush of his skin against hers. His hand traveled along her bare arm as they swayed with the music. She knew he hadn't meant for it to be overly sensual, not while hundreds—thousands—of people surrounded them, but it was definitely sensual.

It was growing late, but Mack didn't want to leave. She could stay out here all evening long.

As if the weather gods read her mind, a crack of thunder rent the air, making the decision for her and all those who had been enjoying the festival and didn't want to go home. Ezra pointed to the darkening sky across the Mississippi River.

"I'd say we have another twenty minutes before that gets here." More thunder cracked. "Maybe not even that long," Ezra amended. "Where's your car? I'll walk you to it."

"I took Uber," Mack said. "I didn't want to have to worry about finding a place to park."

"Wish I'd thought of that," he said with a grin. He hitched his head. "Come on. I'll drop you home."

As they started toward Esplanade Avenue, Mack

learned that Ezra's meteorological skills were nowhere near as sharp as his investigative journalism skills. The twenty minutes he'd predicted they would have before the downpour started was more like eight. They quickened their steps as the raindrops began to fall, and started running faster when the rain gained momentum.

By the time they arrived at Ezra's navy sedan, the rain was falling at a steady pace, and Mack's flimsy peach sundress lay plastered to her skin. She hadn't bothered with a bra, a decision she now regretted. Her nipples poked out like stiff beads underneath the wet material.

Mack slipped into the passenger seat and awkwardly tried to cover her chest.

"You can put your arms down," Ezra said. "I promise not to look."

"Do you?"

"No, I just want you to put your arms down. That looks uncomfortable."

Mack rolled her eyes. "I don't live too far away. I can handle the discomfort for the short drive."

"I've seen breasts before, you know? I haven't seen yours, of course, but are they really that different?"

"Just drive," she said.

Mack kept her arms exactly where they were, moving them only to adjust the air vents once Ezra turned on the heater. The hot summer rain, combined with the warm air blowing from the vents, turned the inside of the car into a sauna. Still, she'd rather be hot and wet than cold and wet.

By the time they arrived at her condo, the thundershower had gained strength. Luckily, Ezra was able to find a parking spot on the street close to the building's main entrance.

"Please tell me you're better than I am at keeping an umbrella in the car?" Mack asked.

He reached behind them, feeling around the backseat and, a moment later, came up with an umbrella. "Stay there. I'll come around to get you."

Sharing the umbrella wasn't ideal, but at least they made it to her apartment building without getting another drenching. Ezra insisted on following her up to her condo. The temperature in the building was, as usual, dialed to frozen tundra, negating the brief relief Mack had achieved from the car's heater.

They got off on her floor and made their way to her front door. Mack was more than aware of Ezra's eyes on her when she had to drop her arms in order to search for her keys.

"You're looking," she said as she fished the keys from her bag.

"Yeah, I think I was wrong about that whole 'seen one set of breasts, seen them all' thing. Yours are amazing."

It was on the tip of her tongue to lay into him, but instead Mack burst out laughing.

"Did what I just say hurt my chances of getting invited in for coffee?" he asked. "Tell me you're not going to send me back out in that rain."

She pushed open the door and gestured for him to enter. "Offering you coffee is the very least I can do after you rescued me from the rain. And for teaching me that newest line dance so I didn't look like a fool out there. And for meeting me at the festival in the first place."

"Damn, I *did* do all of that, didn't I?" He grinned as

he stepped aside so she could turn off the condo's alarm. "I'd say that deserves more than just coffee."

"There's leftover bread pudding from Galatoire's in the fridge," Mack said, tossing the keys on the table next to the door. "You're more than welcome to a bite of it."

"Not even close to what I want a bite of," he murmured. His eyes shot to hers. "I said that out loud, didn't I?"

She nodded and had to swallow the unnamed emotion clogging her throat before she could speak. "Yeah, you did."

That look in his eyes was unmistakable. It caused a shiver that had nothing to do with her wet clothing to travel down Mack's spine. Awareness prickled her skin in response to the blatant desire evident in his gaze.

She pointed toward her room. "I'm…uh…I'm going to change out of this."

Ezra nodded, his gaze still latched on to hers.

Mack raced to her bedroom and closed the door. She leaned her head back on the solid wood and pulled in several deep breaths.

She'd known that they would eventually have to confront this mutual attraction. It was too apparent, too potent, to leave things unsaid in hopes that it would magically go away. There was no escaping this, but Mack wasn't sure she was ready for the conversation just yet. Acknowledging the attraction between them would put it at the forefront, and could very likely prove detrimental to the real goal here: investigating the mayor.

Maybe she could pretend for just a bit longer that the spot between her legs didn't pulse with need every second she was around him.

"Good luck with that," she muttered as she finally pushed away from the door.

She was tempted to jump into the shower, but settled for toweling her damp skin and throwing on one of her favorite loungewear sets. The heather gray leggings and lightweight hooded pullover were soft and comfy, but still presentable. She'd even gone down to the 24-hour drug store in these once.

She sucked in a calming breath, searching for her center of control before leaving the safety of her bedroom. The rich aroma of coffee and chicory hit her the moment she opened the door. She entered the kitchen and found Ezra searching her cabinets.

"Made yourself right at home, didn't you?" Mack asked.

He turned. "Hope you don't mind. I figured I'd get the coffee started. Where do you keep your mugs?"

"You sure you don't know?" Mack teased, pointing to the cabinet just to the right of him. "I was sure you'd searched my condo months ago during your little investigation."

He looked at her over his shoulder and winked. "Breaking and entering goes a bit past my comfort level." He took down two mugs and filled them with steaming coffee.

Mack grabbed the half-and-half, along with the leftover bread pudding, from the fridge. She transferred the bread pudding to a ceramic bowl and zapped it in the microwave for twenty seconds before bringing it, along with two spoons, to where he stood.

"We're sharing," she said, tossing a spoon on the counter in front of him. She dipped her own spoon in the bread pudding, bumping Ezra with her hip as she broke off a healthy chunk. "I hope you feel as special as this situation warrants. I normally wouldn't share my leftover dessert with just anyone."

Oh, good Lord. She was doing it. She was flirting with him! Didn't she just vow to keep this professional not even five minutes ago?

"You should feel pretty special yourself, Councilwoman," he returned. "I don't eat just anyone's dessert."

And just like that, Mack's body lit up like a furnace in the dead of winter.

Maybe she could better handle a game of sexual innuendo tit-for-tat if it hadn't been so damn long since she'd been with a man, but she was in the middle of a year-long drought. Everything out of his mouth had a panty-melting affect.

"So, did you mean for that to sound as dirty as it did?" Mack asked.

"I'm not sure yet," Ezra said. "I'm still trying to figure out how far you'll let my flirting go."

"So you're flirting too?"

His forehead dipped with his frown. "Wait, *you* were flirting?"

Well, hell. Maybe she was even more out of practice than she realized.

"I thought I was. That's what this sharing dessert thing was supposed to be," Mack said. She released a sigh. "But it's probably not a good idea. You know, the whole flirting thing. It would just be a distraction."

"You're right," Ezra said. "Maybe we should just get to the reason I'm here." He tipped his head toward her bedroom. Mack's eyes grew wide, but before she could speak, he said, "You're supposed to show me your copy of *Kindred*, remember?"

Air whooshed from her lungs. "Oh, goodness, yes," she said. Lord, but this overactive imagination was going to drive her insane. "Give me a minute," Mack said.

She dropped her spoon and raced for her bedroom where she kept the book on a handmade bookcase, grateful for a few moments to catch her breath. She pulled the book off the shelf and turned to find Ezra standing at the door. Her heart slammed into her ribcage.

"Can I come in?" he asked.

Mack swallowed the lump of desire that had lodged in her throat. It felt way too intimate to have him in her bedroom, but what could she tell him? No?

She nodded. "Sure. Come in."

He strolled up to her, his hands in his pockets. With a nod toward the book, he asked, "That it?"

She held the book out to him. "Yep. This is it. My prized possession." She shrugged. "I don't read this copy, of course. I have a couple of old, tattered ones I found at a used book store for that."

He flipped to the title page and ran his thumb over Octavia Butler's signature. "This is pretty damn cool."

"I think so too." She smiled up at him and noticed when his eyes dropped to her lips. At the same time, her tongue darted out of her mouth. She licked her lips and Ezra's gaze intensified. Mack figured she had about eight seconds before her heart burst clean out of her chest.

"Our...uh...our coffee will get cold," she said.

"Do you care?" He murmured.

Not one bit. But it was probably better if she got him out of her bedroom.

His eyes narrowed as he looked at something past her shoulder. "What's that?" Ezra asked.

For the first time in a long time Mack experienced true fear when she realized that he was looking in the direction of her dresser, where she kept her vast array of sex toys in the second drawer. Her heart stopped. Had she put the one she'd used last night back in the drawer?

Mack was almost too afraid to turn around. Her shoulders wilted in relief when she finally did turn to find her dresser hot-pink-dildo free.

Ezra walked over to the dresser and picked up the plaque she'd been given by a school she'd visited last month, where she'd served as the keynote speaker for their Honor Roll assembly.

"Oh, wait. This isn't what I thought it was," Ezra said. He held up the plaque. "There's this group of kids and parents in the Carrolton area who have formed something of a club—an unfortunate one. They presented me with a plaque like this for bringing attention to their story years ago. I thought you'd gotten this from them, but the two groups must have used the same trophy maker."

"What did you do to warrant a plaque?" Mack asked. "And why would you call the group unfortunate? That's an odd description."

"Yeah, it is. But, sadly, it's an accurate one."

Mack frowned. "I want to hear the story, but something tells me I won't like it."

Ezra shrugged as he set the plaque on her dresser and perched his backside against it. He folded his arms over his chest and crossed his feet at the ankles. Mack should have been alarmed by how at home he looked in her bedroom. Alarm wasn't what she felt at the moment.

She didn't want to think about what she felt at the moment as she took in his almost too perfect appearance.

"The story starts out pretty bad, but it has a happy ending," Ezra said. "Actually, it started with a friend of mine. He noticed something weird happening with his son. The kid played on one of those neighborhood football teams. The games are all held at Tad Gormley Stadium, but the team Edwin's son played on practiced at a park in their neighborhood." He paused for a moment before continuing. "Joshua—that's Edwin's son—began getting sick a lot, but he'd had asthma as a baby, so Edwin and his wife thought maybe it stemmed from that."

"But it wasn't the asthma," Mack said.

Ezra shook his head. "No. It seems crazy to consider a football injury to be a good thing, but in this case it was. Joshua got hurt and was ordered by his doctor not to play. His mom decided that he should use the time to focus on his school work, so she and Edwin kept him from football—and from the park—for about six months. During that time, Joshua was just fine. As soon as he rejoined the team, the symptoms came back."

"Well, it doesn't take a rocket scientist to figure this one out," Mack said.

"Nope, just your run-of-the-mill investigative reporter," Ezra said with a small smile. "Once I started investigating, I learned that many of the other kids who played at that park were suffering from some of the same symptoms Joshua had experienced."

"Wait, is this the park at Carrolton and Claiborne? I remember when that story broke. It launched an investigation into soil around several parks throughout the city. That was you?"

Ezra nodded. "That was me."

"The story won several awards that year, didn't it?"

Another nod. "It also won me the lead investigative journalist position at the paper. But that was just a bonus," he said. "The accolades and promotion were nice and all, but that story saved a bunch of other kids from getting sick. That's what I'm proudest of."

"The city agreed to pay those families a good amount, didn't it?" Mack asked.

"They received a nice settlement, but you ask any of them and they would much rather that none of this had ever happened."

"Oh, I have no doubt about that," Mack said. "This all happened before I was elected to the city council, but if I had been on it I would have been fighting along with them. It took such courage for them to stand up to the city the way they did. I'd love to meet them one day and just…I don't know…shake their hands and thank them for fighting for their kids."

"I can make that happen," Ezra said. "Tomorrow, in fact."

Mack looked at him with confusion.

"There's an annual event where all the families come together to catch up on how the kids are progressing," he continued. "It just so happens to be tomorrow. You should come with me."

"Are you sure I would be welcomed?"

"Why wouldn't you be?" he asked. "It would be good for the kids and their parents to see a member of the city council there. It would show them that at least someone in power still cares about them."

She nodded slowly as she thought it over and realized he was right. Those families needed to know that the city didn't just toss money their way and forget about them.

"I think I will join you," Mack said. "Thanks for the invitation."

He pushed away from the dresser and took a step toward her. Mack instinctively took a step back, even as the impulse to give in to her body's suddenly ferocious demands threatened to overwhelm her. Thank goodness her need for preservation was stronger than her desire to grab his wrists, bring him over to her bed, and forget about all the reasons sleeping with him would be a bad idea.

But not by much. Which is why she needed to get him out of her room—her home—as soon as possible.

"I…uh…I think the rain has slacked," she said.

The slight grin that edged up the corners of Ezra's lips would haunt her for the rest of the night.

"Is that your not-so-subtle way of throwing me out?"

Yes. And if he didn't leave soon she wasn't going to be subtle about it at all.

Mack latched on to her favorite excuse. "I have court Monday morning and need to prepare for my case, especially if I join you at the picnic tomorrow. I also have to get through some of the transcripts you brought over the other night."

Ezra nodded, but he didn't make an attempt to move. Instead he continued to stare at her with those deep brown eyes. They sparkled with the kind of mischief that told Mack that he saw right through her excuses.

"I guess I'll get out of here then," he said.

Yet he remained in that same spot. His eyes dropped to her mouth as he slowly brushed his thumb across his bottom lip. Fantasies of those lips had occupied her dreams ever since that brief, but intensely satisfying kiss they'd shared.

Except it hadn't really satisfied her. It had only increased her yearning.

Mack tore her eyes away and pivoted toward the door. She needed to break free of the confines of this bedroom before she did something stupid. Like strip Ezra naked and pin him to her bed.

"What time is the event at the park?" Mack called over her shoulder.

Ezra followed her out into the short hallway and to the front door.

"It starts at eleven. I can swing by and pick you up."

She nodded. "Thanks. I know parking can sometimes be an issue in that neighborhood. Especially with all the tourists parking at the foot of the St. Charles Streetcar line."

She opened the front door. Yeah, she was done with being subtle.

Casual amusement flickered in his eyes. With a slight nod of acknowledgment, Ezra started for the door. But before he crossed the threshold, he turned to her.

"If you find anything that causes your antenna to spike as you're going through the transcripts, let me know. Even if it doesn't seem particularly important. If it gives you pause, there's probably something there that you just haven't thought about."

"I'll keep that in mind," she said.

"If you have a question about anything, don't hesitate to call or text. I'm available to you, Mackenna. Any time. Day or night."

Her mind wouldn't allow her to interpret his words in any way but the most hedonistic. At this point he could read his grocery list and her body would probably have this same reaction.

Mack crossed her arms over her chest in an attempt to hide her erect nipples. She cleared her throat and leaned against the doorjamb. "Thanks again for joining me today."

"Thanks for inviting me," he said. He winked. "See you later."

Mack waited until Ezra boarded the elevator before shutting her front door and falling back against it. She slid down to the floor and rested her forearms on her up-drawn knees, hanging her head between them.

"Oh. My. God." She let out on a ragged breath. Then she pushed herself up off the floor and ran to her bedroom, her mind on one thing.

That second drawer.

CHAPTER 8

Ezra pulled into the last remaining parking space along the street where Carrolton and Claiborne Avenues intersected. He waited for a streetcar to pass before crossing the neutral ground—what the rest of the country called the median—that divided the two sides of the street, and continuing on to the park. As he made his way there, he looked around for Mackenna's car. When he'd called earlier to let her know he was on his way, it had gone straight to voicemail. He received a text a minute later, with word that she was in an emergency meeting with a client at the Arts Council and would meet him at the park when she was done.

Even as he'd fought off disappointment at losing out on the chance to pick her up, Ezra knew it was for the best. The more distance that stretched between them, the better. One of the lessons he'd learned yesterday was that, when it came to Mack, his ability to resist temptation was virtually non-existent.

Yesterday had been…interesting.

As he'd stood in her bedroom, Ezra was sure that,

with just a little more effort, he could have convinced Mack to show him much more than just her copy of *Kindred*. He'd seen it in her eyes; they'd held the same desire that pulsed through him every time he so much as thought about her.

His mind was still experiencing whiplash from the complete one-eighty he'd undergone in these last few weeks. For years Mackenna had been an unattainable fantasy he'd admired from afar. From those days when she was that beautiful, brilliant college student who used to visit with Indina, to when she married one of the most recognizable faces in New Orleans, she remained so far out of his reach that Ezra purposely kept his distance. If he knew beforehand that she was joining his family for some type of gathering, he would come up with an excuse for why he couldn't make it. And if they so happened to end up in the same space, he gave her a wide berth.

It was just easier that way. Why put himself through the agony of seeing her when he knew he could never have her?

Once she and Carter divorced it was the fact that she'd become a politician that kept him away. He'd had too many negative experiences with politicians during his career to ever fully trust one. But, over the past few weeks, every minute he spent with Mack created a small fissure in the wall of distrust he instantly erected whenever he encountered a politician.

Because the more he was around her, the harder it was to think of her as a politician. Like the other night, as he sat beside her on the floor in her condo. It had been hard as hell to concentrate on the transcripts he *should* have been reading when what he'd *really* wanted to do was push those papers away and lay her body down on the carpeted floor. He'd envisioned himself running his hand up her shirt, molding his palm over her breast, clutching the perfect mound in his hand while his mouth explored hers.

Ezra groaned. He was less than twenty yards away from a park full of children. Imagining all the deliciously sensual things he wanted to do with Mack was the absolute last thing he should be doing right now.

Good luck with that.

Whatever hopes he had of keeping his thoughts pure were good and thoroughly dashed when he turned to find her striding toward him. There wasn't a man on earth who could fight the impure thoughts this woman elicited with just the sway of her delicate hips. She'd come dressed for the picnic, in soft green pants that stopped a few inches above her ankles, and a pale peach, sleeveless shirt. Her cork-heeled sandals added a couple of inches to her already impressive height, making her nearly as tall as Ezra.

"Sorry I'm late," she said. "A client at the Arts Council is embroiled in a royalty dispute with his record company. It's amazing to me just how many unscrupulous people are out there." She rolled her eyes. "Of course, I was married to one for years, so it shouldn't come as *that* much of a surprise."

"The fact that you're still surprised means that you're still one of the good ones," Ezra said.

The smile that blossomed on her lips was the most gorgeous sight he'd seen in ages.

"Thank you," Mack said. Taking him by the arm, she gestured to the park. "It sounds as if they're having way too much fun without us. Let's go."

They arrived at the picnic much to the excitement of the parents, who were thrilled that one of New Orleans's most popular city council members decided to grace them with her presence. Ezra stood back and watched as Mackenna Arnold, Attorney-at-Law, morphed into Councilmember Arnold right before his eyes. She greeted the families with compassion, listening to their stories of struggle due to not only the soil contamination case, but also issues that had impacted them throughout the years.

Ezra knew that even as a city council member, there was little she could do to alleviate some of their problems, but that didn't stop Mack from giving each and every person her full attention. Sometimes, that's all people needed, to know there was someone willing to listen. As he observed her, Ezra realized this was no politician at work. Her concern was genuine.

She'll make an amazing mayor.

The realization hit him square in the chest. Mack possessed everything this city needed in its mayor. She was tough, but kindhearted; unbelievably smart, but still down to earth. People opened up to her, because in her they saw someone who wouldn't just pay them lip service. Mack had proven in her own district that she was willing to stand up and fight for the people of New Orleans.

She stood there listening to people's stories for the next half hour, until a food truck arrived, grabbing everyone's attention. Hot dogs, nachos, and cotton candy were served, courtesy of the local car dealership that originally sponsored the neighborhood football team. After they'd all filled their bellies with junk food, the games began.

Ezra paired up with Martell Johnson for the three-legged race. Martell had been eleven-years-old and the quarterback for the football team back when Ezra first broke the soil contamination story. Now, Martell was seventeen. Ezra had kept up with him over the years, encouraging the teen as he'd navigated high school, battling a learning impairment that doctors agreed had been exacerbated by the various poisons that had contaminated the soil. It hadn't been easy, but the kid had a drive unlike any Ezra had ever encountered. He'd been humbled and honored several months ago when Martell asked him if he would write him a letter of recommendation for college.

He and Martell came in second in the three-legged race, and Ezra came in an abysmal sixth in horseshoes. An impromptu game of baseball started up, and Mack decide to join in the fun. If he hadn't seen it with his own eyes, Ezra would have never believed a person could be so awful at bat. It was probably for the best. If she *had* managed to actually get a hit, there was no way she'd be able to make it to first base in those sandals.

Once the game ended, everyone was treated to ice cream cones. Ezra got a soft serve for himself and Mack, and together they started down one of the trodden paths around the park.

"Thank you so much for inviting me," she said. "I've had such a wonderful time. These kids are just…just…"

"Amazing," Ezra offered.

"Yes, they're amazing. So are their parents. They've managed to turn a terrible situation into one of the most inspiring displays of courage I've ever witnessed." She looked over at him and smiled. "You're good with them, you know?"

"With who?"

"These kids. I see how much they mean to you. Your eyes light up when you're around them."

Ezra shrugged. "I can't help it," he said, licking melted ice cream from his knuckle. "I've followed their stories for a long time. I know how much they've had to overcome."

"You mean a lot to them too," Mack continued. "It must be incredibly fulfilling to see the impact your work has had on their lives."

Ezra shrugged, but in all honesty, he couldn't speak even if he tried. What more could he say? No other story had gotten to him the way this one had. Some would argue he'd covered more important investigations over the years, those that had resulted in crooked politicians and businessmen eventually serving jail time. But, for Ezra, none of those stories could touch this one.

He'd changed lives with his words. Because of his tenacity and unwillingness to let the story drop, these kids now had futures to look forward to, and many other kids who could have been affected by that contaminated soil had been spared. There was not a single thing he'd done in his adult life that had been more important than this story.

"Thank you for that," Ezra told her. "It means a lot to hear it."

"I can't believe I'm saying this yet again, but thank *you* for being such a bulldog when it comes to your reporting. You're one of the good ones, Ezra Holmes."

Her praise warmed him from the inside out.

"So are you, Councilmember Arnold," Ezra replied.

Their gazes caught and held, and the intensity of the emotions suddenly rushing through him took Ezra's breath away. He'd spent countless hours, days, years, imagining what it would feel like to have Mackenna look at him the way she looked at him this very second. As if she could see herself as more than just a partner in this investigation of the mayor. As if he meant something to her.

As if she'd spent just as much time as he had imagining them together.

Mack was the first to tear her eyes away. She pointed to the trash receptacle. "I probably shouldn't finish this ice cream," she said. "Too many calories."

The haste in which she moved away was telling. So was the amount of time it took her to toss an ice cream cone in the trash. She stood at the garbage can, methodically wiping her hands with a disposable wipe she'd pulled from her purse.

Ezra let her have the time she apparently needed away from the weighty moment that had passed between them. He could use some distance from it himself. There was just one problem. Keeping his distance wasn't working. Nothing was working when it came to fighting this ever-intensifying attraction to her.

Which begged the question: Why fight it?

Don't start this shit.

Ezra knew damn well why he needed to fight it. To say his career hung in the balance wasn't hyperbole. Breaking this story could mean everything to his future. *Everything.* As much as he craved Mackenna, Ezra knew he couldn't allow himself to lose focus.

"So, what's next?" Mack asked as she returned to his side.

Ezra gestured over to where the beanbag toss was set up. "You game?"

She grinned as they made their way to the wooden plank that had been adorned with five bright red targets.

"Fair warning," Mack said. "I'm ridiculously competitive, and I play to win. Are you prepared for this butt whipping?"

He lobbed the beanbag her way. "Bring it."

It only took a few minutes for him to realize that, despite her trash talk, Mack was just as bad at this as she was at baseball. Her hand/eye coordination was so horrible Ezra questioned whether or not she should even be allowed to drive a car. When she tossed the beanbag clear over the target for the third time in a row, he decided to take pity on her.

"No, no, no," Ezra said. "You're putting too much momentum behind the toss. You need a lighter touch." He came up behind her and wrapped his arms around her waist, taking her wrist in his hand. The minute he found himself in that position, Ezra knew he was in trouble. Her backside brushed against his front and he started to harden.

Son of a bitch.

Maybe he should have thought this through before deciding to align his body with that of the woman who'd played a starring role in way too many of his nighttime fantasies. He'd placed himself in an impossible situation. If he remained where he stood, she would definitely feel his arousal within the next thirty seconds. But if he stepped away from her, the current state of affairs in the area behind his zipper would be evident to everyone in the park.

Ezra decided minimizing his embarrassment was the best way to handle this situation. Leaning forward, he whispered in her ear, "Whatever you do, don't move," he said. "And, uh, I'm sorry."

"What for?" Mack asked. But then her body went rigid as things became apparent.

"Before you ask, yes, I am sufficiently embarrassed by my lack of control." Ezra sucked in a deep breath and released it. "But I'm so fucking turned on right now that I can't bring myself to care."

Several beats passed before she cleared her throat and said, "I guess I should applaud your honesty. That must have been hard to admit."

"Was the double entendre on purpose?"

She choked on a laugh. "No, but it kind of works, doesn't it."

Ezra huffed out a gruff laugh. "Just give me a minute." He looked up at the fluffy clouds traveling across the blue skies in an attempt to think about something other than her soft body cushioning his own. After a couple of minutes, he'd finally gotten the situation in his pants under control.

"Everything okay back there?" Mack asked.

"Yeah, although I'm not sure how long that will last."

Her shoulders rose and fell with the deep breath she exhaled. "We already decided we're not doing…you know…*that*."

"My brain knows that. Doesn't mean shit all to another certain part of my anatomy."

Mack turned around, but thankfully, didn't look down. Ezra was convinced his dick would stand at attention the moment her gaze touched it.

"We did make the right choice, right?" she asked, her voice low. "Sleeping together would complicate things. Is that why we thought it wouldn't be a good idea?"

"I can't remember exactly why we thought it wouldn't be a good idea," he said. "Although, now is probably not the best time to ask me, because none of the reasons I'm coming up with make any sense at the moment. Maybe once I've had time for all the blood to rush back to my head instead of where it is right now, I'll be able to think more clearly."

"Whatever the reason, I'm pretty sure it was a good one," Mack said.

He released a sigh. "If you say so."

Her brown eyes captured his in a long, meaningful stare. She was no longer convinced they should fight this either. It was written all over her face.

"It's for the best, Ezra," Mackenna said before walking away.

He could almost believe her. If not for the longing he saw in her eyes, the yearning he heard in her voice, and the magnetic pull pulsing between them that refused to let them go.

~

Ezra waited directly underneath the purple and red P.J.'S Coffee House sign on Annunciation Street. He'd taken a chance seeking out someone in the mayor's office, but he and Mack were running out of time. Although she now claimed it didn't play a significant part, he knew she was basing her decision to run, at least partly, on whether or not they uncovered something with the mayor. Ezra didn't know offhand when the final date to declare candidacy was, but he knew it would be here soon. And after two weeks of digging into the mayor's background, they had yet to find anything on him.

But if the mayor *was* into something shady, Ezra knew of one person in the office who would be willing to talk. He smiled when he spotted her walking toward him.

"How're you doing, Ms. Stella," Ezra said, enveloping the longtime janitor in a hug. "You're looking good."

She looked him up and down. "You looking good too. But you always look good," Ms. Stella said. "You know my daughter is almost single. I can hook you two up."

"*Almost* single?"

"She's gonna leave that rat bastard husband of hers one of these days."

"So maybe you should wait until after she leaves before you offer to hook her up," Ezra said with a laugh. He hooked a thumb at the coffee shop's entrance. "Can I buy you a cup of coffee?"

"I want one of the fancy ones with the caramel drizzle," she said.

"One fancy coffee with caramel drizzle coming up. Why don't you grab us a table and I'll be there in a minute?"

He ordered Ms. Stella's caramel latte, along with a black coffee for himself, then joined her at the table that overlooked the street. From this vantage point, he could see the upper decks of the huge tankers carrying cargo down the Mississippi River.

"I know you only have a few minutes before you

head into work, so I appreciate you meeting up with me. It's been a while," Ezra said.

"I haven't talked to you since you left the paper," she said.

Left the paper. Was fired from the paper. Same difference.

"I didn't realize you were still writing stories." She removed the plastic top from her cup and added five packets of sugar she'd lifted from the condiment bar. Ezra got a toothache just looking at the cascade of crystals filling the cup.

"Yes, I'm still writing," he said. "Not as much as I used to now that I'm teaching at the community college, but I've been working on something and I've run into a brick wall. It's about Mayor Warner."

Usually, when a contact didn't know what he originally contacted them for, it was best to ease into the conversation, but he didn't have to do that with Ms. Stella. She was a straight shooter, something Ezra had always appreciated about her.

"What do you need to know about the mayor?" she asked. "He's not having an affair, if that's what you're thinking. I've offered to hook him up with my daughter too, but he turned me down." She waved a hand as she took a sip of her latte. "Don't matter. Arnette wouldn't go for somebody thirty years older than her."

"This isn't about his personal life," Ezra said. "I want to know if you've seen anything that would make you think he's cut a few deals on the side? Maybe he has some friends in high places that have called in favors?"

Her wrinkled forehead wrinkled even more. "I can't say that I have," she said. "I clean his office every day, so I would know." Ms. Stella had always taken pride in her proximity to the mayor's office. "I haven't noticed anything out of the ordinary."

"You mind keeping an eye out for me?" Ezra asked. "Maybe if some new businessmen are hanging around, you can let me know?"

"Anything for you, gorgeous," Stella said. She raised her cup. "Thanks for the coffee, but I need to get moving if I'm going to clock in on time."

"I hear you," he said. He looked at his watch as he rose from the table. "I've got three classes to teach today. I should get moving myself."

Ms. Stella ran into two separate people she knew in the short time it took them to make their way to the door. This woman probably knew everybody in this city.

"Thanks again for meeting with me," Ezra said as he held the door open for her.

"Anytime. And remember what I said about Arnette," she said with a wink.

He laughed. "Not until after you no longer have a son-in-law."

Ezra got into his car and had to talk himself out of swinging by the Arts Council before heading to class. He'd told Mack about his meeting with a contact from the mayor's office. He could visit her on the pretense of sharing what he'd learned from Ms. Stella, even though he hadn't learned anything from her just yet. No doubt she would see right through that flimsy excuse, but at this point Ezra didn't care.

He wanted to see her. He *always* wanted to see her.

He'd carried the image of her wet sundress plastered to her luscious breasts to bed with him for the past two nights. It had taken a herculean effort to restrain himself when what he'd really wanted to do was dip his head and suck her nipple deep into his mouth, sundress and all.

"Dammit," Ezra whispered underneath his breath. He gripped the steering wheel so hard it hurt his palms, but he didn't let go. Instead, he eased up and caressed it, imagining the smooth leather was Mack's skin. The need to run his hands along her soft body was driving him insane.

Even though he knew that taking it any further than that kiss they'd shared would be reckless, it didn't stop him from wishing for more. It didn't help that whenever he tried to conjure the many reasons he and Mack shouldn't get together, the image of her pebbled nipple against that peach sundress popped up instead.

Yeah, he was going to go insane. He should just accept it as fact.

Ezra managed to bypass the Arts Council building on Gravier Street. It's a good thing he did. He encountered two accidents on the way to the community college and had to take numerous side streets that tacked another twenty-five minutes onto his drive.

He had to hustle after pulling into the faculty parking lot. Ezra didn't worry about grabbing his gym bag from the trunk. Jogging amongst the centuries old oak trees that line the campus was usually the perfect way to clear his mind, but the heat had been so stifling lately that running out here would be akin to suicide. An hour at the gym would have to suffice today.

At the end of his final class of the day, Ezra learned that the gym wouldn't be in his future either. On the way to his car, he got a text from Harrison, asking Ezra if he could swing over to his law office.

His brother shared a practice with Jonathan Campbell, his cousin Toby's college basketball teammate who'd made New Orleans his home years ago. In addition to a successful law practice, Jonathan also owned one of the hottest sports clubs in the city, The Hard Court. They were planning to throw Reid a surprise birthday party there for his thirtieth in a few months.

Ezra drove down Esplanade Avenue, parking not far from where he'd parked this past weekend for Satchmo Fest. As he climbed the steps of the salmon-colored creole cottage with dark green shutters, the front door opened and Jonathan walked out with a gorgeous woman on his arm. It wasn't a surprise to Ezra that it wasn't Kristie, the woman who'd joined Jonathan on the Holmes Family Cruise this past summer. The guy never kept the same girl for more than a few months.

"Hey," Ezra said, pulling him in for a half-arm hug. "Harrison asked me to meet him here."

"He's in there." Jonathan tipped his head toward the front door. "Working late as usual. Maybe you can convince him to get a life while you're in there."

Ezra headed straight for his brother's office, knocking on the partially opened door and poking his head in.

"With the amount of time you spend in this office, one would think you had an unhappy home life," Ezra said by way of greeting. Harrison looked up from whatever he was reading. "*Do* you have an unhappy home life?" Ezra asked. "Indina seems to think so."

Harrison tossed the document on the desk and motioned for Ezra to come in. "Indina needs to mind her own damn business."

"When has Indina ever minded her own damn business?" Ezra asked as he sat in one of the stuffy wingback chairs that faced his brother's desk.

"You're right about that," Harrison said with a derisive snort.

"So, what's up? Is this about mom's foundation, or Reid's surprise party? There's so much in the works these days it's hard to keep up with it all."

"This is about Dad," Harrison said.

Ezra jerked his head back. "What about Dad?"

His brother brought his elbows up on the desk and steepled his fingers. He was pensive, a characteristic Ezra would never normally use to describe his brother.

Fear gripped his chest. "What is it?" Ezra asked again.

"What do you think Dad would say if I invited him to move in with me, Willow and the kids?" Harrison asked.

Not what he'd been expecting. "Where's this coming from?"

Harrison shrugged. "He's in that house by himself. He doesn't need all that room."

"He's had all that room since Reid moved out seven years ago. Mama didn't take up *that* much space."

"You're not concerned about him being alone?"

"Dude, have you seen your father lately? The man still runs three miles every morning and his mind is sharper than mine on most days."

Harrison tapped his pen against the stack of files on his desk. "I've been thinking about him in that house all alone. We've got that little apartment attached to the garage."

"Your man cave? You're willing to give that up?"

"If it means I can keep a better eye on Dad, yeah, I'd give it up," Harrison said.

Ezra leaned back in the chair and ran his hand down his face. "I don't know, man. I guess you can ask him. What does Willow think about all this?"

Harrison's mouth pulled into a frown. "I haven't asked her yet."

Ezra's eyes widened. "Um, don't you think you should ask your wife before inviting another human being to live with you? I know Dad likes her more than he likes you, but still, dude."

Harrison flipped him off.

"I'm being serious here. You can't make this kind of decision without talking it over with Willow first."

"I haven't made any decisions. It was just an idea."

"An idea you haven't talked about with your wife. She should have been the first one you consulted about this."

Harrison ran his palms down his face and shuddered a deep breath. "Things with Willow have been…off," he said.

"Oh, shit. Indina was right."

"Indina isn't right about anything. She doesn't even know what she's talking about."

"So what's going on with you and Willow?" Ezra asked.

When Harrison looked over at him, Ezra was rendered speechless by the look of utter misery teeming in his brother's eyes.

"I have no idea," Harrison choked out.

Ezra cleared his throat. "The two of you have been married sixteen years. You have to have at least a clue."

"I don't." He shook his head. "Granted, with the

hours I work and all the activities Liliana and Athens are into these days, it's not unusual to go the entire day without seeing Willow, but we'd still communicate. These days, we may say two or three words to each other."

"Did you do something to piss her off? Can't you just apologize?"

"It's not as if it just happened all of a sudden," Harrison said. "We just gradually stopped talking things over. It wasn't until that conference I went to in Philly back in March that I realized just how bad things had gotten."

"What happened with the conference?"

"It's not what happened, it's what didn't. I go to that conference every year, and Willow and I would always talk every single day. I realized that I'd been at the conference in Philly for three days and hadn't talked to her once. I'd texted Lily, and FaceTimed with Athens, but Willow and I hadn't spoken a word."

"Did you talk about it when you got back home?" Ezra asked.

He shook his head. "I had a big case to prepare for. I needed to stay focused."

"Harrison, this is your marriage, man. You can't brush it off. You need to talk to your wife."

"I know, I know," he said. "It's just that it's gone on for so long that I don't even know *how* to talk to her about it." His brother shook his head. "I would hear people talk about how couples just drift apart, but I never imagined that shit happening with me and Willow. But that's exactly what's happened, and I don't know what the hell to do about it."

"Staying in the office late every night can't help," Ezra said.

"It's better than climbing in bed next to her and having her turn her back on me," Harrison said. He pushed a stack of files away with more force than necessary, sending a stapler to the floor.

"Damn, man. How long has it been since you got some?" Ezra asked. "That frustration is coming through big time."

"It's been too damn long." His brother pitched his head back and blew out a tired breath toward the ceiling. "I need to figure out what's going on with my wife."

"Yes, you do," Ezra said. "Bringing Dad to live with you will not help. If you want my opinion, what I think you need to do is send the kids to stay with Dad for a weekend so you and Willow can be alone."

"She would just find somewhere else to go. Either to her sister's or on a girl's weekend or something like that."

"*You* need to take her away for the weekend. Don't even tell her where you're going. Just book a room at the Ritz or the Le Pavillion. Hell, drive over to the Beau Rivage in Biloxi. Get out of the city all together. You two can spend all weekend naked and in bed."

"You think that'll just fix everything, huh?" his brother asked with a heavy dose of sarcasm.

"It would work for me," Ezra said.

"Which is why you're not married, and will probably stay that way."

"Don't be so sure of that." The words left Ezra's mouth before he had the chance to rein them in. It was no surprise that Harrison pounced on him.

His brother's brows arched. "You holding back on me? Who has you thinking about marriage?"

"No and nobody," Ezra answered. "Forget I even said that." He stood. "I need to go."

"Oh, no, no, no," Harrison said as he came around the desk. "Who is she?"

"Nobody," Ezra said. Harrison's shrewd stare made him squirm, but Ezra held firm. He poked his brother in the chest with his forefinger. "Don't worry about my love life. You've got enough to worry about with your own."

Harrison snorted. "Thanks for the reminder." He grabbed his suit jacket from the hook behind the door. "I'll follow you out. Maybe if I pick up dinner tonight, it'll put a smile on my wife's face. It's been a while since I saw her with one of those."

The dejection in Harrison's voice pierced Ezra's chest. He loved his sister-in-law dearly. He loved her and Harrison together. The thought of anything happening to their marriage made him feel physically sick.

As they exited the law office, Ezra tapped Harrison on the shoulder.

"Look man, if you need to talk anything out, you know you can always call me, right?"

A barely there smile tipped up the edge of Harrison's mouth. He brought Ezra in for a one-arm hug. "Thanks, man. See you at Dad's for Sunday dinner?"

He nodded. "See you on Sunday."

Mack set her reading glasses on the table and shoved her fingers through her hair, her frustration level fast approaching cataclysmic.

They'd spent the past three hours poring over the newest documents Ezra had received from his Right to Information filing, which was way more documentation than she had been expecting. It made her rethink everything she said and did while in the capacity of a city council member. They kept records of everything.

That should have meant good news for their current investigation, but so far all this reading had not yielded a damn thing. Mack had been so sure the smoking gun was lurking somewhere within the hundreds of memos and meeting minutes that had been unearthed, but there was nothing here. Nada.

She released another frustrated sigh, banging her fist on the table. Ezra reached over and covered her hand.

"Don't get discouraged. We've only scratched the surface with these newest documents." His unflappable calmness helped to put Mack at ease. He looked over at her and grinned. "Did you think this would be easy?"

"Sorta," she admitted. "It always seems to happen so easy in the movies. The characters do a little searching and then, boom, the proof falls right into their laps."

His deep chuckle rippled through the air. "How I wish investigations went as smoothly as they do in the movies," he said. He squeezed the hand he still held and looked into her eyes. "If there's something to be found, we're going to find it. Just stick with it. It's not always on the surface." His thumb brushed back and forth along her wrist, eliciting a bevy of tingles up and down her spine. He took his hand away much too quickly.

No. He took his hand away just in time.

Ezra Holmes-induced tingles were a bad thing. She'd done everything she could to convince herself of that.

"Do you know how long I searched before I found

that connection between your ex and Starlight Enterprises?" Ezra asked. "That took months. Months of painstaking researching and tapping sources I hadn't contacted in well over a year."

Mack grabbed her water bottle and took a large gulp before asking, "How long had you been investigating me?" She tipped her head to the side. "Actually, the better question is *why* were you investigating me at all? What sparked it?"

"An anonymous tip," Ezra answered.

Mack's head jerked back. "*What?* What did the tipster say?"

"She said you were profiting from your position on the council, but never said exactly how. That's why I had to dig."

"It was a woman?"

He nodded. "I still have the message." He took the phone out of his pocket. "I have a calling service that people can use to leave me tips." He dialed into a number and put the phone on speaker.

Mack listened closely as a female voice she didn't recognize encouraged Ezra to look into Mack's background because she had it on good authority that Mack was cutting deals with companies seeking city contracts.

"I never found any evidence of you cutting deals directly with companies seeking city contracts—"

"Because I never have," she interjected.

"I know that now," he continued. "In my searching, I uncovered the stuff on Starlight. Of course, as it turns out, you weren't directly tied to that either. I just figured with you being married to Carter at the time, you had to have known something about it. Because, you know, married couples talk and share and shit."

Mack snorted. "You definitely are a Holmes."

"What's that supposed to mean?"

"I've seen the married couples in the Holmes family. Trust me, that kind of happily wedded bliss isn't always what you get."

Ezra rubbed the back of his neck. "Yeah, well, apparently not all of the Holmes marriages are as happy as they appear either."

Mack frowned, but before she could inquire further, Ezra continued, "So, there you have it. It was that anonymous tip that started my initial investigation."

"Do you remember when this person called?"

"Give me a minute. I can get the exact date for you," he said. "The call service comes with an app that time stamps everything that comes in." He swiped his fingers across the touchscreen. "I got this call back in April."

It only took Mack a couple of seconds before the light bulb went off. "It was April 11th, wasn't it?"

"Yeah." He held the phone out to her. "Just after six o'clock that evening."

"I should have known," she murmured. "I think I know who your anonymous tipster is." She pointed to his phone. "Pull up the message again." Ezra did as she asked. As the nasally voice came through the phone, Mack huffed out a humorless laugh. "I can't believe I didn't recognize her voice the first time around. It's my ex-husband's new wife."

"You sure?"

"Without a doubt," Mack said. "Carter and I had a huge argument that day. He threatened to ruin my reputation in the city."

"Why?"

"Because I refused to give him the boat I got in our

divorce settlement. I didn't take his threat seriously, because I knew I had never done anything inappropriate while in office. I guess siccing you on me was his fiancée's way of helping Carter to get back at me."

"And this is all because of a boat?"

Mack considered the incredulousness in Ezra's voice a sort of vindication for how she'd felt this past year.

"Yes, because of a boat," she said. "And because Carter is an asshole, of course. He could go out and buy a brand new boat tomorrow; he's just upset that the judge awarded this one to me. I don't even want the stupid boat, but I'll be damned if I let him have it."

Ezra's brow arched as his mouth angled upward with a mischievous smile. "I like this side of you, Councilmember Arnold."

"The spiteful bitch side?"

"The no-nonsense side that refuses to take any shit."

"Ah, that one," she said, returning his grin. "It happens to be my best side."

Ezra's gaze traveled from her eyes to her lips, sending a torrent of tingles down Mack's spine and across her skin. The fact that he could set off this kind of reaction within her with a single look didn't bode well for her vow to ignore the attraction pulsing between them. His gaze lingered for several moments more before returning to her eyes.

"Still think it's a bad idea?" Ezra whispered.

Her brain warred with the rest of her body. She'd gone through the litany of reasons why sleeping with Ezra wouldn't be the smartest move, yet the urge to ignore them all was so strong it took everything Mack had within her not to climb onto his lap and attack his mouth.

With a sigh, Mack finally answered, "Yes, it's still a bad idea." Probably. *Maybe?*

"Are you willing to hear my counter argument?" he asked.

"No," she said. She had enough counter arguments of her own.

His lips tipped up in a rueful grin. "Thought so."

"Ezra, we've been over this already."

"I know," he said. He stood and stretched his arm over his head. The motion caused his shirt to rise, revealing two toned rows of a six-pack. Mack barely held in a moan.

"I need more coffee," Ezra stated. "Can I get you some?"

She didn't want coffee. She wanted *him*.

"I'm—" She cleared her throat. "I'm good."

The moment Ezra turned away, Mack dropped her face into her hands and sucked in a breath. How long could a person exist in a state of irrepressible lust before their entire body burst into flames? She had a feeling she would soon find out.

She pulled in several more of those controlled breaths. By the time Ezra returned, she'd managed to tamp down her horniness to a more manageable level.

They resumed their probing, systematically searching through the massive amount of documents. After another hour, Mack tossed the transcript she'd been reading on the table and outright growled.

"I can't do this anymore. My eyes are going to roll out of my head if I try to read one more line." Her shoulders sagged in defeated misery. "I'm starting to feel as if this is hopeless."

"Look, if the mayor manages to keep whatever he's

hiding under wraps in this day and age, he deserves to get away with it. But he won't," Ezra said. "We'll find it."

She looked over at him. "You really think so?"

Ezra nodded. "Uncovering what people want to keep hidden is my job. And I'm damn good at my job."

Once again, his steady, intent gaze found its way to her mouth. He licked his lips.

"Stop looking at me that way," Mack said.

"How am I looking at you?"

"Like you want to eat me alive."

Mack could practically see the shudder that ran through him. His eyes slid shut and he pulled his bottom lip between his teeth. With a deep sigh, Ezra said, "If you only knew how badly I want to eat you."

Oh. My. God.

Mack tried to ignore the instant wetness between her legs. She squeezed her thighs tight as her mind conjured an image of the toys in her bedroom drawer. She didn't want anything to do with those toys tonight. Not when she had the most delectable flesh and blood man right here.

No. She wasn't doing this. She'd told herself over and over again that this could not happen.

With more conviction than she thought she could muster, Mack said. "I'm not going to sleep with you." She paused for a moment before adding, "Tonight."

Ezra's eyes popped open. He pointed to the clock on her microwave. It read 11:59.

"It's almost tomorrow," he said.

Desire pulsed through the air with every second that ticked by. Weeks of pent-up need weighed heavy against Mack's skin, saturating her in a barely suppressed yearning that was impossible to fight. When the clock changed to midnight, Ezra said, "It's tomorrow."

She sucked in a breath and, with a firm nod, said, "Okay, now I'll sleep with you."

Mack reached forward, clamped her hands on either side of his face and pulled his head to hers. She attacked his mouth, plying it with insistent strokes of her tongue, relishing the decadent flavor. Ezra returned her fervency with equal passion. He scooped her up and set her on the table, shoving her knees apart and wedging himself between them.

His eagerness fueled her arousal, the brush of his skin stimulating her every nerve ending. His palms skimmed up and down her sides, before he brought them to her breasts and squeezed.

"Do you know how much I've been dreaming about these?" Ezra asked before dipping his head and covering her breast—shirt, bra and all—with his mouth. Mack eased back and yanked her shirt off. Ezra pulled the cups of her bra down, exposing her breasts to his eyes, lips and tongue. He pounced with relish, lapping her nipple with his tongue, before sucking it into his mouth.

A mewl escaped her throat as she clamped her hands on the back of his head and held him to her breast. She wrapped her legs around his waist and pumped her hips upward, needing to feel him against her center. Needing relief.

"My bed," Mack murmured. "Let's go."

She yelped as Ezra lifted her from the table and carried her to her bedroom. He set her on the mattress and made quick work of his clothes. Mack did the same, stripping off what few pieces of clothing she still wore.

Her mouth watered at the sight of Ezra's heavy

erection. Goodness, but it had been a long time since she'd been treated to something that beautiful. Mack backed herself up on the bed, spread her legs open and crooked her finger.

But Ezra didn't move. He remained at the foot of her bed.

"Not yet," he said.

He reached down, wrapped his palm around his hardening cock and began to stroke. His eyes zeroed in on the spot between her legs and Mack's right hand immediately headed there. She licked the fingers on her left hand and touched herself, rubbing her swollen clit, circling it several times before gliding first one, and then another, finger inside her.

Ezra groaned. So did she.

"Are you going to make me do this all night, or are you going to help me out here?" she asked.

She saw his throat bob with his deep swallow.

"I'll help," he said.

He reached for the pants he'd kicked off and retrieved his wallet from his back pocket. He pulled out a condom, tore off the packaging and rolled it over his stiff erection. Mack was two seconds from spontaneously combusting when he finally walked over to the bed and climbed on top of her.

"I'll try to make this last, but I'm not making any promises," he said.

"I don't care how long it lasts, as long as you make me come."

He covered her mouth with his own, his tongue delving inside, plunging and retreating, swirling around as he explored her mouth. At the same time his erection teased her center, brushing against her slippery lips, pressing lightly against her clit, driving her absolutely insane.

"Ezra, please," Mack breathed. "It's been too damn long for me. I need you inside of me. Now."

He lifted his head and stared down at her, complete and total wonder in his eyes. "You're begging," he whispered.

"Yes, I'm fucking begging. Can you please screw me already?"

That look of awe remained on his face as he slowly shook his head. "Never in my wildest dreams did I ever think Mackenna Arnold would beg me to have sex with her."

"You need to dream bigger," she said with a laugh. "Now, do you want to get started on this making me come thing or what?"

That irresistible grin reappeared. "My pleasure."

With that he drove his long, heavy erection inside her, and Mack experienced her first true relief from the ache that had built up over way too many months of using only battery-operated toys to find sexual pleasure. She concentrated on the slide of his thick length against her inner walls, already coaxing an orgasm from her with every deliberate plunge. He captured her hands and braced them above her head, threading his fingers through hers as he drove deep, over and over and over again.

Ezra bent his head and pulled her right nipple into his mouth while his hips continued to work, the ebb and flow of his strokes enough to light her entire world on fire. Mack squeezed his hands, gripping tightly, needing the steady support he provided as he sent her soaring to new heights of pleasure.

She whimpered when Ezra freed his hands from her grip, but the whimper soon turned into a pleasurable moan when he levered himself up on one elbow while sliding his other hand between them and zeroing in on her clit. He pinched the bundle of nerves between his fingers, rolling it into a tight bud. His tongue worked back and forth in rapid succession over her nipple, while his very strong, very thick, very capable cock continued to drive into her.

Mack locked her ankles at the small of his back and bit down on her bottom lip to stop herself from screaming. She moved with him, thrusting her hips up as he thrust downward.

Just when she thought it couldn't get any better, Ezra changed his angle and lifted her right leg over his shoulder, sliding impossibly deep.

Mack's world lit up like Fourth of July fireworks.

"Oh, my God," she breathed. "More. Please...more."

He drilled into her, pummeling her with powerful lunges, his lips sucking on her nipple, setting off so many incredible sensations within her that Mack just knew she would die from the sheer pleasure. She planted her heels into the mattress and pushed herself up to meet his thrusts, lifting her hips until she and Ezra were practically fused together.

She felt her orgasm began to build deep within her belly. Before she could even grasp what was happening, her entire world erupted in a burst of scorching hot pleasure. It ricocheted off every nerve ending, sending her spiraling to places she had never been before.

She collapsed back onto the bed, her limbs shaking as Ezra continued to pound into her. He braced both hands on either side of her head and quickened his strokes, surging one, two, three times before his arms and back stiffened and he came with a thunderous surge. He fell onto his back and let out a whoosh of air.

"Well, damn," Ezra said. "That was better than I imagined it would be." He looked over at her. "And I've imagined this for a long, *long* time."

Mack released a throaty, exhausted laugh. "Happy I could live up to the fantasy."

He rolled over and captured her mouth in a kiss that had desire stirring within her belly once again. He caressed her bare thigh, rubbing his palm over her damp skin.

Trailing his tongue along her jaw, Ezra whispered, "My fantasies had nothing on the real thing."

CHAPTER 9

EZRA SAT on the edge of his desk, his feet crossed at the ankles, his arms folded over his chest. He was usually eager to get to class and mold tomorrow's journalists. He especially enjoyed his *Ethics in Journalism* class. But today? He just wasn't feeling it.

I wonder why?

He did his best to ignore the annoying inner voice that had badgered him all day, but he should have known better than to think it would be that easy. He'd never been one to turn a deaf ear to his own conscience. This morning, it proved to be impossible to ignore it.

How could he teach his students about ethics when he'd been questioning his own since the moment he'd left Mackenna's bed?

With gargantuan effort, Ezra pushed aside thoughts of Mack and forced himself to concentrate on doing the job that, at the moment, paid his bills. Clapping his hands together, he said, "Last week I asked you all to come up with different scenarios that would present a conflict of interest for a journalist. You each have three minutes to explain your case. As each student presents, the rest of you should consider ways you would handle the situation if you were to ever find yourself involved in it." He pointed to the student in the front row. "Mr. Callahan, the floor is yours."

Ezra sat back and listened as student after student offered their scenarios. The conflicts ranged from accepting money from the subject one is investigating to outing a source. Some students were more eloquent than others, but this assignment was based more on the content rather than style, something Ezra had to remind himself as he assessed their arguments.

Eight students had presented before one hit too close to home.

Jameka Jones, one of the sharpest young minds in his class, blew the discussion wide open with her scenario of a journalist becoming romantically involved with a source.

"There are a number of lines that should never be crossed, but sleeping with a source is one of the most unethical things a journalist could do," she said.

"I don't see what the big deal is," Dexter Callahan said. "As long as the journalist and the source set ground rules, and establish from the get-go that their personal and professional relationships are separate, why should it matter if they hook up?"

The look of sheer repugnance on Jameka's face was priceless. Ezra had to hide his chuckle behind a cough. Her next question, however, punctured his little bubble of amusement.

"Would you say the same if the journalist was sleeping with the subject of an investigation?" Jameka asked.

Dexter stirred in his chair for a moment before he shrugged. "Sure. Why not?"

Jameka's eye-roll was epic. "Even you don't believe that, Dexter. How can you have an unbiased view of someone who you're sleeping with? Once you cross that line, there's no going back."

"What about if you're hooking up with them for the *purpose* of getting a story? And they're boning you because they want their story to be told," Dexter countered. "It could be like a quid pro quo."

"Okay, first of all, that is disgusting," Jameka said. "Secondly, if you have to sleep with a source, you can't trust the source. The same goes for the subject of an investigation. It's just too difficult to separate feelings, unless you're a sociopath," she said, looking markedly at Dexter, who slouched in his seat.

Okay, it was time to break this up. Ezra loudly clapped his hands again.

"Ms. Jones has a point," he said. "There needs to be a separation between journalists and the subject of their story. Full stop. Being romantically involved with someone clouds your judgment. You begin to make excuses for things that you would have previously seen as questionable. It's better to never put yourself in that situation."

It was a miracle that he didn't choke on his own hypocrisy.

How could he stand here in front of these students and lecture them when he could still smell the lavender scent of Mack's bed sheets? It didn't matter that she was more along the lines of a partner now, and no longer the subject of his current investigation. She was still a source. She was his *main* source. She was the impetus behind this entire investigation into the mayor.

If it were not for Mack first coming to him with her hunch, he never would have considered that Lucien Warner could possibly be engaged in questionable conduct—something Ezra was now convinced to be the case.

But, after what they did last night, how could he view anything she told him through an objective lens? How could he look at her at all and not think about the one thing that had been on his mind since he left her bed?

How to get there again.

He wanted to be there again. He *had* to be there again.

But not if it meant compromising this story.

When it came to his career, the stakes had never been higher. Since the moment he'd walked out of the newspaper bureau, clutching a single cardboard box with his belongings to his chest, Ezra had been searching for a story with this kind of blockbuster appeal, something that could catapult him to the next level. It had been handed to him on a silver platter. He should be spending every available minute investigating the mayor.

So why in the hell wasn't he?

Cursing underneath his breath, Ezra wrapped up class early and headed for the small office he had here on campus. He hung the "Unavailable" sign on the hook outside the office and locked the door behind him. He plopped into his chair and dropped his forehead to the desk, the full weight of his actions suddenly overwhelming him.

By sleeping with Mack, he'd allowed himself to lose sight of his primary goal—his *only* goal.

There was only one thing that should be on his mind right now: breaking one of the biggest corruption stories to hit New Orleans in years. Instead, he'd spent much of his morning reliving those hours with Mackenna. Every time he closed his eyes he smelled her coconut-scented hair and felt her soft skin against his. The mayor could come up to him and confess, and Ezra wasn't sure he'd even hear him.

What in the hell was wrong with him? This wasn't just some story. This was *the* story. This was the story that could mold his career into something even he had never allowed himself to envision. Was there anything more important than that?

Yes.

Ezra's head popped up from the desk as a realization he hadn't even contemplated occurred to him. There was something else at stake here. Something that meant even more than seeing his byline on the front page, above the fold of a national newspaper. Something Ezra had been seeking more than anything else.

Redemption.

He'd committed one of the original sins of journalism, trusting the wrong source. Not only had he trusted the wrong source, but he'd ignored his managing editor's warning and nearly destroyed the hundred-plus year reputation of the paper. The chance to redeem himself from the fiasco that could have permanently ruined his career was, without a doubt, the most important thing that could come out of this.

Which was why he needed to remain focused on the mission at hand.

He also needed to think about his integrity as a journalist. Everything Jameka Jones presented in class today was true. How could he remain objective if he became romantically involved with Mack?

He couldn't. It was as simple as that.

Feeling hemmed in by the walls of the small office, Ezra slipped the syllabus he'd been working on last week into his messenger bag and headed for his usual coffee shop. In addition to the syllabus, he still had hundreds of pages of transcripts, meeting minutes and memos from the mayor to read.

He'd just sat down with a cup of black coffee when his phone began to chime. An ache instantly settled in his stomach at the sight of Mack's number illuminating the screen.

Ezra considered letting the call go to voicemail, but he refused to take the coward's way out. He'd have to talk to her eventually. Why not get it over with as quickly as possible?

He answered on the third ring.

"Hello?"

"Hey there," she said. His eyes slid shut at the sound of her voice. How could she make a simple *hey there* sound like sex?

"What's up?" Ezra asked.

"I just found out that the city council has an emergency meeting tonight, but it's on a budget issue that has already been debated so it shouldn't last too long. I'll call you once we're done and you can come over."

"Uh, about that." Ezra hesitated. "I think it's probably better if I don't."

The silence that met him on the other end of the line was deafening.

"If you don't come over?" she finally asked.

He sucked in a deep breath. "Yeah."

More silence. "Um, okay. Well, I understand if you don't want to be out too late tonight. I have a few things to look over at the Arts Council tomorrow morning, but I'm free in the afternoon."

Ezra massaged the bridge of his nose. Damn, this was hard.

"It's probably a good idea if we work independently from now on," he said. "It's safe to say that we've both become a bit distracted when we've worked together. If we're ever going to get to the bottom of this thing with the mayor, we need to devote more time to the actual investigation than to other...stuff."

And there it was again, that horrible, telling silence. It lasted even longer this time, his discomfort ratcheting up with every second that passed. When Mack finally spoke, there was no mistaking the chill in her voice.

"If you think that's best," she said.

No, he didn't think that was best. But he *did* think this was the way it had to be.

"Yeah, it probably is," Ezra answered, not bothering to mask the disappointment in his voice.

"Okay, then." Her curt, no-nonsense tone struck him like a physical blow to the chest. "Email me if you come across anything noteworthy."

She hung up without saying goodbye, and Ezra felt like the dirt being tracked in by every single patron who entered the coffee shop. Why did it suddenly feel as if he'd just made one of the biggest mistakes of his life?

"Because you just did," he muttered underneath his breath.

Ezra knew he'd done the right thing, but he should

have gone about it a better way. He should have been more honest with her and explained that it was his journalistic integrity at stake here. She was a politician. She knew all about integrity. She would have understood that, right?

Ezra brought his elbows up on the table and covered his face with his hands.

Not that it mattered. If the iciness in Mack's voice was anything to go on, none of his reasons would have made a bit of difference anyway.

~

Mack swirled the ice around in her scotch on the rocks, trying to make it last so that she wasn't tempted to have another. She was driving tonight and rarely allowed herself more than one drink, but if she had to sit at this table another ten minutes before having dinner, she was definitely having a second.

Though it wasn't as if the liquor was helping with her mood. If anything, it was making her even more melancholy.

And *that* pissed her off.

She was *not* a wallower. Especially when it came to a man. Hell, she hadn't wallowed when she divorced her husband after fifteen years of marriage. A girl like her didn't grow up to become the woman she was today by allowing her circumstances to get the best of her. She took what life threw at her and did whatever was necessary to make sure she came out on top.

That's what she would do this time.

Her night with Ezra had been exactly what she'd needed. Good sex. Fine, *great* sex. But that's all. It had been a way to blow off some steam. And after going so long without getting any, she appreciated what their time in bed had done for her, both physically and mentally. But it was over. It didn't mean anything to her.

So enough with this self-pity bullshit.

Mack downed the remainder of her scotch in one gulp. Just as she motioned for the waiter, she caught sight of Indina rushing toward her.

"I am *so* sorry," Indina said as she plopped down in the chair across from Mack. "Work has been a complete pain in the ass lately. Today's meeting was supposed to end at five. It went over by two hours."

"It's okay. I haven't been waiting all that long," Mack lied. "What's going on at work? It sounds serious."

"It's very serious. But it's a potential city contract, so we can't talk about it."

"Why not?" Mack shrugged. "Everyone else seems to be using their influence for favors, maybe I should too."

"What are you talking about?" Indina's forehead creased in confusion as the waiter placed the linen napkin in her lap and handed her a menu.

"May I explain tonight's specials?" the young man asked.

"Can you give us a minute?" Indina asked.

"No, we're good," Mack said. She looked up at the waiter. "Go ahead."

Mack ignored Indina's pointed look as she pretended to listen to the waiter. She'd been to this restaurant a dozen times and always ordered the same thing. Once he was done, she said, "I'd like to start with the charbroiled oysters, and for my entree I'll go with the pecan-crusted catfish."

"I'll have the same," Indina said.

"Excellent choices," the waiter said. He took Indina's drink order, then turned to Mack. "Can I get you another scotch?"

She deserved an award for the amount of willpower it took to say, "No, I'll take a Sprite."

The minute the waiter walked away, Indina pounced. "Okay, what was that favors comment about? And what's with the sour look on your face? You look like somebody rolled over your cat."

"I don't like cats," Mack said.

"Mackenna!"

She blew out a weary breath. "It's been a rough week, Indina. Can't we just talk about how great Idris Elba would be as 007 and forget about everything else?"

"We've exhausted that conversation. I'll switch to talking about Morris Chestnut's butt, but only after you explain what's going on. You don't sound like yourself."

"I don't feel like myself," Mack said.

Indina reached across the table and covered her hand. "Talk to me. I haven't seen you like this since your divorce. I'm getting worried."

She knew her friend came from a place of concern, but burdening Indina was the last thing Mack wanted to do. Indina was still in the euphoric stages of early love with Griffin. She deserved to soak in every blissful second, without someone else's problems siphoning away her joy.

But she really needed her friend right now. She decided to be selfish.

Mack started with her suspicions about Mayor Warner. Indina listened with rapt attention, her eyes growing wider with each instance of questionable behavior Mack put forth.

"If it were just two or three times, I'd say it was coincidence, but this goes far beyond mere coincidence," Indina said. "I'm amazed no one else has brought it up."

"If I had not listed it all for you, would any of it have stood out to you?" Indina shook her head. "Exactly," Mack said. "Unless a person is paying close attention, it's not that easy to grasp just how many times the mayor has changed course over the last year. Especially because, for the most part, it isn't on things that will raise many eyebrows."

In a lowered voice, Indian asked, "Is this why you want to run?"

Mack thought about it for only a second before shaking her head. "No. I want to run because I think I can do the job. But all of this does play a part in my timing," she said. She rubbed a water spot from her butter knife. "I had always planned to wait until Lucien was no longer eligible to run. You know how much I admire that man, Indina. I never imagined myself facing him in an election." She hunched her shoulders. "But I can't just sit back and allow corruption to take over this city. And now that it looks as if both Babin and Washington are into some kind of shady business—"

"Wait. *What?*" Indina asked.

Mack blew out a weary breath as she gave Indina the condensed version of her run-in with Russell and Cecil.

"Goodness, Mack. And I thought I was having a shitty Monday."

"You don't know the half of it," Mack muttered.

Indina's eyebrows nearly touched her hairline. "Don't tell me there's more."

Mack hesitated for a moment. She really didn't want to get into this with Indina. Ezra was her brother, after all. But Indina was her best friend. If she couldn't talk to her best friend about this, who could she talk to?

"You know I've been working with Ezra," Mack started.

"I know the two of you have been working on something," Indina said. She dropped her voice to a whisper. "He's helping you to investigate the mayor, isn't he?"

Mack nodded.

"Now it makes sense," Indina said. "I've been wondering what you could possibly have wanted with Ezra ever since you asked me for his number. I hope he hasn't been insufferable."

Mack took a sip of her Sprite and cursed it for not being scotch. "We slept together."

Indina's eyes bucked. Her lips parted in shock, but no words came forth.

"Are you actually speechless?" Mack asked, unable to keep the amusement from her voice. "Never thought I'd see the day."

"But…but…why?" Indina asked. "You two hate each other. Were you drunk?"

"No," Mack answered.

"Was he?"

"No!"

"So how did it happen?"

Mack huffed out an exasperated sigh. "Seriously, Indina, have you seen your brother?"

Her friend held up both hands. "Do *not*. I don't care what other women say about them, when I look at any of my brothers, or even my cousins for that matter, all I see is a bunch of knuckleheads."

"They *are* a bunch of knuckleheads, but they're also fine as hell. Even when I wanted to strangle Ezra while he was investigating me, I still used him as my mental stand-in a few times."

"I thought mental stand-ins were only supposed to be unattainable people, like movie stars?"

"When you go as long as I did without getting any, a mental stand-in is whoever the hell you want it to be." She shrugged. "Ezra did it for me."

Indina's mouth twisted with repugnance. "Gross."

"Shut up," Mack said with a laugh.

"Sorry," she said. "It's just…weird."

The waiter arrived with their oysters. Indina doused hers with hot sauce and slurped up two of them before resuming the conversation. "Okay, so you slept with Ezra," she said. She made a gag motion, sticking her finger down her throat. "Why did that contribute to the shitiness of your Monday? What went wrong?" She held her hands up. "Unless it has something to do with, you know, his performance. I don't want to know."

"Trust me, there was nothing wrong with his performance."

Indina dropped her fork. "Didn't I *just* say I didn't want to know? I could have sworn I *just* said that."

"Sorry," Mack said. She released a sigh. "The truth is, I have no idea what went wrong. Ezra's been over at my place nearly every night for the past three weeks. We've been going over the information he's found on Mayor Warner. Everything was fine, until we slept together." She shrugged. "He all of a sudden decided that we shouldn't work together anymore. That we should still conduct the research, but do it independently."

"What an asshole," Indina said.

"Your sisterly love is so apparent."

"I don't care that he's my brother. That was an asshole move. I need to slap some sense into him."

"No," Mack quickly injected. "Ezra's right." Indina started to speak, but Mack stopped her. "I mean it, Indina. I allowed this attraction to Ezra to distract me from what's really important here." She put her hands up. "Now that I've got it out of my system, I can concentrate on uncovering whatever is going on with the mayor and figuring out whether or not I really want to challenge him in the next mayoral race."

"But that doesn't mean Ezra can give you the wham, bam, thank you ma'am treatment."

"It wasn't like that," Mack said. "Just promise me that you'll stay out of this."

"But—"

"Promise me," Mack said again.

Reluctance emanated from across the table, but Indina finally nodded.

"Fine," she said with a nonchalant wave. "I'll stay out of it." She pointed at Mack. "But don't think I won't punch him the next time I see him. I'll just make up an excuse for why I had to punch him that has nothing to do with you."

Mack laughed. It was the first time she'd done so in three days. "I don't know why it took me so long to tell you this."

"Neither do I," Indina said. "Despite my initial reaction—which, let's face it, is justified seeing that this *is* my brother we're talking about—I'm not as grossed out by the idea of you and Ezra together as I first let on." A smile edged up the corner of her mouth. "Actually, I think I may love it. Just think, if you two were to get married, we'd be sisters."

"For goodness' sake, Indina. Married?" Mack deadpanned. "After what I just told you?"

"Yeah, the fact that he's acting like a complete ass ruins it for me. He wasn't raised that way," Indina said.

"I know that," Mack said. "But it doesn't matter. You know I have no intentions of getting married anytime soon. If ever."

"Well... I said the same thing, and yet?" Indina held her hand up. Mack dropped her fork and her jaw at the same time. "This is just one way I knew something was definitely wrong," Indina continued. "We've been sitting here for twenty minutes and you didn't even notice."

"Holy shit! When did this happen?"

"Today. At work of all places." She rolled her eyes. "He asked me over sushi in my office."

"Oh, Griffin." Mack laughed. "That's probably the most unromantic proposal I've ever heard."

"Yes, he definitely needs work in the romantic gesture department."

Mack reached over and captured her hand. "I am so happy for you, sweetheart. Have the two of you set a date?"

Indina shook her head.

"Good, because I would have been highly pissed if you'd set a date without telling me."

"You know I don't move that fast," Indina said. "The fact that I told him yes so quickly shocked the hell out of both of us. But I already told Griffin that we can't do anything until we've set up my mom's foundation and have it off the ground. He's okay with that. He said he just wanted to see his ring on my finger."

"You found yourself a good one." Mack smiled. "I still can't believe you thought he was only good for sex." Indina had been in a co-workers-with-benefits relationship with her boyfriend—correction: fiancé—for nearly a year before Griffin was able to convince her that they were meant to be together.

"He's still good for that," Indina said. Her eyes fell closed and a huge smiled spread across her face. "Very good."

"Bitch, don't rub it in," Mack said.

Indina's head flew back with her crack of laughter.

As she regarded the sheer bliss on her friend's face, Mack wondered if she would ever find that kind of happiness again.

Again?

When had she *ever* been that happy?

What Indina and Griffin had was real. Mack doubted she'd ever shared that kind of love with Carter. He wasn't the type of man who made himself available for true love.

You could have eventually loved Ezra.

The thought sent a sharp ache through Mack's heart. There was no doubt in her mind that she could have fallen in love with Ezra. But that wasn't in the cards for her, so she'd just have to deal. She was a pro at dealing with whatever life threw her way.

Mack waved her fork at Indina's fingers. "Just because you have that rock on your hand, it doesn't mean you can flaunt it in my face."

"You know I would never do that."

"Sure, just like you never flaunt your smokin' sex life in my face."

"Hey, you can't complain anymore now that your drought is over."

Mack snorted. "One night of sex shouldn't count as the end of my drought."

Indina's smile faltered. "Is it really going to be just one night?"

"Yes," Mack said with a definitive nod. "It was a mistake to begin with."

"Don't say that," Indina said. "I would love it if you and Ezra could actually make something work. He used to be so infatuated with you back when we were in college."

For the second time tonight, Mack's jaw dropped. "You knew about his crush on me?"

"Of course I knew. He's my little brother."

"Why didn't you ever say anything to me about it?"

"Because he was my little brother," Indina repeated. "It wasn't the first time one of my brothers had had a crush on one of my friends. But I must admit that, with you, it seemed to be much more serious, at least for Ezra. That was before you married Carter, of course." She shrugged. "I figured he was over you."

Mack released a deep sigh. "Well, he's definitely over me now."

"I still think you should let me knock him over the head," Indina said.

Mack smiled. "No. Family is too important. I'll be just fine." She picked up the small dessert menu. "But a slice of bourbon pecan pie will make me feel a whole lot better."

"We sharing?" Indina asked.

Mack glared at her. "You touch my pie, you die."

They both burst out laughing, and Mack's heart swelled with gratitude over Indina's enduring friendship.

At least that was one thing she could always count on.

CHAPTER 10

Ezra found himself in familiar territory, standing on the sidewalk in front of Mack's condo building, staring at the outside entrance. But unlike the excitement that pulsed through him the last time he was here, his entire being was consumed with dread.

And…hope.

If he'd ever doubted whether or not he was an optimist, Ezra had his answer. Because despite all the reasons she shouldn't, he held out hope that Mack would be understanding when he explained why he'd been MIA for the past four days.

His eyes traveled up to the seventh floor and over to the third window from the right. The lights were on. She was home.

He sucked in a breath.

He'd taken a chance coming here without calling or texting first, but what in the hell was he supposed to say in a text? Sorry for being an asshole and ignoring you since the moment I left your bed?

Yeah, that would go over real well.

He refused hide behind a text. Ezra figured it was better to speak to her face-to-face. That way, when she told him "screw you," he could gauge how much venom there was behind the words.

He pulled in another reassuring breath before pressing the call button on her doorbell. Several moments passed before Mack's rich voice came through the speaker.

"Who is it?" she asked.

"It's, uh, Ezra. Can I come up?"

His request was met with dead silence. He pressed the button again, but didn't get an answer.

"Shit," Ezra cursed under his breath.

He knew he'd fucked up. He'd come here today to see just how badly he'd fucked up. The fact that she wouldn't even respond was all the answer he needed.

Just as Ezra turned to walk away, the door to the building opened and Mack appeared. The first thing he noticed was how amazing she looked dressed in leggings and an oversized T-shirt; her face devoid of makeup, a silk scarf wrapped around her head. He'd never seen her so casually dressed. He'd never been more attracted to her than he was at this very moment.

"I took a chance on you being here," Ezra said.

"I took a sick day," she answered.

Alarm instantly pierced his chest. "Are you okay?"

"I'm fine. I just needed a day away from everything." She leaned her shoulder against the doorjamb and folded her arms over her chest. "What do you want, Ezra?"

"To apologize," he said.

Her gaze dropped to her feet before returning to his face. "You don't have anything to apologize for."

"Yes, I do."

"Ezra—"

A couple came up behind her, the man pushing a stroller with a sleeping, blond-haired baby snuggling a stuffed unicorn. "Pardon me," the man said.

"I'm sorry," Mack said as she cleared the way for them to pass.

Ezra took the opportunity to step in closer to her. "Can we please go upstairs and talk?"

"I'm not sure we have anything to talk about. Unless you uncovered something else in the investigation that I don't know about."

"Mack, please. Just give me a chance to explain why I…why I did what I did."

Ezra wasn't sure exactly how he planned to do that, but he was good at thinking on his feet. Surely he could come up with something by the time they made it up to her condo.

Mack continued to stare at him, saying nothing. His unease grew with every second that ticked by. Finally, she pushed away from the doorjamb. If he hadn't had all of his attention focused on her, Ezra would have missed the little nudge of her head, inviting him to follow her.

They were silent as they rode the elevator up to her floor. Once they entered her condo, she remained standing in the foyer.

"Do you mind if we sit down?" Ezra asked.

"I'm good right here."

He released a breath and rubbed his hands against his thighs. This wasn't going to be easy, not that he deserved easy. He was lucky she'd agreed to hear him out at all.

"Thursday night spooked me," Ezra started.

The brow over her right eye cocked in inquiry, but she didn't respond.

"Developing feelings for someone who I could potentially have to investigate is a professional hazard for me as a journalist. In the back of my head, I knew it was wrong, but it wasn't until the following day, while teaching my *Ethics in Journalism* class, that it hit me. Actually, it didn't just hit me, it crashed down over my head like a ton of bricks."

She continued her ride on the Stoic and Silent Express, not giving him any cues to what she was thinking. Ezra's heart began to pump faster. Fear that he wasn't getting through to her sent a sharp pain to his chest.

"Do you understand my dilemma, Mackenna? If you decide to run for mayor, how can I ever remain impartial? My journalistic integrity wouldn't be worth shit."

She nodded. "I understand."

"*Do* you?"

"Yes. Of course. Last Thursday was a one-time thing. It won't happen again. We can continue our own separate investigations into Mayor Warner's background and if either of us finds anything, we'll let the other know. Unless you'd rather just forget about the joint investigation entirely."

"No. Dammit, Mack." He tipped his head back and ran both hands down his face. "I don't want to continue on the way we have these past few days. For one thing, it doesn't make sense to work separately. We can find out that we've both been wasting time going down the same path, which would only set us back when time is of the essence."

His eyes connected with hers. "But that's not the only reason I don't want us working apart anymore." He took a step forward and she took one back. Her move was like a physical blow.

He'd made an irrevocable mistake. There was no doubt about that.

Ezra put both hands up. "I won't ask that we just forget about what happened and start over, because I don't want to forget it. That night was…God, Mack, it was the most amazing thing that's happened to me in years."

She folded her arms over her chest and started for the door. "I don't need to hear this," she said.

"Mack, please." Ezra caught her arm. She flinched.

He quickly let go and waited for her to turn before pleading in a pained voice, "Please, just hear me out."

"What do you want from me, Ezra? You're saying that sleeping with me will ruin your career, and at the same time gushing over how it was this magical night. I don't understand what you want. You can't have it both ways."

"I know that," he said.

"Do you think it doesn't compromise me, as well?" Mack asked. "You're the same reporter who was hellbent on ruining *my* career just a few months ago. Do you think it doesn't scare the shit out of me to let my guard down and trust you? How do I know you're not still investigating me and getting in my bed was just another way for you to get closer to me so you can get the real story?"

"You know that's not the case."

"Do I?"

Ezra blew out a frustrated breath. "I'm not investigating you, Mackenna. I now know that the well-being of this city is the most important thing to you."

"But you think if I become mayor, I'll somehow compromise my morals. Is that it?"

"That's not what I'm saying. But let's be real, Mack. It's a legitimate issue. What happens if you become mayor and I have to investigate you?"

Her indifferent expression turned pensive, her forehead creasing slightly.

"I can see how that would be a problem," she finally said. "I guess there's no way to work around that."

"Actually, I came up with a solution. It's a pretty simple one."

She lifted her brows, as if silently asking for further explanation.

"I just wouldn't investigate you," Ezra said. "It wouldn't make me any less of a journalist to step away from any story involving you."

She shook her head. "I wouldn't want you to do that. Your job is a part of who you are, Ezra. It wouldn't be fair to expect you to not be you."

"Let me worry about that," Ezra said. He took the chance of closing the gap between them. It felt like he'd won a victory when she didn't automatically take a step back. "I don't want to stop seeing you. I don't want to stop working with you. I want to see *more* of you. I want to see you not just when we're working together on this investigation, but when you're having dinner, or watching television, or grocery shopping. I want to be with you, Mackenna."

He took her hand in his. "Can we do this? *Really* do

this? Can we start seeing more of each other so that we can at least *try* to see where this leads?"

After several weighty moments passed, she said, "I don't know."

That one statement completely knocked the wind out of Ezra's sails. He'd banked on his plea being enough to win her over.

"What can I do to change your mind?" he asked.

She looked up at him. "Do you know you're the first man I've slept with since divorcing my husband? Only the second man I've slept with since I was twenty-three years old?"

He shook his head and tried to ignore the unwarranted pleasure her admission induced.

"It may have seemed as if it happened all of a sudden, but it didn't, Ezra. I thought long and hard before sleeping with you. It's not something I take lightly."

"I know it isn't," he said.

She slipped her hand out of his hold and took several steps back.

"Well then, you should know that it won't be easy for me to just jump right back into it."

He nodded, mentally acknowledging the sharp ache in his chest. He had to clear his throat before speaking.

"I'm willing to wait," Ezra said. "I knew I'd have to win back your trust." He shoved his hands in his pockets. "So, does this mean we're back on with the investigation as well?"

She hesitated for several moments before nodding. "Meet me at my office in City Hall tomorrow. I'm free any time after two p.m."

Ezra jutted his chin toward her dining room where

they'd worked the other night. "I've got time right now," he said.

"I don't think I'm ready to have you here right now."

And if ever there was a dagger to the heart, that was it.

"Okay," he said. "I won't push."

She nodded. "I appreciate it." Then she turned and opened the door.

Ezra felt as if a ton of lead was tied to his legs as he trudged to the door. Everything within him screamed at him to stay and try to change her mind. But that wouldn't be fair to her. He was the one who'd slept with her, then went radio silent for nearly a week.

He would be happy with whatever crumb of her time she threw his way. At this point, he had no other choice.

~

Mack turned the corner at the end of the hallway and spotted Ezra standing outside the door of her office at City Hall. She cursed her stupid heart for speeding up the way it did just at the sight of him. The man screwed her, and then told her he didn't want to see her again. Not in those exact terms, of course, but that's how it had felt.

He had a legitimate reason.

"Oh, shut up," Mack muttered to that voice in her head that continued to plead Ezra's case. She wasn't ready to give him the benefit of the doubt just yet. But she had to admit it was getting harder to ignore that he'd had a point.

She'd spent much of the night thinking back on the dilemma he'd described. She could see how engaging in an intimate relationship with someone he could potentially have to investigate would put him in an impossible position. If their roles were reversed, would *she* be able to remain impartial if she had to investigate *him*?

No. No way.

All it would take was a reminder of the way his gloriously built body had brought her so much pleasure, and she would be toast. How could she blame him for wanting to hold on to his integrity as a journalist? This was his job. He couldn't compromise his career just because she wanted to continue having amazing sex with him *and* become mayor of this city.

"Hey," Ezra said as she approached her office.

"Hello," Mack returned. She held up her phone. "You can use some work when it comes to telling time. It's only eleven. I said I wouldn't be free until after two p.m."

A slight grin tipped up the corner of his mouth. "This wasn't a planned visit. I'm actually here to support the effort to rename that park on Carrolton after Regina Barton, the mother who first led the fight against Bayou Regional Chemical over the soil contamination. The measure will be on the upcoming agenda the next time the city council meets."

"It has my vote," Mack said. "I can't think of anyone else who would be so worthy of the honor. Except maybe you," she said. "You were the one who broke the story and got it the attention it deserved."

He brushed that off with a shake of his head. "I was just doing my job."

Why must he be both sexy *and* humble? Her irritation over him investigating her had momentarily blinded Mack to his many attributes, but now that he was no longer snooping around, trying to dig up dirt on her, her eyes were wide open. And she liked what she saw.

Ezra Holmes was smart, kind, funny, sexy, engaging, sexy, humble, sexy. Sexy, sexy, sexy. The effort it took to remain indifferent and maintain her distance tested her willpower to the very limit.

Mack tipped her head toward her door. "Do you want to come in?"

Ezra stuffed his hands in his pockets. "I wondered if I could maybe take you out to lunch," he said. "If you were planning to take a lunch break, that is."

Her petty side wanted to turn him down. Yeah, she was still *that* pissed over the way he'd treated her after they slept together. But there was an even stronger side that craved to sit across a table from him and just enjoy his company for an hour. Mack decided to listen to the non-petty side.

"Give me a minute to grab my purse," she said.

They drove to one of the many new restaurants that had popped up in the Mid-City area after Hurricane Katrina. As New Orleans rebuilt itself following the storm, this neighborhood in particular had truly flourished. The spirit of the community could be felt in every eclectic yard sign and colorful flower garden.

They were seated at a wrought-iron sidewalk table under the shady branches of an oak that covered half of Iberville Street. Mack ordered a bowl of gumbo with a side of fried crawfish tails, which she immediately tossed into her gumbo. Ezra opted for the fried catfish po'boy.

"That looks really good," Mack said, eyeing his sandwich.

His eyes sparkled with his wry grin. "I was thinking the same about your gumbo."

They both paused for a moment before quickly switching dishes and taking huge samples of each other's lunch.

"Oh, yeah," Mack said with a moan. "I'll have to come back and get one of these for myself soon."

"I'm usually available for lunch," Ezra said. "If you ever want to make this a standing date."

Despite his casual delivery, Mack couldn't ignore the meaning behind his suggestion. Her answer would be a signal; it would broadcast where she stood when it came to forgiving him for the way he'd treated her this past week.

She dusted the breadcrumbs from her fingers. "I'll think about that."

A brief flash of hope brightened his eyes.

"How about Tuesdays and Thursdays?"

"Ezra—"

He put his hands up. "I'm not pushing," he said. "I promised to give you all the time and space you need, and I'm standing by that." He moved his half-eaten sandwich to the side and reached for her, brushing his thumb back and forth over the back of her hand. "But I want you to know that being with you, even if it's just for lunch, would mean everything to me, Mackenna."

His softly spoken words pitched Mack's heart into a maelstrom of emotions she wasn't ready to acknowledge. She wanted to still be angry, dammit! She *deserved* to be angry with him over the way he'd brushed her off after last Thursday night.

But what would holding onto her anger get her in the end? Another few days of self-righteous indignation?

Self-righteousness wouldn't warm her bed at night. But Ezra could.

Mack covered the hand that was holding hers, and with a smile, said, "Let's play this lunch thing by ear."

His answering smile made him even more handsome. "I'll take it.

"So, you said you were free after two today. That's pretty rare, isn't it?"

"Extremely rare," she said before scooping up the last of her gumbo. She took a sip of iced tea and dabbed at her lips with her napkin. "I had two meetings postponed. I'm so tempted to blow off the next couple of hours, but I'll probably just go back to my office and catch up on email."

"Email? Is that the best you can come up with?" Ezra asked.

"You have a better idea?" Mack asked.

The look he threw her way was part sheepish, part hopeful, and one hundred percent wicked.

An hour later, Mack found herself straddling Ezra's lap, her head pitched back, her eyes closed. She bit down on her bottom lip, but her attempt to hold back her scream crashed and burned when Ezra bucked his hips upward, thrusting his generous length deep inside her.

Mack steadied herself against him, spreading her palms over his muscled chest, seeking purchase as she began to grind with more vigor. She rose and fell, impaling herself on his rigid erection, driving forward with one goal in mind. Reaching the climax she knew awaited her on the other side.

Ezra clamped his hands on either side of her waist and guided her motions. He moved to her backside, his palms spanning her ass as he gripped tight and pulled her down, lifting his hips up to meet her.

The orgasm slammed into her, a wave of pleasure crashing over her, drowning her in the most decadently intense sensations she'd ever felt.

Mack screamed loud enough to wake the dead. She fell forward, crumbling in a heap of satisfaction. Pleasure swept through her veins, cascading along her nerve endings.

"Was that even real?" she murmured against Ezra's chest.

"I think so," he said.

Mack managed to lift her head and look up at him. "I can't believe I just had sex in the middle of a work day."

"Can you think of a better way to spend your free time?" Ezra asked as he scooted up, perching himself against the padded headboard.

She paused for a moment, pretending to think it over while Ezra captured her arms and hauled her up to him.

"Wait, *can* you think of something you would have rather done?" he asked.

She couldn't hold back her grin. She shook her head. "Nope."

"Thank God." He dropped his head back against the headboard. "I would have been devastated if you'd answered that any other way."

She burst out laughing, then twisted around so that her back lay against him, the smattering of hair on his chest grazing her skin. He wrapped his arm around her waist and burrowed his face behind her ear. Mack released a contented sigh. She couldn't remember the last time she'd felt so satisfied, so at peace. As if nothing in the world could touch her.

She'd thought that carefree afternoon at Satchmo Fest was what she'd needed to ease the overwhelming tension that had been bombarding her, but it couldn't hold a candle to what a half hour in bed with Erza did for her stress levels.

"So, if we decide to do the Tuesday and Thursday lunch date, would this be included?" she asked.

"Hell yes," Ezra said against her neck. His head popped up. "But you know we don't have to do it just on Tuesdays and Thursdays, right?"

She laughed. "Good, because I may need to call on you quite often, especially if I decide to run against Lucien."

"Are you still undecided?" he asked. "I would have thought that by now you'd come to terms with the fact that you have to get in this race."

She looked back over her bare shoulder. "I *have* to?"

"Yes, you have to," Ezra said. "It doesn't matter what we find on the mayor. To be honest, it's probably time we accept that we may not find what we're looking for before the deadline to declare your candidacy." He slid his palm over her jaw. "It doesn't matter. You have to run, Mack. There's no one better suited for that job."

She searched his eyes. "What makes you so sure?"

Ezra's fingers gently caressed her skin. "Because I've never met anyone more determined than you," he said. "I don't know where it comes from, but it's one of your most stunning features."

Mack released a wry laugh. "That darn Grandma Geraldine."

"Is that where it comes from? Your grandmother?"

She nodded. "I was raised by my grandparents. My grandfather was pretty laid back, but Grandma Geraldine? She didn't tolerate anyone slacking, especially me."

"How'd you end up with your grandparents? What happened to your parents?"

She stared at him for only a moment before having to break contact with his probing gaze. Mack turned and rested her head against his forearm. She softly stroked his skin, contemplating how much she wanted to tell him.

There were parts of her childhood that she had never shared with her husband; parts she kept to herself because she knew Carter would look down on her if he knew the full story. There were some parts she'd never even told Indina about. Yet, for some reason, the thought of sharing it with Ezra didn't send her into an instant panic. Mack didn't want to think about what that meant. She wasn't sure she was ready for that kind of introspection.

"My mom was in and out of jail," she said. "She would get picked up every other month for writing bad checks, stealing from the cash register at whatever convenience store job she managed to get, identity fraud. You name it."

The room was silent for several moments before Ezra finally asked in a soft whisper, "Was it drugs?"

"No." Mack shook her head. "She just loved buying shit. As I got older, I started to believe that she truly suffered from a mental illness. It was as if she couldn't control it. She would steal so that she could buy the latest designer jeans, or a gold watch. She even bought a double-wide trailer once in one of her bosses' names. Forged the woman's signature and everything. That's the one that sent her to prison, and caused my grandmother to cut her out of our lives for good."

Ezra tightened his hold on her. "What about your dad?"

Mack snorted. "Your guess is as good as mine. I never even tried to solve that mystery." She shrugged. "I have an idea of who my little sister's dad is, but—"

"Wait. You have a sister?" Ezra asked, cutting her off.

"Yes. Alicia. Now *she's* the drug addict of the family," Mack said with a laugh that turn into a painful hiccup. She'd tried for flippant, but couldn't pull it off. Hurt pierced her chest just at the thought of her younger sister. Mack remembered the way she looked the last time she saw her, hair caked with dirt, eyes hollow, skin marred with dime-sized bruises from needle pricks. She sucked in a shuddering breath.

"I'm sorry," Ezra said.

She shook her head and forced herself to speak. "I've done everything I can do to help her. I could have bought a house over in English Turn with the amount of money I've spent on rehab. She'll stay clean for a few months—as long as a year one time. But she always slips back into that awful lifestyle. At this point I'm just waiting for a call from the sheriff up in Shreveport telling me that they've found her body somewhere."

She wiped a tear on Ezra's bicep, then eased her grip on his forearm. She hadn't realized just how tight she'd been holding onto him. When he covered her hand with his and squeezed, as if telling her to hold on as tightly as she needed to, Mack nearly cried with gratitude. She'd been alone in her pain for so long. She no longer had to suffer alone.

"There has to be something more that can be done," Ezra whispered.

She shook her head and sniffed. "I've done everything. So has my grandmother. She gave up on Alicia even before I did. I just *knew* if I tried hard enough, I could get her clean, but nothing worked. There came a point where I had to decide whether I would continue to try to help her—and likely kill myself in the process—or just let her go. I decided to let her go. It was the hardest thing I've ever done."

"God, I'm so sorry, Mack." Ezra kissed the top of her head.

They lay there in contented silence for several long minutes, with nothing but the hum of the air conditioner and their matching breaths piercing the quietness. After a couple more moments drifted by, Ezra spoke, his voice cautious.

"You *do* know this is likely to come out if you decide to run, don't you? Somebody will find her. You can bet Mayor Warner's team will have people dispatched up there to dig up dirt on your past as soon as you declare your candidacy."

"Let them," Mack said. "I've never tried to hide Alicia or my mother's past. I just haven't share it all that much. With anyone," she emphasized, wondering if he would catch on to what she was trying to tell him.

"Not even with Carter?"

She shook her head. "Not with Indina either."

Ezra scooped his arm underneath her and turned her fully around to face him. His eyes searched her face. "Why me?" he asked.

"Because I trust you with the information," Mack answered. "I trust you not to turn around and use it against me."

His hands slid up to hold both sides of her face. He leaned forward and captured her lips, pressing a deep, soulful kiss to her mouth.

"Thank you for saying that." He brushed his thumbs along her cheeks. "I don't know where this will go, Mack. I'm not sure what it will look like two years—hell two *months*—from now. You may get tired of me by next week. But at this very moment, there is nothing in this world I want more than to be with you."

Her chest expanded with the deep breath she pulled in.

Mack's first instinct was to resist. His behavior after the first time they slept together had only worked to fuel her distrust in relationships that had developed following her divorce.

But Mack fought against the overwhelming urge to push away. She would not allow fear of what *could* happen to deny her the pleasure of what lay right in front of her.

She wrapped her arms around Ezra's neck and pulled him to her.

"I want that too," she said. "I want *you*."

She opened her mouth over his and lost herself in his kiss.

CHAPTER 11

MACK WALKED up to the receptionist's desk at the Arts Council and picked up the clipboard that held the sign-in sheets. She flipped back to Tuesday, searching for the full name of the harpist who'd come in with a complaint about a wedding venue in Metairie that had reneged on a longstanding contract.

"Elizabeth, do you know if Seth Middleton plans to stop by today?" she asked the receptionist. "I tried emailing him, but he hasn't responded."

"Didn't you hear?"

"Hear what?" Mack asked.

"He quit."

"Quit?" Mack frowned. "But he just started doing pro bono work a few months ago."

"He didn't just quit the pro bono work, he quit everything. His practice, his marriage, everything."

"*What?*"

Elizabeth nodded enthusiastically, her eyes taking on that shimmer they got when she had juicy gossip to share.

"So, I take spin class with one of the paralegals in his law practice, and she said Mr. Middleton came in one day last week and said that he was tired of this life. He couldn't handle the stress of the job anymore and he was tired of his wife sleeping around with one of the partners in the firm—something that's been going on for a couple of years, by the way. He said that he was done and moving to a horse farm in Wyoming."

"Well, damn," Mack said. "I know who wins this year's prize for overkill."

"Right?" Elizabeth laughed.

Though, to be honest, Mack couldn't blame the guy. Hell, just over a year ago she'd been in that exact same place. She never considered a horse farm in Wyoming, but she *had* researched several homes in the Phoenix area. She didn't know anyone in Phoenix. Had never seen anything other than the city's airport on a few layovers while flying to the West Coast. But for about three days, she'd been determined to get there.

It was two days after Carter's new girlfriend moved in with him. Mack had been in the library on Loyola's campus, preparing materials for her upcoming class. She'd walked up to a map that hung on the wall, closed her eyes, and pointed. When she opened her eyes, Phoenix had been the closest big city to her finger. She'd decided that's where she would start her brand new life. A life away from the pain and humiliation Carter had subjected her to during their divorce.

Now? Thoughts of those days were permanently in her rearview mirror. The past two weeks with Ezra had helped assuage some of the hurt and embarrassment Mack had refused to admit still lingered.

No, she didn't want her ex-husband. She'd been over

their marriage even before it had officially ended. But she had still felt shame at the way it ended. She no longer harbored that shame.

The door to the Art Council's office suite opened and John Darbonne walked in.

"Hey you," Mack said, walking over and giving him a hug. "Were we scheduled to meet today?"

"No," he said. "But I just got through a mediation on Poydras and thought I'd stop over." He took a couple of Hershey's Kisses from the bowl on Elizabeth's desk and winked at her. The receptionist's pale skin turned bright red.

"Stop flirting with the staff and come on back to my office," Mack said.

"It's okay if he flirts," Elizabeth said with a dreamy sigh. "The staff doesn't mind."

"He's happily married," Mack called over her shoulder as she led John to her office. "You want coffee?" she asked him, going to the single-cup brewer on the tiny table in the corner and popping in a pod.

John waved off her offer. "I'm trying to cut back. Pretty sure I have an ulcer forming."

"Have you been to the doctor?"

He gave her a look that said *are you kidding me?*

"What is it with men and doctors?" Mack asked, shaking her head.

"I don't know about all men, but the men in my family simply don't go. They prefer to just drop dead before the age of forty-five."

Mack pointed a finger at him. "You better not drop dead. I'll still be in the mayor's office when we're forty-five. I'll need you as my legal counsel."

John leaned back in his chair and crossed his ankle

over his knee, a cagey smile breaking out over his handsome face. "So, you've finally made up your mind."

Taking her mug in her hands, Mack opted for the chair next to John's instead of the one behind her desk. "I'm ninety-nine percent sure I'm going to run," she said.

"What's the one-percent that's holding you back?"

She hunched her shoulders. "I'm still clinging to a little drop of loyalty. There's a part of me that still hates the thought of running against Lucien."

"Tell that part of you to take a hike," John said. "This is your calling, Mackenna."

"I wouldn't go that far," she said, trying to brush off his heavy words with a wave of her hand.

"I would. Look at all you've done for District D in the four years you've been their representative on the city council. You've accomplished more than the past three council members who represented that district combined. When I think about what someone with your mind, your drive, your *heart* can do for this entire city…" John released a low whistle. "You were meant to do this. Whatever doubts you have, just put them away. New Orleans needs you."

"Wow. No pressure there," Mack said with an uneasy laugh.

"I've known you long enough to know that you do best under pressure," John said.

Mack smiled at him over the rim of her coffee mug. "So," she said, after taking a sip. "If I *do* run, are you still willing to be my campaign manager?"

John took out his phone, swiped his finger across it, then held it up to her. "Already designed your official campaign sign. I can't wait to see it on that huge billboard next to the Super Dome where Carter has been advertising his law firm."

Mack threw her head back with her laugh. "You are definitely the best man for the job."

"I'm ready to get you elected mayor of this city. Are you ready to say that you're one hundred percent in?"

Mack sucked in a deep breath and tamped down the panic that started to rise in her throat.

She could do this. She *would* do this.

"Yes," she said. "The Honorable Mackenna Arnold sounds too damn good not to at least try."

John slapped his hands on his thighs before standing. "Damn right it does." He hauled Mack out of her chair and wrapped her up in a bear hug. "This is going to be epic."

After John left, Mack tried to catch up on all the work that had been piling up since she started looking into the current mayor's background, but her brain wouldn't allow it. She tossed her pen on the desk, brought her elbows up on her blotter, and ran both hands down her face.

She was at a loss when it came to what to do about Lucien. Either he was a master at hiding whatever shady dealings he was into, or his hands were clean. Mack couldn't be sure. But she had serious doubts that she and Ezra would find that smoking gun before the qualifying period for the mayor's race began.

Speaking of…

She would have to carve out some time over the next four days to prepare the paperwork for the upcoming race. Now that she'd officially made her decision, being a mayoral candidate was about to become her full-time job.

As much as she'd hedged over the last few weeks, she was shockingly at peace with her decision. The anxiety she'd been prepared to feel had been a fleeting thing. Now, she was all about getting to work.

She couldn't wait to tell Ezra about her decision. Mack picked up her phone to text him, but immediately set it back on the desk. This wasn't news she wanted to share over a text. She wanted to tell him face-to-face.

No, she wouldn't *tell* him at all. She would *show* him. She would present him with her candidate declaration papers.

Just as she clicked on the folder where she'd saved a PDF of the declaration form, alerts rang out on both her personal and city council-provided cell phones. She answered the business phone, while scanning the text messages coming to her personal phone.

"Hello?" Mack answered.

"Hello, Councilmember Arnold." It was Cecil Washington. "The council needs to convene for an emergency meeting. Are you available to meet at five p.m.?"

"Absolutely," Mack answered. She looked at the clock on her computer. It was a quarter to four. "What are we meeting on?"

"The vehicles-for-hire issue," he said.

Her head reared back. "I thought we'd already settled that issue."

There had been a huge fight over the introduction of app-based drivers-for-hire services in New Orleans, mostly from the taxi cab companies who were afraid they would be priced out of business. The council had voted to allow only certain vehicle sizes for hire, and agreed to require a minimum amount that must be charged so that the taxi companies, which all had significantly higher overhead, wouldn't be put out of business. The issue, as far as Mack knew, had been put to bed.

"There have been new developments," Cecil said. "We're convening at five. I'll see you there."

Once she ended the call with Cecil, she answered the text messages from fellow council members who wanted to know if she had any insight into what had changed with the vehicles-for-hire issue. Mack found it interesting that the only members who'd texted her were the ones on the side of the taxi companies.

She arrived at City Hall ten minutes before they were set to meet. She found Juliette Cannon waiting just outside the council's chambers.

"So, do you know what this is about?" Juliette asked.

Mack shook her head. "I have no idea. But I guess we're about to find out."

The hum of busy chatter could be heard before they even opened the doors to the chamber. When they did, Mack was taken aback by the number of people crowding the large room. She definitely hadn't expected this many spectators, especially for an emergency meeting.

"You think someone tipped off the taxi companies?" Juliette murmured.

"Sure looks that way," Mack said.

Not that she could blame them for wanting to be here. This was their livelihood.

Cecil called the meeting to order and the parliamentarian conducted the roll call.

"This emergency meeting of the New Orleans City Council has been called to conduct business specifically related to Chapter 162, Article 8 of the New Orleans

City Charter. Previously, the council agreed to a fifteen-dollar minimum charge for all rides to and from Louis Armstrong International Airport. That measure is now up for reconsideration."

"By whom?" Mack asked.

Cecil banged his gavel. "Out of order, Councilmember Arnold."

Mack bit back the curse she nearly spewed and motioned to the parliamentarian to put her on the list of speakers. By the time it was her turn to speak, several council members had already voiced their displeasure and disagreement over this particular subject being raised again, especially after the amount of time the council had spent on it earlier this year. Still, Mack would not yield the floor without letting her voice be heard. She needed the taxi drivers to know that she was one hundred percent behind them.

"When this measure was put in place, it was not with the intention of harming individuals looking to capitalize on new technologies," Mack said. "App-based car services are here to stay, but we have to make sure they're operating on a level playing field. It isn't fair that taxi drivers must adhere to a certain set of rules, while others don't have to."

That set off a huge round of applause throughout the chamber. Cecil's gavel did little to silence it. The taxi drivers were fed up, and so was Mack.

"I don't understand why this item is being revisited at all," she said. "The entire council was in agreement, as well as the mayor's office."

"The mayor's office supports revisiting the measure," Cecil said. "Mayor Warner is now of the understanding that the city must rethink the way it deals with this issue.

We don't want to be left behind when it comes to new technologies."

Not again.

Mack was thunderstruck at the realization that Lucien had flip-flopped yet again on an issue he'd been vehemently against just a few months ago.

"Are you done, Councilmember Arnold?" Cecil asked.

She nodded and relinquished the floor back to the parliamentarian. She didn't have anything else to say on this matter. There was only one person she needed to speak to.

It was time she had a talk with her old mentor.

~

Ezra sat on the front stoop of his shotgun house in the Bywater neighborhood, waiting for Mack to arrive. His knee bobbed rapidly up and down, a byproduct of the anxiety that had been rippling through him since he ended the call with her twenty minutes ago. Something had upset her. She didn't say what, but Ezra could hear it in her voice.

He spotted her car at the stop sign two houses down, and started down the steps. By the time she pulled up to the curb, Ezra was waiting for her. He opened the car door and his heart lurched within his chest at the sight of her. The look of utter defeat on her face nearly did him in.

Ezra dropped to his haunches, taking her hand.

"You want to talk about it?" he asked.

"Not out here," she said. "Let's go inside first."

He helped her out of the car, and guided her into

the house. She stood in the middle of his living room, her eyes roaming the space.

"This is my first time coming here," she said.

"You want a tour?" Ezra asked. His house wasn't as spectacular as that mansion she once lived in over in Old Metairie—or even her condo—but it was comfortable, and it was his.

She turned to him. "After sex. Right now, I just need some long, slow medicinal sex."

He nodded. "I can help with that."

The small smile that lifted up the corner of her mouth didn't reach her eyes. It caused the anxiety Ezra had been trying to fight off to intensify. He had no idea what was going on, but whatever it was, it had affected her in a bad way. He squelched the urge to try to get her to talk it out, and instead gave her what she'd asked for.

Guiding her to his bedroom, he worshipfully made love to her, concentrating on doing the things he'd learned over the last two weeks brought her the most pleasure. As she lay prone on his bed, he peppered her spine with kisses, trailing his tongue along the dip at the small of her back. He urged her to lift her hips and, using his thumbs, spread her open and pressed a deep kiss to her center.

Her low moan told Ezra he was doing something right.

He tongued her with single-minded determination, quickening his strokes until she was nearly on the brink of orgasm, then slowing down before she reached the peak. It wasn't until she called out his name in a tortured, pleading voice that he finally relented, moving his tongue rapidly back and forth over the delicate nub at the apex of her sex. He slid two fingers inside her and pumped to the same rhythm of his tongue's strokes until he brought her to completion.

While her limbs still trembled from that first climax, Ezra embarked on the next. He slipped underneath her, fitting her moist thighs on either side of his waist. Cradling her hips in his hands, he guided her onto his stiff cock, thrusting upward to meet her. Mack's head fell back. Her breasts swayed with her gentle rock as she moved up and down his length, massaging him with her hot, wet flesh. Her body milking him with every deep dive of her hips.

A heavy sensation started to build at the base of his spine, and Ezra knew he was seconds from exploding. He reached down and pressed his thumb against her clit. Her arms stiffened and she erupted seconds before he found his own release.

When she collapsed onto his chest, Ezra was once against stunned by how perfectly she fit there. It was as if their bodies were made to fit together.

He kissed the top of her head and wrapped his arms around her.

After several minutes passed, Ezra quietly whispered, "Are you ready to talk about whatever had you seeking medicinal sex?"

She released a deep sigh and nodded, but she didn't speak.

"Mack?"

"There was an emergency city council meeting," she finally shared. "Lucien flip-flopped yet again. This time on vehicles-for-hire. He reneged on a promise he made to the cab companies." She huffed out a humorless laugh. "It'll be hard enough to fight the construction of that damn gas turbine. Now I have to take up this fight again too."

"Think you can handle it?" Ezra asked.

"I know I can." She twisted around and faced him. "I'm running."

"Officially?"

She nodded. "I was actually planning to surprise you with my fully completed declaration form when I got a call about the emergency meeting. First thing tomorrow morning, I'm going to request to meet with Lucien. I want to tell him to his face that I'm coming for his job."

"So the cabbies were the last straw, huh?"

She shook her head. "I'd decided to make it official even before this evening's meeting. It's not about Lucien anymore. It's about *me*. I'm the right person for this job."

"God, you're sexy when you're being all confident and bad ass."

She chuckled. "Be prepared to see a lot more of it. This is my usual *modus operandi*."

"Lucien Warner won't know what hit him."

He dipped his head and seized her lips in a long, slow kiss. As much as he'd enjoyed spending the last couple of weeks at her condo, he hadn't realized just how much he wanted her in *his* bed until this very moment.

"Do you want to practice what you'll say to the mayor?" Ezra asked.

She put her finger to his lips. "I don't even want to think about it right now. But I do need to come up with a non-sex related distraction while my body recovers."

"How long will this recovery take?"

She burst out laughing. "Not that long, but I need more than ten minutes between bouts."

"Actually, I may have a distraction for you. I received some good news today," Ezra said.

"Share!" she said. She propped herself up on her elbows. "I can use some good news for a change."

Ezra was blown away by the picture she presented. She was so damn gorgeous. Her hair stuck out at different angles, wild and disheveled after their tumble between the sheets. Her firm breasts were practically in his face, the pert nipples abrading his chest. For a moment he forgot what he was about to say, his entire focus centered on the sexy woman in his bed.

"Ezra?" Mackenna asked. "Where's my good news."

"Oh, right," he said. His mouth quirked up in a smile. "Sorry, I got distracted."

"No? Really?" she said with mocked surprise. She thumped his chest. "Give me my good news."

"I got a call today from Martell Johnson, the kid I introduced you to at the picnic a few weeks ago."

"The one you wrote the college letter of recommendation for?"

"Yep. He got his letter of acceptance to Nicholls State University today," Ezra said. He couldn't staunch the flow of pride suddenly rushing through his veins. He'd been on cloud nine since the minute Martell called to share the news.

"Ezra, that's phenomenal," Mack said. "You must be so proud."

"I think the only ones more proud are his parents, but I'm running a close second. I've seen how hard this kid has worked over the years. Despite all the setbacks he's faced, he was able to make this dream happen. He's remarkable. All of those kids are remarkable."

Mack's hand came to rest on his jaw. "Do you know how much your face lights up when you talk about them?"

"I can't help it," Ezra said. "They are some of the most amazing human beings I've ever met. Not just the kids, but their entire families. If you heard some of the stories of what they've had to endure, and how they've managed to rise above it all. It's unbelievable how strong they are."

"So why aren't you telling their stories, Ezra?"

His head jerked back. "Me?"

"Well, duh. You're the writer. You know their stories better than any writer out there. Who better to tell their stories than the person who first gave voice to their problem?"

"That's more human interest. It's not the kind of writing I do. I'm an *investigative* reporter."

"You're more than just an investigative reporter, Ezra. After that picnic a few weeks ago, I went back and read the initial story you wrote about that contaminated soil. You could have focused on the company and their corruption, but instead you chose to focus on the children."

"The children were the important subject in that story," he said.

"Because you *chose* to make them important. Not every reporter would have. And you didn't just make them the focal point of the story, but you wrote them in a way that made each child more than just a name on a page. You made them real. You gave a face to the faceless."

"But—"

She put up a hand. "Just hear me out. When it comes to your work as a reporter, I have first-hand knowledge of how tenacious you are. But in all the time I've watch you investigating first me, then Mayor Warner, I never saw you as excited as you were when you're discussing those kids. You've spent your career doing amazing investigative journalism, but maybe you should give this kind of writing a chance."

Ezra's initial thought was to dismiss her suggestion. He reported the tough, hard-hitting stories that made headlines. That's who he was; it's what had defined him throughout his career.

Yet, when he thought back on all the articles he'd written over the years, he couldn't deny that it was the soil contamination story that generated the most pride. Not because of the awards he'd won or the accolades the story had garnered from his colleagues, but because of the help those kids had received because of his reporting. Something he'd written had made a difference in their lives. How many more lives could he change with his words?

Ezra's chest tightened with a combination of anxiety and hope. Could he do this?

Hell yes, you can do this!

So what if his Pulitzer wouldn't be the result of uncovering some salacious political scandal. Changing the focus of his reporting didn't mean he had to abandon his dream of winning journalism's top prize, or even making it to a national outlet.

He considered the stories he'd run across throughout the years that he'd wanted to sink his teeth into, but instead, had backed away from because he thought they were too soft for a hard-nose investigative reporter. What he wouldn't give to be able to write those stories.

When he'd set out to be a reporter, he'd done so with the goal of making the world a better place. A more honest place. He still remembered the talk he had with his mother—a talk no one else in his family knew about. When his friends and coaches, and even his own dad and brothers, were telling him that he should pursue a career in the NFL, it was his mother who told him to follow his heart.

His heart told him this was the right move.

"You're pretty quiet," Mack murmured. She lifted her head from where she'd laid it on his chest and pressed a kiss to his skin. "I hope I wasn't too bossy."

Ezra looked down at her and grinned. "I kinda like it when you're bossy."

She pinched his nipple.

"Ouch," he yelped. "Okay, maybe I'm not ready for the whole BDSM scene."

"Would you stop it already," Mack said with a laugh. She kissed the nipple she'd just assaulted. "I don't want you to think that I don't value the work you've been doing. That's not why I suggested changing up the stories you write," she said. "I just see how excited you get when you talk about those kids."

"I know," he said. "I appreciate it. You've given me something to think about."

He wasn't ready to commit just yet. He still had to think it over and figure out how this new focus would fit into his work schedule. But he could feel the excitement building within his chest just at the thought of bringing a story like Martell's and the other kids' to light.

And he had the woman in his bed to thank for it. God, but she was good for him.

Ezra gave her bare backside a healthy pat. "Are you sure you don't want to practice what you're going to say to the mayor tomorrow? It may help."

"I don't want to overthink it," Mack replied with a firm head shake. "I just want to go in there and tell him from the heart why I think I would be a better mayor than he is."

"Are you going to say anything about the investigation?"

"I don't know. If I say anything to tip him off, we may never uncover whatever it is he's been up to."

"Want to know what I think?" Ezra asked. "I think you can win the mayor's office by a landslide *even if* we never find anything on Lucien. The people of New Orleans will see that you're good for this city."

She levered up on her elbows and pressed a kiss to his lips. "You are amazingly good for my ego, Mr. Holmes."

"You're welcome," he said.

She threw her head back and laughed. "Maybe I should have said thank you first."

He cupped her ass and nudged her upward until their pelvises met. His thickening erection brushed against her soft, wet center.

"I don't need to hear the words," he said. "Let me show you a better way to thank me."

CHAPTER 12

MACK TRIED to ignore the steadily ticking clock as she read through the emails in her inbox. She was scheduled to meet with Mayor Warner in less than an hour, and of all the things she had not been looking forward to in her life, this one ranked up there with gallbladder surgery.

She figured reading about the concerns of her constituents was the best way to take her mind off the impending meeting. The other council members had assistants to wade through their emails before forwarding the ones deemed most important, but Mack didn't trust anyone else to decide what was an important matter and what wasn't. She didn't care if it was a pothole, or a broken streetlight, or a complaint about the coleslaw someone's kid was served in the school cafeteria. If a citizen thought it was important enough to break into their busy day to write an email, it was important enough to her to read said email, and if necessary, send a personal response.

Mack thought about how that would most likely change if she became mayor. She often struggled to get through the dozens—sometimes *hundreds*—of weekly emails she received from the people in her district alone, often sacrificing the minimal amount of TV time she treated herself to in order to get through them. There was no way she'd be able to field emails from the entire city. The thought saddened her.

She hadn't fully contemplated all the changes a mayoralty would mean to her life. She'd considered the big changes, of course. She would have to give up her pro bono work with the Arts Council, and the classes she taught at Loyola. She could forget about meeting Indina for happy hour once a week. She would be lucky if she saw her friend once a month after she moved into that much bigger office here in City Hall.

"It will all be worth it," Mack reassured herself.

She had a vision for New Orleans—one that would bring prosperity to *all* citizens—not just those who could afford the big mansions on St. Charles Avenue. Her vision wasn't tied to low-paying tourists industry jobs for the city's residents, either. New Orleans would always be a tourist destination. It was one of the country's gems. But *her* New Orleans would be so much more. *Her* New Orleans would be a model for other cities that needed to turn their economies around. She was ready to bring in new industries, strengthen the education system, and lower crime.

Mack felt the familiar excitement building within her chest. It was the excitement she felt whenever she thought about the changes she had in store for her adopted hometown. She was *so* ready to get to work.

The one downside was having to push out her mentor in order to do it. She knew it had to be done, but knowing it didn't make it any easier. Whether or not she found proof of whatever Lucien had gotten himself tied up in, she would have to have this conversation with him. She would have to tell this man who meant so much to her that she was set to become his opponent.

Mack glanced at the clock and had to do a double-take. Where had the last forty minutes gone?

She tried to tamp down the dread that suddenly filled her stomach. It was more than the impending conversation that had her belly in a whirlwind, it was the unknown. She had no idea how Lucien would react. Would he be disappointed in her? Would he be angry? Was there a chance he would be proud that his former student aspired to such lofty heights?

Okay, so she was reaching with that one.

But it didn't really matter what Lucien thought. This was the path she'd chosen, and she wasn't turning back.

Mack nearly jumped clear out of her chair when the alert she'd set on her phone went off, letting her know that she had fifteen minutes before her scheduled meeting with the mayor. His office was just down the hallway, but she wanted to arrive a few minutes early. She locked her computer screen, set her phone to silent, and walked out of her office.

Mack's heart beat faster with each step that brought her closer to Lucien's office. Her nerves were as tangled as the box of hair balls her grandmother used to put in her hair when she was a kid, and her palms were so sweaty she was certain she wouldn't be able to turn the doorknob.

She stopped in the middle of the corridor.

This was *not* the Mackenna Arnold she'd grown into. She didn't cower. She didn't scare easily. Especially when she was right. And, on this subject, she was right.

When she reached the mayor's suite, Mack stood before the door for a moment to take it all in with fresh eyes. She'd visited this office countless times over the past four years, but this was the first time she'd come here and pictured herself as its main resident. This could be *her* office next year, if the people of New Orleans deemed her worthy enough to lead them into the future.

They will.

Mack entered the office and was greeted by the mayor's receptionist.

"He'll be ready for you in just a few minutes, Councilmember Arnold."

"Thanks, Lynda," Mack answered. She went over to take a seat on one of the armchairs lining the wall, but before she could sit, the door to the mayor's personal office opened and Lucien stepped out, a jovial grin creasing his lips as he greeted her.

Mack's stomach pitched yet again.

This man, with his handsome face, ever-present smile, and wonderful attitude had meant so much to her over the years. His hair was white now, and the lines on his face more pronounced, but behind those few marks of aging stood the professor who'd taught her so much about the law, including how it could be abused by those in power. The fact that he'd allowed himself to become one of those who'd abused his power broke Mack's heart in two.

"It's great to see you, Mackenna," Lucien said as he guided her into his office. "One would think we would run into each other more often being that we're in the same building, but that doesn't seem to happen."

"No, it doesn't," Mack said. She took the seat he offered. "It's a pretty big building, and we're both busy."

"Absolutely," he said. "I'm happy you were able to carve out some time to see me. I know things have been contentious on the city council. I've been meaning to check in and see how you're handling it."

He folded his hands over his desk, and Mack was struck by the memories that pose conjured. She was suddenly back at Tulane, and he was sitting behind his desk during office hours, patiently waiting to hear what kind of dilemma his strong-willed student had found herself in this time.

She had to remind herself that she was no longer his student. And this wasn't school. They were colleagues now. And it was time for her to state her case.

"I wanted to be the first to tell you that I plan to file my candidacy for the mayoral race next week."

The silence that followed her statement was one of the most uncomfortable Mack had ever experienced. Lucien stared at her for several moments before he began to chuckle.

"You can't be serious," he said, leaning back in his chair.

"I am, sir. I'm running against you for mayor."

"You're only a few months into your second term. You don't have enough experience with holding public office to run."

"I disagree."

"What makes you think the people of New Orleans would vote for a one-term city council member over me?"

Mack crossed her legs and folded her hands over her knee. "That's part of my job as a candidate, selling myself as the best person for the job, which I believe I am."

"You really think you're up for this job? You have no idea what it takes to do this job," the mayor said. "How much it requires of your time, your heart, everything."

"I'm ready to devote whatever is necessary to make sure this city has someone who has its best interests at heart at the helm."

"And you don't think I have this city's best interest at heart?"

"I believe you used to," Mack said. "But you're no longer the man I once knew." She swallowed down the emotion welling up in her throat. "I'm not sure what happened to you, Lucien, but over this past year you have changed your position on so many things—things I thought you strongly believed in—that I could only come to one conclusion. Some outside force is pressuring you to change them."

The mayor slapped both hands on his desk and leaned forward.

"Are you accusing me of corruption?" he barked.

Mack maintained her calm.

"Answer me," he growled.

"I haven't found any evidence," Mack said. "And now that I've shared my suspicions, I doubt I'll ever find any. You're a smart man, and if you *are* doing something illegal, you'll definitely cover your tracks now."

"How dare you, Mackenna Arnold." The hurt in his voice pierced Mack's soul. "After the years I spent teaching you, mentoring you, molding you into the legal mind you are today. That you can say such a thing—could even *think* such a thing of me—is the ultimate slap in the face. It's clear you don't know nearly as much about me as I thought you did."

She took a much-needed moment to calm herself down.

"And if you think it was easy for me to come in here and say these things to you, then you don't know much about me, either," she said, cursing the emotion she couldn't keep out of her voice.

"Why?" Lucien asked. "Why would you think I was on the take, Mackenna?"

"Why wouldn't I?" she asked. Mack started counting items off on her fingers, listing all the times the mayor had flip-flopped.

"What am I supposed to think when you've gone back on your word so many times this past year, and especially on things like the cab drivers and the gas turbine. I stood in this very office and told you how detrimental that utility plant would be to my district, and you agreed."

"I still feel that way," he said.

Mack's eyes widened. "Really? Well, maybe you should tell that to Cecil Washington and Russell Babin," she said. "And while you're at it, ask Cecil why he forged an electronic memo from your office stating the opposite." She scrolled through her email on her phone and held it out for him to see. "According to this, you're now in favor of the gas turbine. Are you flip-flopping again?"

Lucien squinted at her phone, confusion flashing across his face.

"Mr. Mayor?" Mack said.

His head jerked back and he blinked rapidly several times. He cleared his throat as he sat back in his chair and folded his hands over his stomach.

"You've stated your case," he said. "If you feel you are the better person for this job, I'll see you in the first debate. Now, if you'll excuse me, I have a number of meetings to prepare for today. It's a big part of my job as mayor."

Mack stood, but she didn't leave. She'd prepared herself for the possibility of this conversation completely annihilating her relationship with her long-time mentor, but she didn't want to walk away from it like this.

"Lucien," she said.

"Good day, Ms. Arnold," he said without looking up from the document he'd started reading.

His dismissal was like a punch to the gut.

With a silent nod, she turned and walked out of the office, and then out of the suite. She fought the urge to slip into the restroom and treat herself to a nice, healthy cry-fest. Instead, Mack sucked in a deep breath, collected herself, and surged forward with more determination than she'd felt in months.

The past twenty minutes had been difficult, but if she was going to take on the job of mayor of a major U.S. city, she would have a lot more difficult moments ahead of her. This was just the beginning.

"Bring it on," Mack said as she slipped behind her desk.

She located John Darbonne's phone number in her contacts list. When he answered, Mack said, "Okay, Campaign Manager. Let's do this."

*E*zra pulled in behind Reid's massive pickup truck in the circular driveway at Harrison's. Indina had called earlier, asking if he could come over to sign some papers regarding the setup of the foundation, which was moving at lightning speed now that they'd agreed on the basics.

Actually, it was after they'd all agreed to let Indina handle everything that things started happening, but for once, Ezra was thankful for his sister's bossy ways and take charge attitude. He'd been too busy these past few weeks to contribute much of anything. He vowed to be more useful in the upcoming months. At least he'd come up with the idea of presenting the idea to his dad on his 70th birthday, which was a few weeks away. They'd planned to give it to him a month ago, on their mother's birthday, but turned out there was a lot more to setting up a foundation than any of them realized.

As he rounded Reid's truck, Ezra had hoped to find his sister-in-law's car in the driveway, but Willow's gray Camry was nowhere to be found.

He cursed underneath his breath.

He missed the days of being clueless about whatever the hell was going on between his brother and Willow. Now, every time Harrison's number showed up on his phone's screen, Ezra was afraid it was his brother calling to tell him that he and his wife had decided to call it quits. He wasn't sure if it was time for an intervention or what. All he knew was that those two needed to get their shit together, because anything other than a long, happy marriage between the two of them was unacceptable.

Ezra rapped twice on the front door. His knees

nearly buckled in relief when it opened and Willow appeared on the other side.

"Hey you," she greeted. "I wondered where you were. Everyone else is here already."

"Wills! Damn, it's good to see you."

Ezra enclosed her in a bear hug, holding on longer than necessary. He couldn't help himself. He loved this woman. He loved her for what she'd brought to his family. He needed her to *remain* a member of this family. Forever.

He pulled back slightly, but didn't release her. "Where's your car?" he asked.

"Liliana has it. One of the other parents at the school took her and her best friend out for a driving lesson."

"Oh, shit," Ezra said. "And I thought the gray hair I found yesterday made me feel old. That's nothing compared to the thought of seeing Lily behind the wheel of a car."

Willow chuckled. "I think Harrison may have a heart attack before she gets her actual license."

"So, you two are talking again?" Ezra asked.

The light in his sister-in-law's eyes immediately dimmed. She broke away from his hold.

Shit!

"I mean—" he started, but Willow cut him off.

"It's okay, Ezra," she said with a wave of her hand.

She turned, but Ezra caught her by the shoulder. He tugged gently until she turned back to face him. Every drop of the joy that had sparkled in her eyes a minute ago was gone. Pain gripped his chest.

"Wills, you know you can talk to me, right?" Ezra

offered. "I won't automatically side with Harrison just because he's my brother. I know how he is."

"There are no sides to take," she said. "We're fine. Stop worrying about me and your brother."

"You're fine? Is that why Harrison's working late every night because he's not sure if he's welcomed at home?"

Her head reared back slightly. "Is that what he said?"

"Not in those exact words, but he's clueless, Wills. He's not sure what's going on either."

She snorted. "Typical."

Ezra captured her upper arms and dipped his head so that he could look her in the eyes. "Willow, please. Whatever it is, you guys need to work it out. I love you both too much to just sit back and watch your marriage crumble."

She cupped his jaw and, with a sad smile, said, "Our marriage isn't crumbling. I promise, Harrison and I will be okay." She gave his cheek a pat. "Now, please, go on into the kitchen. Your sister and brothers are in there. Indina has some great ideas for a logo for the new foundation."

"Aren't you coming?" he asked. Willow had been instrumental in first getting the idea for their mom's foundation off the ground.

"I'll be there in a minute," she said. "I just need to check in on Athens. He's upstairs working on his math."

"Not my strong suit."

"I'm learning that third-grade math is a lot harder than I remembered," she said with a laugh, but it didn't reach her eyes.

Ezra stood there for a moment, watching as his sister-in-law ascended the stairs. He was at a loss. Neither she nor Harrison seemed willing to talk about whatever was going on between them. Though, to be honest, Ezra didn't know how much help he could be. It wasn't as if he had ever been married. In fact, there was a time when just *thinking* of the "M word" was enough to make him panic. Marriage was for people more settled, like his older brother. Ezra had decided long ago that bachelorhood suited him just fine.

Now? Yeah, he could see himself married.

He shook his head, amazed at how quickly life changed. Just a few months ago the only place he wanted to see Mackenna was in someone's jail. Now, he could easily envision her as his wife.

He entered the kitchen to find his siblings engrossed in whatever was happening on their various electronics. Indina and Harrison were seated at the breakfast table, both with laptops opened in front of them. Reid stood at the bar, reading something on an iPad.

"I like the light blue one," Reid said. "That was mama's favorite color."

"Her favorite color was brown," Indina said.

"No, it wasn't," Reid said.

"Yes, it was," Harrison, Ezra and Indina said at the same time. They all looked over at Ezra and greeted him with a wave and nod before returning to their electronic screens.

"All this time I thought Mama's favorite color was light blue," Reid said. "Whenever I bought her something, that's the color I always got. She never said anything."

"Probably because she didn't want to hurt your feelings," Indina said with a laugh. She turned her laptop around so that it faced Ezra. "We're debating logos for the foundation. Harrison likes the book, but Reid and I both like the church hat since it was mama's signature on Sundays."

"Mama did like her church hats," Ezra said.

"I've changed my mind," Harrison said. "I figured the book worked because we were giving academic scholarships, but who's to say the foundation won't expand beyond that. The hat is more versatile."

"Good point," Indina said. "So that hat it is."

"Oh, you all decided on the church hat?" Willow said, returning to the kitchen. She opted for the seat next to Harrison's instead of across from him. Ezra took that as a good sign.

She peered at her husband's computer screen. "Good, that's the one I liked too."

"So why didn't you say that when I asked which one you thought would work the best?" Indina asked her.

Willow shrugged. "This is up to you and your brothers to decide. My opinion shouldn't sway things one way or the other."

"Girl, please." Indina snorted. "You know my mama would have picked you over all of these fools combined."

"True dat," Reid said. "Mama loved her some Willow."

"What's not to love?" Harrison said.

Willow responded to that with an eye roll, to which Harrison responded with one of his own.

Well, this was awkward. And hard as hell to witness.

Reid looked at both Harrison and Willow and asked, "Am I missing something?"

Indina cleared her throat. "Now that we've decided

on a logo, I propose that we get some T-shirts printed. We can pass them out at Daddy's birthday party."

"Birthday party?" Ezra asked. "Who said anything about a party? Dad hates birthday parties."

"I'm not talking fireworks and a ten-piece band," his sister said. "Just a small gathering with family and a few friends. It's his 70th. We can't let that pass without celebrating it."

Ezra put his hands up. "If you say so. Just try not to get your feelings hurt when he's not all that excited. You know Dad doesn't like people making a fuss over him."

"Well, that's too bad," Indina said. "If you're lucky enough to see seventy years on this earth, you deserve to be fussed over."

Ezra knew there was no changing Indina's mind when she got like this, so he let the subject drop.

The discussion moved to the application process they planned to institute for students wanting a shot at winning a scholarship from the new foundation. There were two more awkward exchanges between Harrison and Willow, but then—surprise, surprise—she actually smiled at something his brother said.

There were no longer any doubts that these two were going through a rough patch, but that one smile gave Ezra hope.

Just as Reid announced that he would die of starvation if he didn't eat within the next five minutes, Ezra's phone chirped. He looked at the screen to find a text from Mack, asking if he would be on his way soon.

"Hey, I'll have to pass on pizza," Ezra said.

"Oh, really?" Indina asked, her brows hiked high enough to need clearance from the FAA. "Where're you off to?"

"To mind my own business," he answered.

"Boy, don't think you're fooling anybody. I know you and Mack are seeing each other."

"Say what?" Reid said.

"No way!" Harrison added.

Willow clapped excitedly, her smile huge. "I love it. I've always thought you two would make the cutest couple."

"Really?" Harrison asked.

"Of course," Indina chimed in.

"But she sent the cops after him," Reid said. "Now they're dating? What kind of twisted shit is that?"

Indina rolled her eyes. "You are *so* clueless when it comes to women."

"*Me?* I know everything there is to know about women."

"I'm leaving," Ezra announced as he backed out of the kitchen, although he didn't think any of them noticed. Reid and Indina were so deep into their argument, they wouldn't notice a herd of elephants running through the living room.

Ezra backed out of the driveway and headed straight for Mack's. He'd planned to stop in at her favorite taqueria on the way to her condo, but the urgency he'd read in her words compelled him to lay all his previous plans to rest. He needed to see her with his own eyes; he needed to make sure she was okay. He'd called earlier to ask how her meeting with the mayor went, but she'd been on her way to her class and couldn't talk. All she'd told him was that it could have gone better.

When he texted her an hour later, once he figured she was done with her class, and asked if she wanted him to come over, she'd responded with a single word: Please.

Ezra just wanted to hold her for the rest of the night. He'd known today would be tough on her.

When he arrived at the condo, Mack still wore the gray skirt and pale pink shirt she'd dressed in before leaving for work this morning. She lounged on her sofa, her stockinged feet crossed atop the coffee table. One hand cradled a glass half-filled with golden brown liquid.

"That kind of day, huh?" Ezra asked, nodding toward the glass.

"I opened up the Macallan 1824."

"I'm not a scotch drinker, so I don't know what that means."

"It means today was bad enough that I'm drowning my sorrows in four hundred dollar scotch."

He winced and went over to the sofa. She made room for him. Ezra gathered her in his arms so that she could rest her back against his chest. He pressed a kiss to her temple. "You did what you had to do," he said.

"It wasn't easy."

"I know," he said. "Did you bring up your suspicions?"

She nodded.

"How did he react?"

"It's safe to say I'm no longer his favorite former student."

Ezra rubbed his palm back and forth over her forearm. "If it makes you feel any better, I was never a favorite student to any of my teachers. My old Home Economics teacher actually told me that she hated me."

"She was probably a former band member," Mack said with a laugh.

"Probably," he teased. He rested his chin on her shoulder. "You do realize we'll never find any evidence of wrongdoing now, don't you? Whatever was out there has now been obliterated."

"I know," Mack said with a weary sigh. She peered over at him. "But if I win, it won't matter. From this moment on, it's all about making sure the best person is in the mayor's office. I just have to make sure *I'm* that person."

"You will be," Ezra said. He kissed her. "I'm proud of you. I know it wasn't easy to have that conversation with someone who meant so much to you."

"I'm just disappointed that I had to have it at all," Mack said.

"Did he deny any wrongdoing?"

"No. To be honest, he looked more shocked than guilty. It was hard to read him."

"You did the right thing," Ezra reiterated. "Never forget that."

She nodded, then drain the rest of her scotch. She held the glass up to him. "Take this away from me. This stuff is too expensive to waste it on drowning my sorrows." Then she pushed up from the sofa. "If you give me a few minutes, we can go out to dinner."

"I'm okay with ordering in if you are," Ezra said.

Her entire body seemed to wilt with relief. "Thank God. I was so not in the mood to go out tonight." Her lips tilted up in a grateful smile. "You probably sensed that."

He held his forefinger and thumb a couple of millimeters apart. "Just a little." Ezra stood and pressed a kiss to her forehead. "Why don't you go change out of those clothes, and I'll order flautas from Filipe's."

She moaned in agreement. "With chips, salsa and extra guac, please."

She hadn't taken two steps before her phone began to dance on the coffee table.

"Let it go to voicemail," Ezra said. "It's probably Indina calling to gloat because she figured out that we're seeing each other."

Mack picked up the phone and frowned. "No, it isn't Indina," she said. She answered the phone with a cautious, "Hello?"

Unease slid down Ezra's spine as he witnessed the emotions playing across her face. The crease in her forehead deepened the longer she listened to the person on the other line.

He walked over to her and rubbed his hand up and down her arm.

"Yes," Mack said. "Okay. I'll be there in an hour." She disconnected the call but continued to stare at the phone, her expression tinged with confusion and reservation.

"Everything okay?" Ezra asked.

"I'm not sure," she said. "That was Liza Warner, the mayor's wife. She asked if I could come over." She looked up at him. "They want to talk about Lucien endorsing me as a candidate for mayor."

~

As she approached the imposing glass doors of the two-story brick home Lucien shared with his wife in the Eastover Country Club neighborhood in New Orleans East, Mack couldn't help but notice how different this felt from the countless times she'd been here before. She'd attended her share of Christmas parties and other get-togethers in this house. It had always felt so warm and welcoming. But something about this evening made it feel ominous, as if her mere presence here was a threat.

She looked over at Ezra. "Thank you for coming with me," she said as he knocked on the front door.

He stuck his hands in his pockets. "Let's just hope the mayor doesn't ask me to leave." He looked over at her, a smirk tipping up the corner of his mouth. "Politicians aren't always fond of reporters showing up at their doors."

"You don't say," Mack returned with mock surprise. "You're not here in a work capacity. You're here to support me. We'll make sure both he and Liza know that."

The door opened and Shelly, the Warner's long-time housekeeper, answered.

"Hello Ms. Arnold," Shelly greeted. "The mayor and Mrs. Warner are in the study. They're expecting you. Can I get you and your guest a drink?"

"I'm good," Ezra declined.

"So am I," Mack said. "But thank you."

When they entered the study, they found Liza Warner standing at a window, looking out at the side lawn where the gazebo was located. When they held outdoor events, that's usually where the caterer set up the food. Lucien sat behind his desk. His eyes were closed, his head pitched back on the headrest of his leather desk chair.

"The councilwoman is here," Shelly announced.

They both snapped to attention. Liza's smile was

genuine as she walked over to Mack and captured her hands.

"How are you doing, Mackenna," the woman greeted. Her kind eyes always put Mack at ease.

"Fine," she answered. "And you?"

"Things are...well," Liza replied.

There was an awkward pause before Mack said, "I hope you don't mind that I brought a friend. This is Ezra Holmes."

"I know the byline," Lucien said. He stood and came around his desk. He shook Ezra's hand and nodded at Mack. "Thank you for coming."

"You're welcome," Mack said. "Although, I must admit that I'm a bit confused as to why I'm here."

Liza pointed to a dark brown leather couch. "Please, sit down. Did Shelly offer you something to drink?"

"She did, but we're good," Mack answered.

Lucien walked over to a rich, Cherrywood sideboard that held a decanter and several cut-crystal tumblers. He poured two drinks, then came to where they were all seated. He handed Mack one of the glasses. "I know you," he said. "I taught you the finer points of drinking a good scotch, remember?"

Mack gave him a sad smile as she took the glass and nodded. She took a sip, knowing the scotch would be rich, smoky and smooth before it ever touched her lips. Lucien Warner knew how to pick a perfect scotch.

"Lucien told me about your meeting today," Liza opened. "That took guts, Mackenna."

"I hate that it was necessary," Mack said.

"I'm not involved in any corruption or scandal," the mayor opened. He took a sip of his drink. Liza slipped her hand in his and gave it a squeeze. He peered over at his wife and sent her a sad smile, then his eyes returned to Mack's.

"I have dementia," Lucien stated.

Mack couldn't have been more stunned if he'd knocked the art books off the coffee table and started breakdancing on it. She tried to speak, but nothing came out.

"I started to suspect something was wrong nearly two years ago," Liza said. "I noticed Lucien would repeat things he'd told me just a few minutes before, or I'd walk into a room to find him looking around as if he was trying to find something, but when I asked what he was looking for, he couldn't tell me. I Googled the symptoms, as one does these days, but kept telling myself that I was just blowing things out of proportion." She sucked in a deep breath. "But it's become too dangerous to ignore."

"Dangerous?" Mack asked.

Liza bit her bottom lip. "Lucien got lost on his way home earlier this week. He drove all the way to Pascagoula, Mississippi before he realized something was wrong."

"My God," Mack gasped.

"I was out of my mind with worry," Liza said. "But I…I couldn't call for help, because he didn't want anyone to know."

"I wasn't planning to run for another term," Lucien said. "I know my time is up."

"Your time in the *mayor's office* is up," Liza said, squeezing his hand. "You're not leaving me any time soon."

"No, I'm not," Lucien said to his wife. He looked over at Mack. "I think you would make a fine mayor,

Mackenna. In fact, I can't think of anyone who would be better for the job."

Mack told herself not to cry. She would cry later, when she was alone and could bawl like a baby. Or, better yet, when she was in Ezra's arms and could sob against his chest. Right now, she would be the strong person Lucien Warner had help mold her into.

"Are you planning to step down?" she asked him.

"Yes," he said with a nod. "I was hoping I could serve out the rest of my term, but that's selfishness on my part. It's better for everyone—for the entire city—if I step down," he said.

He let out a shuddering breath. Liza patted his hand.

The light bulb finally went off in Mack's head. "This is why you've flip-flopped on so many things this year."

He nodded. "I've been battling bouts of confusion all year. I'll remember looking at a certain matter one way, but then days—sometimes hours later—forget how I felt about it."

Mack's heart broke in two. She'd never seen a look of such utter defeat on Lucien Warner's face. It pained her to see him this way.

"I wish I had known sooner," Mack said.

"I should have told someone. I should have stepped down months ago," he said.

"It's okay," Liza told him.

"But it isn't," Lucien said. "We both know that. I keep thinking about what could have happened if I'd wandered further than Pascagoula and couldn't find my way home. Or if I'd been stopped by a sheriff's deputy and couldn't explain who I was or where I was going. Can you imagine the headlines?" He shook his head. "I don't want something like that to be my legacy. I want to leave office with dignity."

"Then do it on your own terms, in your own words," Ezra said.

They all turned to him.

Ezra nodded reassuringly at Mack before turning his attention to the mayor. "Mayor Warner, how would you feel about an open letter to the people of New Orleans, where you explain exactly what's happening and why you're stepping down?"

"That's a compelling idea," Mack said. "This way you would control the narrative."

"Exactly," Ezra said. "We could begin with what it has meant for you to be the mayor of this city, and then explain the need to step down. You would have a say in how citizens learn about your condition, without having to fear that it will be sensationalized."

Liza Warner walked around the chair and placed her hands on her husband's shoulders. "I think you should consider this, Lucien. Like he said, this would be you stepping down on your own terms. We wouldn't have to hide it anymore, or worry about what would happen if someone found out."

He looked at Mack. "Or have someone I love and respect believe that I've turned into a corrupt politician."

"I'm sorry," Mack said, her voice cracking over the words. Ezra caught her right hand and brought it to his lips.

"What do you say, Lucien?" Liza asked.

With his eyes on his wife, the mayor nodded. "Okay. I'll do it." He turned to Ezra and Mack. "But I want this to happen quickly. Within weeks, not months. I want this to be my resignation letter."

"I'm available to get started whenever you are," Ezra said. "I'll make the time."

Mack rose and walked over to her mentor. He stood, and after a moment, wrapped his arms around her. "You will make an excellent mayor, Mackenna Arnold. And you make sure they don't put that gas turbine in District D. I want you to give Cecil and Russell hell."

She laughed, but it came out as more of a sob. "I will. I promise," she said. Still holding onto Lucien, she reached over and grabbed Liza's hand. "You both know you can call on me at any time, right? Do not hesitate. I mean that."

"I know you do," Liza said. "I'm going to take good care of him. I've already found several promising clinical studies around the country, and plan to get him into one of them as soon as possible."

They said their goodbyes, with Ezra making a promise to return in a couple of days to begin his interview of the mayor.

Mack could feel the emotional tidal wave approaching with each step she took toward her car. She sat in the passenger seat and broke down. Convulsive sobs tore through her with such force her shoulders began to ache.

Ezra sat behind the wheel, gently caressing her back while softly whispering that it would be okay over and over again. Even if she had all the time in the world, it wouldn't be enough time to express how grateful she was to have him here with her right now. At this very moment, Mack could see herself falling in love with him. She was halfway there already.

Once she was over the worst of her crying jag, she pressed the heels of her hands to her eyes and released a deep sigh. "I don't know if I'm crying because I'm sad or relieved."

"Probably a little of both," Ezra said.

She nodded. "I can't even describe how much of a relief it is to learn that Lucien was never involved in any kind of corruption. But dementia? Nothing like that ever entered my mind."

"Why would it?" Ezra asked. "He's still relatively young, and in tremendous shape."

She looked over at him. "I'm not sure how I should feel. It would be different if he had to leave office because he was wrapped up in something shady, but now that I know he's being forced out because of this. I feel…guilty."

"Don't," Ezra said. "You have his blessing. And his support. You have nothing to feel guilty about, Mack." He slid his hand to her neck and began to massage it. Then he nudged her head, encouraging her to turn his way. "He was right, you know? You're going to make one fine mayor, Mackenna Arnold." He winked. "In more ways than one."

Mack burst out laughing.

She leaned over and captured his jaw, then went in for a quick, but deep kiss. "At least I know I have one reporter I can trust in my corner," she said.

His brow hitched up, along with one corner of his mouth. "What makes you so sure about that?"

"Because you've proven it," she answered in all seriousness, hoping he heard the genuine sincerity of her words.

He took possession of her lips once more, trea

her to the kind of kiss that would have led to her stripping herself bare…if they weren't still sitting in her old law professor's driveway.

With one last swipe of his tongue, Ezra released her from his kiss and whispered, "And I'll continue to prove it to you every single day."

EPILOGUE

EZRA PULLED his cap further down on his head as he made a break for it, running from his car to his father's front door. The rainstorm had been brutal all day and didn't look to be letting up anytime soon.

He entered the house and found his entire family in the living room, including Mackenna, who'd come earlier with Indina.

"I guess it's a good thing we didn't have that party, huh?" he asked.

Their dad had caught wind of Indina's plans for a surprise party and put the kibosh on it, much to his sister's disappointment. He had, however, agreed to a nice family dinner with his kids and grandkids.

"That's okay," Indina said. "Mack got Daddy to agree to have a party at the lake," she said.

Ezra's eyes widened as he looked over at his dad. "*You* agreed to a party? You?"

Clark Holmes shrugged his broad shoulders. "She said we could take her speedboat out on the lake. I couldn't pass it up."

Mack gave a shrug of her own. "It's just sitting there. Why not put it to use?"

"That's going to piss someone off," Ezra said.

She grinned. "An added bonus."

"Sounds like a plan to me," Reid said. His brother walked over to him and gave Ezra a one-arm hug. "Congrats on the story, bro. It's been blowing up my timeline on Facebook all day. "

"You're on Facebook, Uncle Reid?" Athens asked.

"Of course he is," Liliana said. "That's where all the old people go to waste their time."

"Hey," Reid said. "I'm not old."

"You turn thirty next month," Ezra reminded him.

"Yeah, definitely old," Liliana said.

"Harrison, come get your kids," Reid said. "And your brother and sister. I'm done with all of them."

Mack greeted Ezra with a smile, hug and kiss. "I've been following the noise about the article. It's getting hailed in some of the major news outlets around the country."

His profile on Lucien Warner, *In His Own Words*, had taken political circles by storm. It was rare for the mayor of a large city to step down. Mayor Warner had been applauded for doing so in such a dignified manner. Ezra had, in turn, received calls from a number of news organizations around the country.

In fact, he was late to his dad's because he'd had a conference call with one of the nation's largest online news magazines. The editorial board wanted him to join their team as their southeastern region reporter. The call had ended with a promise from Ezra to get back with them after he finished up calls with several other outlets.

It felt damn good to be wanted.

"I was going to buy a cake from the bakery, but Liliana and Willow decided to make your favorite," Indina said, carrying a double layer cake into the dining room. "Yellow cake with chocolate buttercream icing and coconut filling."

"Now, you see here. This here is all I need," their dad said.

"Well, that's too bad, because there's more," Willow said. She actually smiled at Harrison as he handed her a wrapped gift, and said, "Thanks, honey."

Ezra had to stop himself from giving them both a high five. It looked as if they were making some progress.

"Now, you children know how I feel about presents," his dad said in that warning tone he'd been using since they were kids. It didn't have the same effect on them it once did, but it was pretty damn close. Ezra nearly took a step back so that he wasn't within smacking distance.

"Well, this gift isn't only for you," Willow said as she set the box on the table in front of him. "It's our hope that many of the people in this city will benefit from this gift for years to come."

Their dad looked suspiciously at them all as he tore the paper from the box and took off the top. "What the…" He lifted the T-shirt from the box. "The Diane Holmes Foundation?"

His dad's shocked, befuddled expression made Ezra smile.

"We want Mama's legacy to live on by helping young girls in New Orleans go to medical school to study heart disease in the black community," Harrison explained. "Maybe, one day, one of those girls will be the one who cures it. Mama will have played a part."

Ezra stood there in shock as he witnessed something he'd never seen before, a tear rolling down his father's face.

Clark wiped his face and cleared his throat. "I guess we did a good job raising y'all after all." He stood and gave them each a hug.

Reid cracked a stupid joke, breaking up the emotional tension filling the air. At the same time, Griffin showed up, and Indina suggested they cut the cake so they could all get out of their dad's hair.

A few minutes later, Mack came over to the chair where Ezra sat in the living room and parked herself on his lap. "This cake is amazing," she said. "Willow should open a bakery."

"You plan to share?"

She jerked her plate away from him. "You'd better get your own slice. And be quick about it, because Reid is already on his third piece." She nudged him with her shoulder. "How did you stop yourself from crying when your dad opened his gift? I was ready to bawl."

"I ran baseball statistics from the All-Star game in my head," he said.

Mack rolled her eyes. "Just so you'll know for future reference, I find a man that shows a little emotion sexy," she said.

"Is that so?" Ezra asked, running his hand along her firm thigh. "In that case, why don't we go back to your place. We'll throw on one of those chick flicks and I'll give you all the emotion you can handle. I'm talking about crying, kicking, screaming. You name it."

She threw her head back with a laugh. Then she leaned over and whispered in his ear, "What do you say we skip the movie and I give you another reason to scream?"

He immediately took the plate from her hand and set it on the coffee table. Nudging her from his lap, he took her by the hand and hauled her out of the living room.

"Where y'all going?" Reid called.

"Mack just got wind of an emergency meeting," Ezra said. "We'll see you all later."

Once they were on the front porch, Mack stopped him. "Umm, don't you think they'll find it suspicious when they find out there was no emergency meeting at City Hall," she asked.

"Did I say anything about the meeting being at City Hall?" Ezra slapped her on the ass. "Now let's get out of here, councilwoman. We've got a meeting in your bedroom to get to."

CHASE ME

BOOK FOUR IN THE HOLMES BROTHERS SERIES

WHAT WAS SHE THINKING?

The last thing Indina Holmes needs in her life is three days on the open seas with her loving but nosy family. But that's exactly what she's in store for her when her brother guilts her into joining the Holmes family reunion cruise. When she needs a cabin mate at the last minute, her only option is the co-worker she's been sleeping with for the past year. Now, she just has to keep her family from trying to play matchmaker.

WHAT WAS HE THINKING?

For the past eight months, Griffin Sims has pretended to be okay with the co-worker-with-benefits arrangement he's had going with Indina, but he wants more than just her body. He wants a real relationship. Indina's invitation to join her on a cruise is exactly the opportunity Griffin has been looking for to prove to the woman who has been sharing his bed that it's time for her to share her heart.

Chapter One

Squinting against the sun's vibrant rays peeking annoyingly through the mahogany custom-made blinds, Indina Holmes executed a full body stretch across the silky 1000 thread count sheets. Her previously tense muscles were now loose and languid after the early morning workout she'd just been subjected to in this bed. Thank God for that particular kind of workout. She'd needed it like a man roaming the desert needed water.

It had been dark when she'd arrived nearly an hour ago, but judging by the dawn's insistent intrusion on her postcoital relaxation, it was past time for her to go.

"I don't want to," Indina half groaned, half whined as her eyes focused on the ceiling fan twirling lazily above her.

You can't stay in this bed all day.

Especially not today, when the culmination of countless meetings, hours of field research, and more time at her design desk than Indina wanted to think about, would finally be put forth before the executive committee responsible for several new federal and state buildings that would be built in the city of New Orleans. Her team's performance today would determine if they landed a billion-dollar contract.

And just like that, the tension was back. Too bad she didn't have time to go for another round between the sheets.

Indina sucked in an uneasy breath as she glanced over at the digital clock on the nightstand.

Shit.

If she didn't get out of here soon she would be late for work. She cursed herself for not bringing her work clothes with her when she left her house earlier this morning.

With one last stretch across the king-size bed, Indina pushed herself up into a sitting position. She could hear the shower's powerful jets coming from just beyond the bathroom door, and cursed herself again. Five minutes in that shower would get rid of the lingering tension in her muscles, with or without the water.

Tossing her legs over the edge of the bed, she walked over to the sitting area and picked up her bra and panties from the chair where she normally dropped them whenever she was here, which had been more often than usual in the past month. Between work and family, her stress levels were at an all-time high. Thank the ever-loving Lord she had a reliable outlet to expend the nervous energy constantly flowing through her bloodstream these days.

Indina slipped her panties on and threaded her arms through the bra's straps, clasping it in the back. Just as she reached for the cotton shirtdress she'd thrown on before coming over, her cell phone rang. She walked back over to where she'd left it on the nightstand, and rolled her eyes when she noticed her brother's name on the screen.

With a sigh, Indina sat on the edge of the bed and swept her thumb across the green button.

"Is there a reason you're calling me before eight a.m.?" she spoke into the phone.

"Good morning to you too," her older brother replied.

She ignored the reprimand in his voice.

"What do you need, Harrison? And there had better be a good reason for you calling me at this time of the morning."

"I need the final head count for the Holmes family reunion cruise. Are you in or are you out? And before you answer that, I want you to think about your newly widowed father and how heartbroken he would be if his only daughter did not participate in this reunion."

She released a disgusted breath. "I hate you so much."

"That was very convincing. It's a good thing I know you don't mean it."

"I mean it," she said.

"Would you just give me the go-ahead to mark you down on the list so I can send the names to the travel agent?" Her brother's harassed voice made her feel marginally better. But only marginally.

Indina massaged the bridge of her nose. She loved her family, but these days she could only take them in small doses. She visited her dad at least once during the week—even more if she could—and tried to make as many Sunday dinners as possible, but that was only a few hours out of her day, and once her brothers started eating, there was very little talking. Could she survive being stuck on a cruise ship with them for three days without going straight-up insane?

And it wasn't limited to her pesky brothers this time around. The entire Holmes clan would be there. Her late Uncle Wesley's three sons, Alexander, Elijah and Tobias, along with their wives and their ever-growing brood of children were all going. And if her boys would be there, Indina knew her Aunt Margo would be there too, along with her husband, Gerald Mitchell.

There would be Holmeses galore. That poor cruise ship had no idea what it was in store for.

"Indina!" Harrison's voice startled her. "Are you coming on the cruise or not? Wait, let me rephrase that. Are you going to break your father's heart or not?"

"Stop it with the guilt trip."

"I'm just saying."

"I've never been on a cruise before," she pointed out. "What if I get seasick?"

"You can wear one of those patches behind your ear. And if that doesn't work there's medicine you can take," Harrison said. "I'll tell Eli to bring you some."

Great. That's what she got for having a cousin who was a doctor, and who also happened to be married to a doctor.

"You got any more excuses you need me to shoot down before I head to my office?" her brother asked.

"I really do hate you right now," Indina said. She rubbed her temple as she came to terms with the fact that there was no way out of this. "Fine, I'll come on the damn cruise."

"I'd already marked you down as a yes," Harrison replied. "I just called to make sure *you* knew that you were going."

"Asshole," she said.

"I love you too. By the way, I put you in the cabin with Lily and Jasmine."

"Lily and Jasmine?" Indina sat up straight. "You do realize I'm forty-two years old, don't you? Why would I want to room with a couple of teenagers?"

No, make that a teenager and a pre-teen. Her cousin Alex's daughter, Jasmine, was only twelve.

"Because everyone else is paired up and the cabin rates are based on double occupancy," he explained. "If I didn't put you in the girls' room you'd have to pay an upcharge because you're a single."

A single. As if it was some kind of diseased designation she wore on her chest.

"And just why would you think I would be alone?" Indina asked.

"Why wouldn't I?" The incredulousness in his voice made her want to slap him through the phone. "When was the last time you brought anyone around?"

Indina ignored that question. It had been nearly two years since she'd been in a bring-him-over-to-meet-the-family kind of relationship. That didn't mean her brother had to throw it in her face. Just for that, she would pluck his insensitive ass right between the eyebrows next time she saw him.

"I won't have the cabin for myself," Indina said. "I'm bringing someone."

"Who?" Harrison asked.

"None of your business."

"I need the name for the travel agent."

"I'll text you the name later. Now leave me alone. I need to get going."

The shower stopped the minute she disconnected the call. Moments later, the bathroom door opened and Griffin Sims walked out, wiping his face with a plush cranberry-colored towel. There was another towel wrapped around his waist, hanging low on his hips. His chiseled dark brown chest glistened with specks of moisture. Indina tracked a water droplet that traveled down his torso to the smattering of curly hair that trailed from his belly button to below the towel.

She pulled her bottom lip between her teeth and damn near whimpered.

Griffin stopped short when he spotted her.

"You're still here?"

"I'm sorry," Indina said, rising from where she'd sat on the edge of his bed. "I got a phone call that I had to take just as I started getting dressed."

"No need to apologize. It's just that you're usually gone by the time I get out of the shower."

Her eyes roamed over his muscular back and shoulders as he walked over to the dresser. She didn't know where he found the time to go to the gym, but she appreciated the way he took care of his body.

"Are you still nervous about today?" Griffin asked.

He turned to her, holding the pair of heather gray boxer briefs he'd retrieved from the dresser. He dropped the towel and Indina couldn't hold back the whimper this time.

She had explored the heavy weight between his legs with her tongue just an hour ago, yet her mouth still watered at the sight of it. She just stood there and marveled at his beauty as he pulled the briefs up his well-toned legs.

"Indina," Griffin called.

She blinked several times. "Wait. What?"

A knowing grin curled up the side of his mouth. "I asked if you were still nervous about today?"

"A little, but at least I'm no longer tense."

"Happy I could help with that," he said. His deep

chuckle reverberated along her nerve endings, straight down to that spot between her legs he'd pleasured this morning.

Over the last eight months, she'd relied on Griffin for that particular kind of pleasurable help on a regular basis. They'd met a little over a year ago, when Indina decided to move away from residential interior design and concentrate on the more lucrative industrial sector. She began freelancing with the structural engineering firm where Griffin worked after one of the owners sought her out.

Griffin was the lead engineer on the very first project she worked on with Sykes-Wilcox. The physical attraction had been there from the moment she walked into a conference room and saw him braced over a set of blueprints, his shirtsleeves rolled up on his strong arms. Indina decided not to act on that attraction until several months later, after she learned through the office grapevine that Griffin was divorced and not necessarily looking for a relationship.

She knew all about that. Not the being divorced part, but being burnt out on relationships?

Hell yes, she knew about that.

But there were only so many *Top Ten Self-Pleasuring Tips* articles a girl could be expected to read. And she'd read them. *All* of them. She needed the real deal. The way Indina saw it she and Griffin were in the perfect position to provide each other with some much needed sexual relief.

She could still remember how her fingers had trembled as she'd typed the text, asking Griffin if he was up for a little casual, no-strings-attached sex. She wasn't sure how she would have handled working with him if he had turned down her bold invitation to meet her at the Bourbon Orleans Hotel in the French Quarter.

He'd arrived at the hotel even before she did, and with that one afternoon, they'd embarked upon a coworkers with benefits arrangement that never failed to leave her body satisfied and her mind free of relationship drama.

Her phone beeped. It was a text from Harrison with the travel agent's name and phone number, and a reminder to send the name of the person who would be sharing her cabin.

Indina looked over at Griffin. He'd just put on a gingham blue dress shirt, but hadn't bothered to button it up yet. Her mouth watered again at the expanse of exposed skin.

He looked up from the neckties he'd been contemplating.

"Everything okay?" he asked.

Indina nodded and decided not to ask the question that had been on the tip of her tongue. Hadn't she just acknowledged that what she and Griffin had going was perfect? Why would she jeopardize it by asking him to come with her on this damn cruise?

She slipped her dress over her head, then picked up her wristlet and keys from where she'd dropped them on the dresser.

In a real relationship this is where they would kiss each other goodbye. But this wasn't a real relationship. It wasn't how she and Griffin rolled.

And that was just fine with her.

"See you in a few hours," Indina said, gripping the

handle on the bedroom door. "I'll lock the front door on my way out."

Read Indina and Griffin's story! Pick up your copy of Chase Me.

ACKNOWLEDGMENTS

Big thanks to Bettina and Donald for allowing me to use your engagement photo for the cover of **Trust Me**. You both bring Mackenna and Ezra to life. Blessings for a long and happy marriage!

ABOUT THE AUTHOR

A native of south Louisiana, Farrah Rochon officially began her writing career while waiting in between classes in the student lounge at Xavier University of Louisiana. After earning her Bachelors of Science degree and a Masters of Arts from Southeastern Louisiana University, Farrah decided to pursue her lifelong dream of becoming a published novelist. She was named *Shades of Romance Magazine*'s Best New Author of 2007. Her debut novel garnered rave reviews, earning Farrah several SORMAG Readers' Choice Awards. *I'll Catch You*, the second book in her New York Sabers series for Harlequin Kimani, was a 2012 RITA ® Award finalist. Yours Forever, the third book in her Bayou Dreams series, is a 2015 RITA® Award finalist.

When she is not writing in her favorite coffee shop, Farrah spends most of her time reading her favorite romance novels or seeing as many Broadway shows as possible. An admitted sports fanatic, Farrah feeds her addiction to football by watching New Orleans Saints games on Sunday afternoons.

Learn more about my books:
www.farrahrochon.com
farrah@farrahrochon.com